'*The Intuitionist* is the story of a love affair with the steel and stone, machinery and architecture of the city. It's not a pretty love, but a working-class passion for the stench of humanity that its heroine, Lila Mae Watson, has made her own. But as always with love there is betrayal. This extraordinary novel is first voice in a powerful chorus to come'   Walter Mosley

'*The Intuitionist* is a facinating novel, full of quirky insights and beautifully imagined characters'   Gary Indiana

'An enormously accomplished first novel, a meditation on race and technology and imagination that is absolutely dazzling'
Susan Isaacs in *Brave Dames and Wimpettes*

'Colson Whitehead's debut novel is part urban thriller, part meditation on race—and all vigorous language and supple imagination'   *The Oregonian*

'This splendid novel reads as though a stray line in Pynchon or Millhauser had been meticulously unfolded to reveal an entire world, one of spooky, stylish alternate-Americana, as rich and haunted as our own. The care and confidence of the prose, the visionary metaphor beating like a heart at the center—these do not outweigh the poignance and humor, the human presence here. *The Intuitionist* rises someplace new, and very special'

Jonathan Lethem

'The world of *The Intuitionist* is an unforgettable universe'
Seattle Post-Intelligencer

'Brilliant . . . Whitehead carves out an exclusive space for himself in America's literary canon . . . his imagination and writing skills always keep the story fresh and will undoubtedly keep you guessing'   *Washington Post Book World*

D1323686

Colson Whitehead is the *New York Times* bestselling author of *The Underground Railroad*, which won the National Book Award in 2016; *The Noble Hustle*; *Zone One*; *Sag Harbor*; *The Intuitionist*; *John Henry Days*; *Apex Hides the Hurt* and one collection of essays, *The Colossus of New York*. A Pulitzer Prize finalist and a recipient of MacArthur and Guggenheim fellowships, he lives in New York City.

The

INTUITIONIST

The INTUITIONIST

Colson Whitehead

FLEET

2017

FLEET

First published in the United States in 1999 by Anchor Books
First published in Great Britain in 1999 by Granta
This paperback edition published in 2017 by Fleet

1 3 5 7 9 10 8 6 4 2

A CIP catalogue record for this book
is available from the British Library.

ISBN 978-0-7088-9847-5

Printed and bound in Great Britain by
Clays Ltd, St Ives plc

Papers used by Fleet are from well-managed forests
and other responsible sources.

Fleet
An imprint of
Little, Brown Book Group
Carmelite House
50 Victoria Embankment
London EC4Y 0DZ

An Hachette UK Company
www.hachette.co.uk

www.littlebrown.co.uk

for my parents

A c k n o w l e d g m e n t s

A boy should never leave home without a copy of *American Standard Practice for the Inspection of Elevators*, not unless he wants to get into trouble. Shout outs: Gary Dauphin, Wesley Jones, Valerie Burgher, Dan Schrecker, Darren Aronofsky, Sue Johnson, Ari Handel, Hugh Garvey, Jed Weintrob, Bill Parsons, Jim Macintosh, Jeannette Draper. Thanks to Kevin Young for encouragement and the title. Nicole Aragi, my agent, is awesome. Tina Pohlman, my editor, is a woman of wealth and taste. I couldn't have done this without the love and support of my family and Natasha Stovall, the best partner a boy could have.

DOWN

Part **ONE**

It's a new elevator, freshly pressed to the rails, and it's not built to fall this fast.

*   *   *

She doesn't know what to do with her eyes. The front door of the building is too scarred and gouged to look at, and the street behind her is improbably empty, as if the city had been evacuated and she's the only one who didn't hear about it. There is always the game at moments like this to distract her. She opens her leather field binder and props it on her chest. The game gets harder the farther back she goes. Most of the inspectors from the last decade or so are still with the Guild and are easy to identify: LMT, MG, BP, JW. So far she doesn't particularly like the men who have preceded her at 125 Walker. Martin Gruber chews with his mouth open and likes to juggle his glass eye. Big Billy Porter is one of the Old Dogs, and proud of it. On many occasions Lila Mae has returned to the Pit from an errand only to hear Big Billy

1

Porter regaling the boys about the glory days of the Guild, before. While his comments are never specific, it is clear to everyone just what and who Big Billy is referring to in his croaking, muddy voice. Rebellious among the bureaucratic rows of the Pit, Big Billy's oak desk juts out into the aisle so he can seat his bulk directly beneath one of the ceiling fans. He says he overheats easily and on the hottest days of the summer his remaining hair slides away from how he's combed it, the strands easing into nautilus whorls. It's a slow process and watching it is like waiting for a new hour. But it happens eventually.

All the inspectors who have visited 125 Walker in the past have been Empiricists. As far as she can tell. When she gets fifteen years back in the record there are no more faces to put to the initials. She recognizes the initials from the inspection records of other elevators in other buildings but has never met the people they belong to. JM, for example, is also listed in the inspection record of the elevator Lila Mae departed just half an hour ago, and EH, she's learned over time, has a thing for worn guide shoes, something no one ever looks at except the real stickler types. Checking guide shoes is a losing proposition. Some of the initial men must be in the pictures along the walls of the Pit. The men in those pictures sport the regulation haircuts the Guild required back then, respectable haircuts fit for men of duty and responsibility. The haircuts are utilitarian mishaps that project honor, fidelity, brotherhood unto death. The barber shop two doors down from the Guild, the one that always has big band music coming from inside, used to specialize. Or so they say. Some of the younger inspectors have started wearing the haircut again. It's called a Safety. Lila Mae's hair parts in the middle and cups her round face like a thousand hungry fingers.

The light at this hour, on this street, is the secondhand gray of ghetto twilight, a dull mercury color. She rings the superintendent again and hears a tinny bleating sound. Down twenty years in the record she finds one of the treasures that make the game real:

James Fulton and Frank Chancre inspected 125 Walker within six months of each other. From Lila Mae's vantage, it is easy to read into this coincidence the passing of the crown. Not clear why Fulton left his office to hit the field again, though. Twenty years ago he would have been Dean of the Institute and long past making the rounds of the buildings, ringing superintendents, waiting on worn and ugly stoops. Then she remembers Fulton liked to go into the field every now and again so he wouldn't forget. Fulton with his mahogany cane, rapping impatiently on one of the three windows set in the front door of 125 Walker. Perhaps they weren't cracked then. Perhaps he cracked them. Across from his initials the inspection record notes a problem with the limit switch, a 387. She recognizes the handwriting from Fulton's room at the Institute, from the tall wooden display cases where his most famous papers are kept behind glass, in controlled atmospheres.

As for Chancre, he would have been a young and rising inspector back then. A little thinner, fewer exploded capillaries in his nose. He wouldn't have been able to afford his double-breasted navy suits on a rookie's salary, but his position has changed since those days. Lila Mae sees Chancre swallowing the super's hands with his oversized mitts in faltering camaraderie. It takes a long time to become a politician, but he was born with the smile. You can't fake smiles like that. Nice building you got here, chum. Nice to see a man who takes pride in his craft. Sometimes you walk into these places, you never know what you're going to see, bless my heart. You want to say to yourself, how can people live like this, but then we are all dealt differently and you have to play what you're dealt. Back home, we . . . He gave 125 Walker a clean bill. Lots on his mind, lots on his mind.

The wind is trapped in one of Walker Street's secret nooks, pushing through, whistling. The elevator is an Arbo Smooth-Glide, popular with residential building contractors when 125 went up. Lila Mae remembers from an Institute class on elevator marketing that Arbo spent millions promoting the Smooth-Glide in the trades and at conventions. They were the first to understand the dark powers of the bikini. On a revolving platform festooned with red, white and blue streamers, slender fingers fan the air, summoning the contractors hither. The models have perfect American navels and the air is stuffy in the old convention hall. A placard overlooked for red-blooded distraction details in silver script Arbo's patented QuarterPoint CounterWeight System. Has this ever happened to you? You've just put the finishing touches on your latest assignment and are proud as a peacock to show off for your client. As you ride to the top floor, the Brand X elevator stops and refuses to budge. You won't be working with *them* anymore! Say goodbye to sticky, stubborn counterweights with the new Smooth-Glide Residential Elevator from Arbo. Over two million Arbo elevators are in use worldwide. Going up?

A bald head girdled by loose curls of red hair appears at the door's window. The man squints at Lila Mae and opens the door, hiding his body behind the gray metal. He leaves it to her to speak.

"Lila Mae Watson," she says. "I've come to inspect your elevator."

The man's lips arch up toward his nose and Lila Mae understands that he's never seen an elevator inspector like her before. Lila Mae has pinpointed a spot as the locus of metropolitan disaffection. A zero-point. It is situated in the heart of the city, on a streetcorner that clots with busy, milling citizens during the day and empties completely at night except for prostitutes and lost encyclopedia salesmen. It's a two-minute walk from the office. With that zero-point as reference, she can predict just how much suspicion, curiosity and anger she will rouse in her cases. 125 Walker is at the outer edges of the city, near the bank of the polluted river that keeps the skyscrapers at bay from the suburbs, and quite a distance from the streetcorner: He doesn't like her. "Let me see your badge," the man says, but Lila Mae's hand is already fishing in her jacket pocket. She flips open her identification and holds it up to the man's face. He doesn't bother to look at it. He just asked for effect.

The hallway smells of burning animal fat and obscure gravies boiling to slag. Half the ceiling lights are cracked open or missing. "Back here," he says. The superintendent seems to be melting as he leads Lila Mae across the grime-caulked black and white hexagonal tile. His bulbous head dissolves into shoulders, then spreads into a broad pool of torso and legs. "How come Jimmy didn't come this time?" the super asks. "Jimmy's good people." Lila Mae doesn't answer him. Dark oil streaks his forearms and clouds his green T-shirt. A door bangs open upstairs and a loud female voice yells something in the chafing tones reserved for disciplining children and pets.

The lumpy, pitted texture of the cab's door tells her that management has painted it over a few times, but Lila Mae still recognizes the unusually wide dimensions of an Arbo Smooth-Glide door. Taking their cue from the early days of passenger-response criticism, Arbo equipped their newest model with an oversized door to foster the illusion of space, to distract the passenger from what every passenger feels acutely about elevators. That they ride in a box on a rope in a pit. That they are in the void. If the super doesn't strip the old paint the next time he renovates, it will eventually impede the movement of the door. (Of course a lot of graffiti in this neighborhood.) Already the elevator door halts in its furrows when it opens. A violation waiting to be born, the nascent outlines of a 787. Lila Mae decides against saying anything to the super. It's not her job. "You'll want to start in the machine room, I guess," the super says. He's fixated on the ideal triangularity of Lila Mae's tie knot, its grid of purple and blue squares. The tie disappears near her bosom, gliding beneath the buttons of her dark blue suit.

Lila Mae does not answer him. She leans against the dorsal wall of the elevator and listens. 125 Walker is only twelve floors high, and the vibration of the idling drive doesn't diminish that much as it swims through the gritty loop of the diverting pulley, descends down the cables, navigates the suspension gear, and grasps the car. Lila Mae can feel the idling in her back. She hears the door operator click above her in the dark well and then the door shuts, halting a small degree as the strata of paint chafes. Three Gemco helical springs are standard-issue buffers on Arbo elevators. They wait fifteen feet below her like stalagmites. "Press twelve," Lila Mae orders the super. Even with her eyes closed she could have done it herself, but she's trying to concentrate on the vibrations massaging her back. She can almost see them now. This elevator's vibrations are resolving themselves in her mind as an aqua-blue cone. Her pen rests in her palm and her grip loosens. It might fall. She shuts out the sound of the super's breathing, which is a low rumble lilting into a wheeze at the ultimate convexity of his exhalation. That's noise. The elevator moves. The elevator moves upward in the well, toward the grunting in the machine room, and Lila Mae turns that into a picture, too. The ascension is a red spike circling around the blue cone, which doubles in size and wobbles as the elevator starts climbing. You don't pick the shapes and their behavior. Everyone has their own set of genies. Depends on how your brain works. Lila Mae has always had a thing for geometric forms. As the elevator reaches the fifth floor landing, an orange octagon cartwheels into her mind's frame. It hops up and down, incongruous with the annular aggression of the red spike. Cubes and parallelograms emerge around the eighth floor, but they're satisfied with half-hearted little jigs and don't disrupt the proceedings like the mischievous orange octagon. The octagon ricochets into the foreground, famished for attention. She knows what it is. The triad of helical buffers recedes farther from her, ten stories down at the dusty and dark floor of the well. No need to continue. Just before she opens her eyes she tries to think of what the super's expression must be. She doesn't come close, save for that peculiar arching of his lips, but that doesn't count because she already saw that from when he opened the front door.

The super's eyes are two black lines that withdraw indistinguishably into the skein of his hieroglyphic squint. His lips push up so far that his nostrils seem to suck them in. "I'm going to have to cite you for a faulty overspeed governor," Lila Mae says. The door opens slowly in its track and the drive's idling vibration is full and strong, up here so close to the machine room.

"But you haven't even looked at it," the super says. "You haven't even seen it." He is confused, and tiny pricks of blood speckle his pink cheeks.

"I'm going to have to cite you for a faulty overspeed governor," Lila Mae repeats. She's removing the tiny screws from the glass inspection plate on the left anterior wall of the elevator. The side of her screwdriver reads, PROPERTY OF THE DEPARTMENT OF ELEVATOR INSPECTORS. "It catches every six meters or so," Lila Mae adds as she withdraws the inspection slip from beneath the glass. "If you want, I can get my handbook from the car and you can see the regulations for yourself."

"I don't want to look at the damn book," the super says. He runs his thumbs animatedly across his fingers as she signs the slip and replaces the plate. "I know what the book says. I want you to look at the damn thing yourself. It's running fine. You haven't even been upstairs."

"Nevertheless," Lila Mae says. She opens her field binder and writes her initials at the bottom of the ID column. Even from the twelfth floor, she can still hear the woman downstairs yelling at her children, or what Lila Mae supposes to be children. You never know these days.

"You aren't one of those voodoo inspectors, are you? Don't need to see anything, you just feel it, right? I heard Jimmy make jokes about you witch doctors."

She says, "Intuitionist." Lila Mae rubs the ballpoint of the pen to get the ink flowing. The *W* of her initials belongs to a ghost alphabet.

The super grins. "If that's the game you want to play," he says,

7

"I guess you got me on the ropes." There are three twenty-dollar bills in his oily palm. He leans over to Lila Mae and places the money in her breast pocket. Pats it down. "I haven't ever seen a woman elevator inspector before, let alone a colored one, but I guess they teach you all the same tricks."

The door of apartment 12-A cracks behind Lila Mae. "What's all this noise in the hall?" a high, reedy voice asks. "Who's that hanging out there? What you want?"

The super pulls 12-A's door firmly shut and says, "You just mind your own business, Missus LaFleur. It's just me." He turns back to Lila Mae and smiles again. He sticks his tongue into the hole where his two front teeth used to be. Arbo didn't lie about their QuarterPoint CounterWeight System. It rarely fails. A regrettable incident in Atlanta kicked up a lot of fuss in the trades a few years back, but an inquiry later absolved Arbo of any wrongdoing. As they say. The model's overspeed governors are another matter, though, notoriously unreliable, and probability says their famous manufacturing defect should have emerged long ago. Sixty bucks is sixty bucks.

"You'll get a copy of the official citation in a few days in the mail, and it'll inform you how much the fine is," Lila Mae says. She writes *333* in 125 Walker's inspection record.

The super slaps the door of 12-A with his big hand. "But I just gave you sixty dollars! Nobody has ever squeezed me for more than sixty." He's having trouble keeping his trembling arms still at his chest. No, he wouldn't mind taking a swipe at her.

"You placed sixty dollars in my pocket. I don't think I implied by my behavior that I wanted you to bribe me, nor have I made any statement or gesture, such as an outstretched palm, for example, saying that I would change my report because you gave me money. If you want to give away your hard-earned money"—Lila Mae waves her hand toward a concentration of graffiti—"I see it as a curious, although in this case fortuitous, habit of yours that has nothing whatsoever to do with me. Or why I'm here." Lila Mae

8

starts down the stairs. After riding elevators all day, she looks forward to walking down stairs. "If you want to try and take your sixty dollars off me, you're welcome to try, and if you want to challenge my findings and have another person double-check the overspeed governor, that's your right as a representative of this building. But I'm correct." Lila Mae abandons the super on the twelfth floor with the Arbo Smooth-Glide. The super cusses. She is right about the overspeed governor. She is never wrong.

She doesn't know yet.

* * *

All of the Department's cars are algae green and shine like algae, thanks to the diligent ministrations of the motor pool. On the night of his inauguration Chancre gripped the lectern with his sausage fingers and announced his Ten Point Plan. The gold badge of his office hung over his shoulders by a long, patriotic ribbon. "Department vehicles," he thundered, "must be kept in a condition befitting the Department." To much applause in the dim banquet room of the Albatross Hotel. Those seated at the long oval tables, gathered around Mrs. Chancre's unholy floral arrangements, easily translated Point Number Seven to the more succinct "Those colored boys better put a shine on those cars." One of the mechanics, Jimmy, has a secret crush on Lila Mae. Not completely secret: Lila Mae's sedan is the only one that gets vacuumed daily, and each morning when she leaves the garage for the field the rearview mirror has been adjusted from the night shift's contortions, to just the way she likes it. Jimmy is a slender character among the burly crew of the motor pool, and the youngest. The calluses on his hands are still tiny pebbles in his flesh.

The traffic at quitting time is a bother. Radio station WCAM equips men with binoculars and positions them at strategic overpasses to describe the gnarls and tangles. Lila Mae is never able to differentiate these men from the meandering isolates who linger at the margins of freeways. All of them make obscure, furtive gestures, all share a certain stooped posture that says they lack substantive reasons for being where they are, at the side of the road. Impossible to distinguish a walkie-talkie from a bottle of cheap wine at such distances.

They don't have alibis, Lila Mae appraises the men at the side of the road.

Her sedan limps through black glue. The WCAM sentry warns of an accident up ahead: A schoolbus has overturned, and as the passing commuters rubberneck and bless themselves, the traffic clots.

Over here, honks a woman in a red compact. The light trilling of her car horn reveals its foreign birth, cribside cooing in alien tongues. Lila Mae thinks car horns work backward: they don't prod and urge the laggard ahead but summon those behind, come up, follow me. Lila Mae listens to the sporadic summons, listens to the news reports of WCAM, the red brake lights smoldering on the road ahead. Each of the announcer's words have the routine elegance, the blank purity Lila Mae associates with geometry. The announcer says that a low-pressure system is rolling east. The announcer says that there's been an accident at the Fanny Briggs Memorial Building. An elevator has fallen.

Now we're cooking.

Lila Mae turns on her Department radio and hears the dispatcher call her inspector's code. "Come in, Z34. Report Zulu-three-four."

"This is Z34 reporting to base," Lila Mae says.

"Why haven't you reported back, Z34?" Contrary to prevailing notions, the elevator inspector dispatch room is not filled with long consoles staffed by an able company who furiously plug and unplug wires from myriad inputs, busily routing. The dispatch room is a small box on the top floor of the office and there's only one person on duty at a time. It is very neat and has no windows. Craig's on dispatch now, and in Lila Mae's imagination he is a skinny man with brown hair who withers in his revolving chair, dressed in suspendered slacks and a sleeveless undershirt. She's never seen a dispatcher, and she's only seen their room once, on her first day of work. He must have been in the bathroom, or making coffee.

"I was on a call," Lila Mae responds. "125 Walker. I just stepped in the car." No one is going to catch her in that lie. Lila Mae always turns off the radio when she's finished for the day. Occasionally one of the night shift calls in sick and Craig wants her to fill in for a few hours. Until the city and the Department work out their overtime policies there's no way Lila Mae is going to fill in for the night shift. If you haven't killed your hangover by six o'clock, you should take your lumps, is what she thinks.

"You're to report back to HQ immediately," Craig says. Then he adds, "Zulu-thirty-four."

"What's this crap about the Briggs building?" Lila Mae asks.

"You're to report back here immediately, Z34. Chancre wants to talk to you. And I don't think I have to quote you Department regs on profanity over city frequencies. Dispatch out."

Lila Mae returns to WCAM, hoping for more details. For some reason Craig's being a hardass, and that's not good. She considers steering over to the shoulder to bypass the traffic, brandishing her inspector credentials should a policeman stop her. But the police and the elevator inspectors have a difficult past, and it's doubtful a cop would let her off the hook, even for city business. Of course the city has never answered Chancre's repeated requests for sirens. No one outside the Guild seems to think they're necessary for some reason. Over the radio, one of the WCAM sentries ahead comments on how long it's taking the emergency techs to remove the children from the schoolbus.

Lila Mae once delivered an oral report on Fanny Briggs in the third grade. Fanny Briggs was in the newer encyclopedias. Some even had her picture. Fanny Briggs looked tired in the marginalia; her eyelids drooped and her jowls oozed down from her cheekbones. Lila Mae stood in front of Ms. Parker's third-grade class and trembled as she started her report. She preferred to fade into the back rows, next to the rabbit cages, beneath the awkward pastels of the spring art project. There she was at Ms. Parker's desk, and her index cards shook in her tiny hands.

"Fanny Briggs was a slave who taught herself how to read."

One time a radio program featured Dorothy Beechum, the most famous colored actress in country, reading parts of Fanny Brigg's account of her escape North. Lila Mae's mother called her into the drawing room. Lila Mae's legs dangled over her mother's lap as she leaned toward the brown mesh of the radio speaker. The actress's voice was iron and strong and did not fail to summon applause from the more liberal quarters of her audience, who murmured about noble struggle. Tiny particles of darkness pressed beyond the cracked, wheaty mesh of the speaker, the kind of unsettling darkness Lila Mae would later associate with the elevator well. Of course she'd do her oral report on Fanny Briggs. Who else was there?

Not much progress in this traffic.

The times are changing. In a city with an increasingly vocal colored population—who are not above staging tiresome demonstrations for the lowlier tabloids, or throwing tomatoes and rotten cabbages during otherwise perfectly orchestrated speeches and rallies—it only makes sense to name the new municipal building after one of their heroes. The Mayor is not stupid; you don't become the ruler of a city this large and insane by being stupid. The Mayor is shrewd and understands that this city is not a Southern city, it is not an old money city or a new money city but the most famous city in the world, and the rules are different here. The new municipal building has been named the Fanny Briggs Memorial Building, and there have been few complaints, and fewer tomatoes.

When Lila Mae was assigned the Fanny Briggs Memorial

Building, she thought nothing of it. It made sense that it would be either her or Pompey, the only two colored inspectors in the Department. Chancre's no fool. There are, after all, election years in the Elevator Guild too, and this is one of them, and all sorts of unexpected things have been happening. The Department-wide $1.25 raise, for example, which according to Chancre really adds up to a pretty penny after a while. Not that the elevator inspectors, civil-servant to the core despite their maverick reputations and occasionally flashy antics, needed to be convinced of the importance of a $1.25 raise. A government job is a government job, whether it's inspecting elevators or railroad cars full of hanging meat, and anything that brings their salaries into closer proportion to their contributions to the American good are accepted cheerfully, election-year ploy or no. Same thing with the screwdrivers. When a memo circulating soon after the raises announced that the new screwdrivers were on their way, few cared that the Guild Chair was so naked in his attempt to score points with the electorate. For the new screwdrivers were quite beautiful. Ever since the city granted license to the Department, bulky and ungainly screwdrivers had poked and bulged in the jacket pockets of the elevator inspectors, completely ruining any attempts at dapperness and savoir faire. It's difficult to look official and imposing while listing to one side. The new screwdrivers have mother-of-pearl handles and heads the exact width of an inspection-plate screw. They fold out like jackknives and lend themselves to baroque fantasies about spies and secret missions. And who can argue with that?

So when the word spread that Lila Mae had been assigned the 18-deep elevator stack in the Fanny Briggs Memorial Building (18-deep!), a career-making case for any inspector, few were surprised and whatever ground Chancre lost among the Old Dogs of the Guild was more than compensated for by the goodwill generated by the raise and the new mother-of-pearl jackknife screwdrivers. Lila Mae knew when she got the assignment that it was

13

meant to draw attention from Chancre's opponent in the race for the Guild Chair, the liberal Orville Lever, who apparently thinks that only Intuitionists are capable of building coalitions, shaking hands with fundamentally different people, etc. Lila Mae (who, by the way, is still not making much headway in the evening traffic) may be an Intuitionist, but she is a colored woman, which is more to the point. Chancre's assistant left a note on her desk: *Your good service won't be forgotten after the election.* As if she needed to be bribed with a vague promise of promotion (and probably a lie anyway). It's her job. She's taken an oath and such things are to be taken seriously. Lila Mae held the note in her small hands, and even though she did not look up from her desk she knew that all of them, the Old Dogs and the New Guys in their retrograde Safety haircuts, were looking at her. The way the gossip flows in the Pit (Lila Mae is situated quite far downstream), they probably knew she got the case before she did. Probably skinny Ned, that vapor, that meandering cumulus masquerading as a man, sentenced to desk duty after the infamous Johnson Towers debacle, talked to a guy who talked to a guy in Chancre's inner circle and the word came down: the colored gal gets the job. Not any of them, not Pompey. There are no surprises in election years, just a bit more static.

And here's Chancre now, arms struts at the tails of his signature double-breasted suit, twenty feet tall on a billboard for the United Elevator Co. Lila Mae's car creeps through the bottleneck at the entrance to the tunnel so there's no missing him. No more honking for this glum procession—they can see the tunnel now, and there is always the mandatory period of pensive anticipation on entering the tunnel. ALL SAFE declares the copy across his feet, a play on Otis's famous declaration at the 1853 Crystal Palace Exposition. The reference doesn't mean much to the people in the cars around Lila Mae—elevator ads probably only register in civilian heads as a dim affirmation of modernity, happy progress to be taken for granted and subconsciously cherished—but Otis's phrase is the hoist pulling her and her fellow inspectors out of bed each morning. The sacred motto.

Even long observers of the mysterious ways of corporate vanity are hard-pressed to understand the sudden ubiquity of elevator ads. In addition to billboards like the one towering over Lila Mae right now, the elevator industry's advertisements line park benches, adorn the buses and subways of the city's transit system, brace the outfield walls of baseball stadiums, bright non sequiturs. Other places, too. One time before the start of a double feature at her favorite movie house—the Marquee on Twenty-third Street, notorious among those in the know for its free popcorn refills—Lila Mae sat astonished as a thirty-second movie reel introduced American Elevator's new frictionless drive. From time to time Lila Mae still catches herself humming the spot's elastic doo-wop chorus, never mind that the frictionless drive in question is just American's old 240–60 drive in a smart new housing. It's a relatively recent phenomenon, the vocality of the international short-range vertical transport industry, and there's no one to explain it. How much Chancre makes in endorsements each year is anyone's guess, but it goes without saying that he has a lot riding on his reelection to Guild Chair. Just look at him up there. So far Lila Mae thinks her role in the campaign is limited to window dressing—evidence for the new, progressive face of the Elevator Guild, and by extension, city government.

She doesn't know yet.

She's almost inside the tunnel when WCAM finally decides to update the situation at the Fanny Briggs Memorial Building. The yellow tiles inside the tunnel glisten and Lila Mae sees a long throat strangled by mucus. In his geometric voice, so full of planes, WCAM's radio announcer says that Chancre and the Mayor will be holding a press conference to discuss what transpired at the new municipal building early this afternoon. But before he can say something more, something tangible that Lila Mae can use to prepare herself, the tunnel eats the transmission. Like that. Then there's just the agitated scratch of static inside her sedan and the earnest humming of multiple tires on the tunnel floor outside. Near silence, to better contemplate the engineering marvel they travel through, the age of miracles they live in. The air is poisonous.

Something happened. It was her case. Lila Mae drums her fingers on the steering wheel and relives her call to the Briggs building the day before. Those looking for a correlative to Fanny Briggs's powerful, lumpy body in the shape of the building dedicated to her will have to bear in mind the will to squat that roosts in the soul of every city architect. Government buildings are generally squat rather than tall, presumably to better accommodate deep file drawers of triplicate ephemera. So it has been for generations. But who can resist the seductions of elevators these days, those stepping stones to Heaven, which make relentless verticality so alluring? While the architects understand that the future is up, the future is in how high you can go, it is difficult to shake old habits. Habits clamp down on the ankle and resist all entreaties, no matter how logical. As it is in politics, the only victor in the end was ugly compromise. The Fanny Briggs Memorial Building hunkers down on the northern edge of Federal Plaza in the renovated section of downtown, burly and squat for five floors before launching into space with another forty stories of pure, unsullied steel. The net effect is chrysalid, a photograph of a glass insect emerging from a stone cocoon. When Lila Mae first walked up the broad stone steps of the building, she looked up at the monolith above and felt a trembling instant of vertigo: It was a big responsibility. The mandatory Latinate motto was engraved above the entrance.

Lila Mae is outside the tunnel now and can't think of what she did wrong. She needs a plan.

Keep cool, Lila Mae.

The weird thing about the tunnel is that on the world-side, the city's skyline is merely one incident among many on the horizon. From the world's side of the tunnel the skyline is a row of broken teeth, an angry serration gnawing at the atmosphere, but there's a lot of other stuff going on, dirty water and more land beyond that dirty water, the humble metropolitan outpost just departed, a crop of weedy smokestacks, lots of stuff, 360 degrees to choose from and the generous illusion of choice. Then the tunnel, and no more sky. Nothing but teeth. The drivers mellow once they hit the city because they remember again what the city is like and get exhausted, one by one as they exit the tunnel, and can't remember why they were in such a hurry to get there. The internecine system of one-way streets and prohibited U-turns makes retreat a difficult enterprise. This is on purpose.

As she turns the corner to Headquarters, Lila Mae sees that the press conference is under way, although it takes her a few seconds to put two and two together. Remarkable pinstripes on the newspapermen and radio reporters; if the city fathers could only regulate construction, keep tabs on how this place looks from afar, maybe the city could be those pinstripes: uniform, doubtless, regimented. The thicket of fedoraed men is such that initially she can't make out Chancre and the Mayor, but then Lila Mae sees the strange red halation that forms around Chancre's Irish face when all the blood rushes into it, when the incumbent Guild Chair is set for one of his eruptions. She feels exposed, a voyeur in full moonlight on the clearest night of summer. Because they are talking about her, because she is implicated in all this—she knows this much, if not the specifics. The press conference bows around the entrance to Headquarters, and the garage ramp is mercifully unimpeded. The flashbulbs crackle and pop like dry brush beneath the feet of hunters.

City buildings may be deficient in adequate staple supplies, comfortable chairs and quality toilet paper, but never in fluorescent lights. Lila Mae eases her sedan into the rank gloom of the garage and past the observation window of the mechanics' office. The six-man crew in their dark green uniforms crane over their office's old, reliable radio and Lila Mae prays she will make it safe past them, be spared the customary frowns and code-nods. Dicty college woman. This space in the garage is what the Department has allowed the colored men—it is underground, there are no windows permitting sky, and the sick light is all the more enervating for it—but the mechanics have done their best to make it their own. For example: A close inspection of Chancre's campaign posters, which are taped to every other cement column despite regulations against campaign literature within a hundred yards of Headquarters, reveals myriad tiny insurrections, such as counterclockwise swirls in the middle of Chancre's pupils, an allusion to his famous nocturnal dipsomania. You have to stand up real close to the posters to see the swirls, and even then they're easy to miss: Lila Mae had to have Jimmy point them out to her. Horns, boiling cysts, the occasional cussword inked in across Chancre's slat teeth—they add up after a while, somehow more personal and meaningful than the usual cartoons and pinups of office homesteading. No one notices them but they're there, near-invisible, and count for something.

Lila Mae closes the door and squeezes between the cars: it's past seven and none of the night shift have left yet, which hasn't happened in the three years she's been with the Department. She doesn't have a plan yet, figures she has at least until the press conference is over before she has to meet Chancre, and that much time to get her story straight. Unfortunately, Lila Mae realizes, she turned in her inspection report on the Briggs building yesterday afternoon, and even if she could think of a way to sneak into Processing, past Miss Bally and her girls, they would have already removed it. As evidence. How long before they pull in Internal Affairs, if they haven't already? No one owes her any favors. After three years she doesn't owe any favors and no one owes her any back, which was how she liked it up 'til now. She is reconsidering her position. Maybe Chuck.

"How's she running today?" Jimmy asks. The young mechanic always says that when Lila Mae comes in from the field, figuring that his consistency and friendly shop talk will one day seem worth it, fondly recollected as a period of prehistoric innocence in their romance. He didn't sneak up on her really—Lila Mae was just too preoccupied to notice his wiry body canter out of the office across the cement. She's not too preoccupied, however, to notice that his daily query sounds uncertain today, the usual ambiguity over whether he is asking about Lila Mae or the Department sedan even more confused. He is smiling, however, and Lila Mae thinks maybe things aren't that bad after all.

Lila Mae asks, "What are all these cars still doing here?"

"They're all listening to Chancre and the Mayor talk about the building." He's not sure how much to say, or how to say it. He pulls his rag from the back pocket of his overalls and twists and bends it.

It's going to be like pulling teeth. After all this time, Lila Mae is not sure if Jimmy is just shy or dim-witted. Whenever she decides for sure one way, Jimmy does something to make her reconsider, initiating another few months' speculation. "They're talking about the Fanny Briggs building, right?"

"Yes," Jimmy says.

"And what happened to it?" She's taking it step by step. She is very aware that her time is running out.

"Something happened and the elevator fell. There's been a lot of fuss about it and—everybody—in the garage—is saying that you did it." Sucks in his breath: "And that's what they're saying on the radio, too."

"It's okay, Jimmy. Just one more thing—is the day shift upstairs or are they in O'Connor's?"

"I heard some of them say they were going over to O'Connor's to listen to Chancre." The poor kid is shaking. He stopped smiling some time ago.

"Thank you, Jimmy," Lila Mae says. Up the ramp, out onto the street, and it's three stores over to O'Connor's. She can probably make it without being seen by the people at the entrance. If Chuck is there. On her way out, Lila Mae grabs Jimmy's shoulder and tells him she's running fine. Fibbing of course.

* * *

Lila Mae has one friend in the Department and his name is Chuck. Chuck's red hair is chopped and coaxed into a prim Safety, which helps him fit in with the younger inspectors in the Department. According to Chuck, the haircut is mandatory at the Midwestern Institute for Vertical Transport, his alma mater as of last spring. Item one (or close to it) in the *Handbook for Students.* Even the female students have to wear Safeties, making for so many confused, wrenching swivels that Midwestern's physician christened the resulting campus-wide epidemic of bruised spinal muscles "Safety Neck." Chuck's theory is that the Safety's reemergence is part of an oozing conservatism observable in every facet of the elevator industry, from this season's minimalist cab designs to the return of the sturdy T-rail after the ill-fated flirtation with round, European guardrails. Says he. Been too many changes in the Guild over the last few years—just look at the messy rise of Intuitionism, or the growing numbers of women and colored people in the Guild, shoot, just look at Lila Mae, flux itself, three times cursed. Inevitably the cycle's got to come back around to what the Old Dogs want. "Innovation and regression," Chuck likes to tell Lila Mae over lunch, lunch usually being a brown-bag negotiation over squeezed knees in the dirty atrium of the Metzger Building a few blocks from the office. "Back and forth, back and forth." Or up and down, Lila Mae adds to herself.

Chuck maintains that after a quick tour of duty running the

streets, he intends to park himself at a Department desk job for a while and then pack it up to teach escalators at the Institute. Chuck's a shrewd one. Given elevator inspection's undeniable macho cachet and preferential treatment within the Guild, it takes a unique personality to specialize in escalators, the lowliest conveyance on the totem pole. Escalator safety has never received its due respect, probably because inspecting the revolving creatures is so monotonous that few have the fortitude, the stomach for vertigo, necessary to stare at the cascading teeth all day. But Chuck can live with the obscurity and disrespect and occasional migraines. Specialization means job security, and there's a nationwide lack of escalator professors in the Institutes, so Chuck figures he's a shoo-in for a teaching job. And once he's in there, drawing a bead on tenure, he can branch out from escalators and teach whatever he wants. He probably even has his dream syllabus tucked in his pocket at this very moment, scratched on a cheap napkin. A general survey course on the history of hydraulic elevators, for example—Chuck's kooky for hydraulics, from Edoux's 1867 direct-action monstrosity to the latest rumors on the hybrids Arbo Labs has planned for next year's fall line. Or hypothetical elevators; hypothetical elevator studies is bound to come back into vogue again, now that the furor has died down. Chuck's assured Lila Mae that even though he is a staunch Empiricist, he'll throw in the Intuitionist counterarguments where necessary. His students should be acquainted with the entire body of elevator knowledge, not just the canon. Chuck feels his future in the Guild is assured. For now, in one ear and out the other with all the "tread jockey" jokes.

No jokes or other forms of gentle and not-so-gentle ribbing right now, however: Chuck has been more or less accepted by the rest of the Department after a brief period of imperceptible hazing (imperceptible to New Guys like Chuck and perennial outsiders like Lila Mae on account that most of it consists of secret code words and birdlike hand gestures only members recognize, let

21

alone notice), and besides, tonight everyone's crowded around the radio listening to the press conference. The big news. Lila Mae, having crept out of the garage and walked over to O'Connor's so tentatively that anyone watching her would have thought her to have just that morning discovered her legs, is not surprised to find her colleagues listening to the radio describe an event unfolding a scant hundred yards away. They could have easily joined the newsmen outside the front of HQ, but that would have been too direct. The trip is everything to elevator inspectors—the bumps and shudders, not the banalities of departure and destination—and if the radio waves must first amble from the reporters' microphones to the receiver atop the WCAM Building and dally there a bit before returning (nearly) to the humble spot of their nativity, so much the better. The intrinsic circuitousness of inspecting appeases certain dustier quarters of her and her colleagues' mentalities, the very neighborhoods, it turns out, where the key and foundational character deficits reside. Nobody's quite up to investigating those localities, or prepared to acknowledge or remark upon them anyway; to do so would lead to instructive, yes, but no doubt devastating revelations about their jobs, about themselves. They're that important. Really. The first one to suggest they go over to O'Connor's to hear Chancre and the Mayor, the one who made it easy for them to indulge their widening array of avoidances and circumabulations, is probably drinking free all night.

The day shift and the night shift are firmly installed in slouching semicircles around O'Connor's radio, which is enshrined behind the bar underneath an emerald neon shamrock. She spots Chuck's red hair halfway into the pack. The wolves are intent on the sounds. On the radio, the Mayor says we'll get to the bottom of this affair, pillory the guilty parties, launch a full-scale investigation into the terrible accident at the Fanny Briggs building, dedicated to one of our country's most distinguished daughters.

"Do you think that a party or parties resistant to colored progress may be responsible?" a reporter asks the Mayor, to much furious murmuring in O'Connor's. Everyone thinks, as they must, of last summer's riots, of how strange it was to live in a metropolis such as this (magnificent elevated trains, five daily newspapers, two baseball stadiums) and yet be too afraid to leave the house. How quickly things can fall into medieval disorder.

"Right now we're hesitant to speculate on who may or may not be responsible," the Mayor says. "We don't want to inflame any emotions or incite the baser impulses. I was present at the scene and all I know is that there was a great clanging, a loud clang-alang, and much confusion, and I knew that something terrible had transpired at the Fanny Briggs Memorial Building. Right now we're concentrating on the facts at hand, such as the inspection records. But Mr. Chancre, the Chair of the Department of Elevator Inspectors, will be handling those questions. Mr. Chancre?"

Needless to say, Lila Mae doesn't frequent O'Connor's very often, usually just on the Department's bowling nights, when it's just her and Chuck and the resident alcoholics, this latter party posing no threat except to clean floors. Because her father taught her that white folks can turn on you at any moment. She fears for her life in O'Connor's because she believes that the unexpected scrape of a chair across the floor or a voice's sudden intensity contains the potentiality of a fight. On the few occasions Lila Mae has been in O'Connor's during the broadcast of a baseball game or a boxing match, every cheer sent her looking for makeshift weapons. It doesn't help matters that the bartender rings a large brass bell when a patron doesn't tip; she jumps every time. Jumps at that sound and at the starter's pistol they fire to quell disagreements, heated exchanges over the various merits and drawbacks of heat dispersal in United Elevator's braking systems, say. They can turn rabid at any second; this is the true result of gathering integration: the replacement of sure violence with deferred sure violence. Her position is precarious in the office, she understands that, and in O'Connor's as well; she's a lost tourist among heavy vowels, the crude maps of ancestral homelands, and the family crests of near-exterminated clans. Her position is precarious everywhere she goes in this city, for that matter, but she's trained dread to keep invisible in its ubiquity, like fire hydrants and gum trod into black sidewalk spackle. Makeshift weapons include shoes, keys and broken bottles. Pool cues if they're handy.

"I'll bet you ten dollars Chancre makes a campaign speech."

"Sucker bet."

Peril tonight especially. Imagine it like this: Everything known is now different.

"She really put her foot in it now."

"Her and the rest of that bunch, by Roland."

"Chancre's a cinch now."

Never mind that Lila Mae hasn't been in a fight since the third grade, when a young blonde girl with horse teeth asked her, *Why do niggers have curly hair?*

"That's what happens when you let freaks and misfits into the Guild."

"Shut up—I want to hear the man."

The first thing a colored person does when she enters a white bar is look for other colored people. There is only one other colored person besides Lila Mae who ever ventures past the sneering leprechaun who cavorts on O'Connor's door, and that's Pompey, who's here tonight, elbows on the bar, sipping whiskey daintily as if it were the Caliph's tea, the cuffs of his shirt bold out of sad and comically short jacket sleeves. The bartender sweeps away empty glasses with a clockhand's impatience so there's no estimating the margin of safety. For Lila Mae, not Pompey. These men would never hurt Pompey, little Pompey, who surely would have commanded some limp mare at the racetrack had he not found his illustrious vocation. (Or it found him, for there's something akin to fatal resignation in the inspectors' attitude toward their life's work.) Here's a story about Pompey that's true or not true: it doesn't matter. One time George Holt, Chancre's predecessor, called Pompey into his office near quitting time. The Guild

24

Chair's office is on the executive floor above the Pit, and since reprimands and termination notices arrive in official Department interoffice mail envelopes, invitations upstairs are universally regarded as omens of good fortune. Promotions, plum assignments, keys to the better sedans. Again: Pompey, the first colored elevator inspector in the city, is summoned up to see Holt for the first time, after putting in four years on the streets. The difficulty of all colored "firsts" is well documented or at the very least easily imaginable, and need not be elaborated except to say that Pompey had an exceedingly hard time of things. When Holt called him upstairs, Pompey believed his appallingly obsequious nature, cultivated to exceptional degree during his time in the Department, had finally served him well. Holt had never spoken to him before and Pompey found him surprisingly affable. Holt offered him a cigar, the scent of which Pompey was well acquainted with, as it lingered in random pockets of the Department's hallways and offices, marking where Holt had walked and surveyed, an acrid reminder of authority: bodiless, unseen, everywhere. Pompey brushed his tongue across the inside of his cheeks to forage the residue of the faintly cinnamon smoke, the very wisps of Holt's esteem. He expected confidences; Holt told him he was going to kick him in the ass. Pompey laughed (this executive humor was going to take a little getting used to) and went along with the joke, even after Holt told him to bend over. Which he did. Pompey continued to chortle until Holt kicked him in the left ass cheek with the arrowhead of one of his burgundy wingtips (Pompey's angle of vision precluded determination of exactly which shoe). Then Holt told him to leave his office. The next day a small memo appeared on Pompey's desk informing him of his promotion to Inspector Second Grade. True, Holt didn't first ask him to shine the shoe. And he got to keep the cigar.

Lila Mae hadn't heard the story until Chuck told her about it. Far from explaining Pompey's animus toward her, the story merely obscured matters. Did Pompey resent Lila Mae for presenting them with a more exotic token, thus diluting their hatred toward him, the hatred that had calcified over time into something he came to cherish and savor as friendship; or were his haughty stares and keen disparagements his attempt at a warning against becoming him, and thus an aspect of racial love? Pompey says now, "She's finally getting what's been coming to her for a long time now," and Halitosis Harry smacks him on the back in agreement. Nobody's spotted her yet except for the bartender, who's too much of a pro to say anything. She's not hiding exactly, but most of her body is secreted behind a pillar conveniently situated between the door and the crowd at the radio. The same leering leprechaun on the front door of O'Connor's shimmies on the pillar in triplicate. Or maybe she is hiding. She's not sure. She doesn't know how to get Chuck's attention. He's been quiet through all of it. One of her colleagues lets fly a rolling rebel yell at something Chancre just said.

"Is it true that the inspector was an Intuitionist?" a reporter asks.

"Yes, the inspector of the Fanny Briggs building, a Miss Lila Mae Watson, is an Intuitionist. I'm real reluctant to turn this terrible affair into a political matter, but I'm sure most of you are well aware that my opponent in the election for Guild Chair is also an Intuitionist."

Lila Mae realizes that the time she spent thinking about how to navigate O'Connor's would have been better spent listening to the radio or simply going up to Chuck and grabbing him out of the mob. That would have surprised them. But now she's no more wiser than when she entered.

"Do you think that Intuitionist methods, which in the past you have described as 'heretical and downright voodoo,' may have played a part in today's crash?"

"Right now Internal Affairs is looking into that very possibility. We have a copy of the building's inspection report and believe me, we are scrutinizing and cogitating as I speak. Gentlemen, it's just these very kinds of occurrences I have been trying to eradicate in my four years as Guild Chair, and I don't think I'm being immodest when I tell you I think I've made a pretty good go of it. Our Department sedans are shiny as never before and morale has never been so high. It's almost scary. Sometimes people ask me how I made this Department the crown jewel, the very pearl of city services. I tell them that sometimes the old ways are the best ways. Why hold truck with the uppity and newfangled when Empiricism has always been the steering light of reason? Just like it was in our fathers' day, and our fathers' fathers'. Today's incident is just the kind of unfortunate mishap that can happen when you kowtow to the latest fashions from overseas. We're going to get to the bottom of this, gentlemen, I can give you my blood oath on that little crawdaddy."

It occurs to her that now she doesn't have an alibi either, just like the anonymous wraiths on the side of the highway. No one knows who they are.

*   *   *

Not that Lila Mae couldn't use some excitement in her life, as the two men searching her apartment are discovering through items and effects. Jim's on his knees in Lila Mae's closet, forcing his plump fingers into her shoes and testing the heels for secret hiding places. She has one pair of worn sneakers, left over from when she first moved to the city and spent long hours on trudging marches between the buildings. Each time she came to the city's edges and saw the churning brown rivers beyond, Lila Mae would hit a right angle and turn back into the buildings, deeper in. She'd never experienced anonymity like that: it's as if the place stimulates enzymes that form a carapace. The walks petered out about a year ago. Now she sits. The rest of her footwear consists of Department-reg wingtips, shined to obsessive gleam in the wake of Chancre's image crusade. She has five pairs of them, arranged to the days of the work week. Friday's pair is missing.

Jim's already searched every pocket of her clothes, traced every stitch. Find it, is his motto. Jim's the more obvious of this duo, sworn to his day's specific orders. Today's are "get evidence." John's the philosophically inclined one, prone to staring moodily out of the attic window of the house he lives in with his parents. Continuing to stare out even after Louisa, his next-door neighbor, has finished undressing and turned out the lights. John needs patterns, and labors after them even when circumstances betray him. Because there must be patterns, experience is recursive, and if the pattern has not announced itself yet, it will, eloquent and emphatic in a mild-mannered sort of way. He's still searching for a concordance between the loss of his virginity (purchased) and an ankle sprain (accidental) exactly three years later, give or take an hour. John is sure it will come, awaiting another item in the series or a new perspective on the extant ones. No matter. For now he satisfies himself with an appraisal of Lila Mae's clothes, which gently brush over Jim's bent back. Very few casual clothes, and what there are of them favor autumnal spectra: damp browns, rust, brittle grays. Her four dark blue suits (one, again, is missing) are identical, describing, John thinks, a pathological affinity for regularity, the constant and true. An attempt to fit in that unavoidably calls attention to itself. It appeases John's societal schemata that Lila Mae is of the colored persuasion.

Jim and John are white, and thanks to the vagaries of statistical distribution, average citizens of this country. Contrary to the universal constant of partners, Jim and John are not tall and short, fat and skinny, jaunting into comic dissimilarity. They look alike, and look like a great number of other people. Their fraternity glut the police files of known assailants; they reach for the grocer's last box of cereal to prevent the next customer from enjoying it, and don't even like cereal. Banks are full of them, and movie theaters

28

and public transport. The invisible everymen, the true citizens. Lila Mae counts few people in this world as friends. Jim and John are the rest. Dusty brown clumps of hair, prow jaws, complexions quick to blood. Eaters of steak, fat gobblers, belchers. (The Department of Elevator Inspectors is overflowing with men like this, but don't be fooled by their officious demeanors and methodical bent: these guys aren't Department.) Hot dogs and mustard is Jim's favorite meal, mustard being a discreet element and not mere condiment. John likes hamburgers with ketchup—fine distinctions are not lost on John, who is the sort that prides himself on knowing what is what. With regards to their present duty, what's what is that they haven't found what they are looking for.

Two rooms: a main room with just enough space to prevent Lila Mae from being trampled by herself, and a smaller cube that barely accommodates a bed and dresser. A plant, a piggy bank, a plastic pear. Her few possessions are aloof in their perches, on sills and tables, confident that their ranks will not grow and that the competition for Lila Mae's attention (or lack thereof) will remain as it has been for some time. What strikes John the most is the studied appearance of habitation. She is trying to convince other people that she lives here, but the impression instead is that of slow moving-out, piece by piece. Nothing rattles in the piggy bank.

"This place must get a lot of light," John says. Outside of Lila Mae's window, the red bulb on top of a radio tower blinks slow as a lizard.

"A lot of light," Jim replies.

"How much do you think she pays for this place?"

"I wouldn't live in this neighborhood if you paid me," Jim says without regret.

The neighborhood is tidal, receding and dilating according to the exigencies of the city. Years before, a rich man decided to erect a monument to himself, an elevated train that traversed the city, even in neighborhoods, like this one, which were not even neighborhoods yet, but stubborn farmland scattered with the wooden houses of optimistic citizens. Pig pens and goats. To justify the trains and the rich man's romance, speculators assembled dreary and sturdy tenements and directed immigrants' inquiries north, to the new territory. The train justified itself in due course and the speculators did quite well for themselves—there was a destination now, the harbor disgorged hundreds daily, and they had to live somewhere. The neighborhood named itself, created a persona: optimistic, scrabbling, indebted to the grand new country of which it was merely a small and insignificant part. Then the coloreds surged and dreamed of the north, too. They had been told something and believed it. One by one, the lights in the windows of the Poles' and Russians' apartments extinguished, and when the windows blazed again, it was a colored light that burned within them. The neighborhood retained its old name, but it meant something very different. Never mind that a few Poles and Russians continued to operate grocery and butcher stores and occasionally extend credit; no one doubted that the neighborhood's new meaning prevailed, for the Poles and Russians turned out the lights in their stores at nightfall and scurried back on the elevated trains to their new neighborhood. The neighborhood is changing again. Its meaning blurs at the edges as white people return, obeying the city's rules of teeming density and insidious rents. Only the real estate agents, who understand that meaning is elastic, know the borders of the neighborhood for sure, modulating their sales pitches to reassure their clients that they are not moving into the colored neighborhood, but into the farther reaches of the adjacent white neighborhood. None of this impresses Jim, who would not move into the neighborhood if you paid him.

There is no elevator in Lila Mae's building. She has two paintings on the walls of her gloomy abode, amateur landscape watercolors. Like the art in motel rooms: fits in with the general atmosphere of Lila Mae's apartment. John picks up the one photograph in the apartment, which rests on the end table next to Lila Mae's grim, scarecrow couch. Right now Lila Mae is only a few blocks away from her apartment, but when her father shot the picture ten years before, she stood on the porch of her childhood home with her mother, skinny and quiet. The denuded light and sad lethargy of the tableau says late summer: the cold months are coming. Lila Mae seems comfortable with this knowledge. Hers is essentially a sad face, inward-tending and declivitous, a face that draws the unwary into the slope of its melancholy. Something in the bones, and inherited, John decides after an appraisal of her mother. Children are doomed to reiterate the mistakes in their parents' physiognomies, as if trapped by curses that mark generations and wait for unknowable acts of atonement. Jim's parents are obviously close kin, and if you ask him he won't deny it.

At one point she got a bird, but it died.

John notices Jim rubbing his jaw. "Tooth still hurting you?" he asks.

Jim nods solemnly.

"You better go to the dentist tomorrow," John advises. "No use walking around in pain if you don't have to be."

John discovers Lila Mae's books in a ziggurat stack beneath the end table. They're all work books, the standard texts: Zither's *An Introduction to Counterweights*, *Elisha Otis: The Man and His Times* and so on. She has all of Fulton's books, from the groundbreaking *Towards a System of Vertical Transport*, to the more blasphemous parts of his oeuvre, *Theoretical Elevators* Volumes One and Two. So far their information has been correct, as it always is.

"Looks like a real blue-ribbon type," John decides, flipping through *Guidebook to Elevator Safety* for incriminating papers.

"You always call 'em," Jim says.

"She's got all the right books."

"You always call 'em," Jim says.

Jim and John are neat ransackers. When their cases return to their homes, they suffer only the vaguest sense of loss, a nagging perplexity, and with so many other possible causes of that sense of loss, few suspect that these two men have been pawing their things. John sees himself as a crucial gear in the city's mechanism, a freelance poltergeist of metropolitan disquiet. Jim and John's employers are proud of them, and when they receive their briefing on tonight's activities, Jim and John will not be reprimanded for failure. The particular organization they work for can afford to forgive, as long as that forgiveness is tracked and tabulated like absenteeism, pencil theft, fire damage (accident, insurance fraud), and at the end of each quarter, the books tally.

What Jim and John are missing is the safe behind the somber painting of haystacks. Where she keeps all of her important things. Perhaps John would have found the safe eventually if Lila Mae hadn't disturbed their search. It takes her a few attempts to realize that the reason she can't unlock her door is because it is already unlocked. Jim and John do not take the time allowed by Lila Mae's clicking and fumbling to clamber down the fire escape, or hide in the closet, or pull out their guns and recline on Lila Mae's couch in a rather labored we've-got-you-covered pose, no, they continue to shake the joint down and that's how Lila Mae finds them, John scrutinizing a pile of receipts from the middle left hand drawer of Lila Mae's sad afterthought of a kitchenette— you never know what notations can be encrypted into a seemingly innocuous phrase such as "Bob's Grocery: A Place to Shop" or in the numerical fortress of "prices" and "taxes"—and Jim scraping a finger through the jar of peach preserves Lila Mae received last Christmas from her mother's sister, checking for little treasures like bus station locker keys and microfilm, microfilm, which Jim has never encountered in all his searches through so many apartments, but will one day, he's sure of it. That's how Lila Mae finds them, John peering, one big eye, through a magnifying glass and Jim licking his fingers. Given obscenity's remarkable gallop into conversational speech, colorful epithets are to be expected in Lila Mae's address to the two strangers lurking about her apartment.

But it is John who is the first to speak. He says, "You're the little lady."

*   *   *

The counterweight, conscripted into service by the accident, rockets into the aerie of the shaft, angry with new velocity.

*   *   *

Only Chuck knows for sure whether it is his congenitally weak bladder (family lore tells of three aunts and a cousin with the same affliction) or his distaste for Chancre's unabashed politicking that makes him rise from his leatherette stool and pad over to O'Connor's scary toilet facilities. Chancre is still spinning out today's accident into a stump speech on the accomplishments of his four years as Guild—and hence Department—Chair. The election is just around the corner, after all, and Chuck (a clever man, but not precocious about it) knows Chancre's game. This press conference allows Chancre to reach members of the Elevator Inspectors Guild who no longer work for the city, the "unactives" who have retired from the lonesome life running the streets, have secluded themselves behind the ivy gates of the Institute for Vertical Transport or entered into the private sector, consulting the dolts from United and American and Arbo on what elevators are really about, the secrets the shafts have to tell to those who know how to listen. The men in the Department are Chancre's, mostly Empiricists, he's seen to that, but the unactives are a mercurial bunch, tending to cranky, nonpartisan dispositions. And they vote. Anyone who's a member of the EIG votes every four years on the new Guild Chair, and the Guild Chair automatically becomes the head of the city's Department of Elevator (and escalator, Chuck adds) Inspectors. Chuck still doesn't know how this arrangement between the Guild and the city came about, and when he asks one of the Old Dogs about it, they change the subject and look nervous. Chuck hasn't been able to find anything on paper about it, not even in the silent archives of the Institute, not a single precedent, but nevertheless: the Guild members elect their Chair, and the Chair gets a nice government job. Chuck supposes that if an incumbent lost his reelection bid, he could conceivably refuse to budge and cling to his cushy leather chair for dear life, but that's never happened. Chuck can see Chancre doing it, though, and as he walks into the alcove in front of O'Connor's bathrooms he wonders what would happen then.

She pulls him into the ladies' room before he knows what happened. The ladies' room in O'Connor's was designed to accommodate one person. Two people is cozy, and three is scandalous, but that's how many are in there now: Chuck, Lila Mae and Piefaced Annie. Piefaced Annie, she of the gravely mug, is passed out on the toilet, as she always is at this time of day. O'Connor's lone female alcoholic, Piefaced Annie puts in a long day and needs this time to rest up for the long final lap of the day's drinking. She doesn't look passed out so much as eerily blissful, almost as if . . . Lila Mae has already taken her pulse just in case. It was a short scurry from her flimsy hiding place in the bar to the bathrooms; she started when she saw Chuck rise and made it around the corner before he'd even escaped the crowd. In the spirit of decency, Lila Mae pushed Piefaced Annie's legs together from their aerated generosity.

Chuck is equally disturbed by three things: the ease of his kidnapping, which insults his sense of alertness; the unfamiliarity of being in a ladies' bathroom, which brings to his mind an unsettling flash of his mother squatting; and the surety that Lila Mae is going to drag him into this deplorable business about the Fanny Briggs building. "Lila Mae," he says, "I don't think this is very appropriate." He can feel the wet sink dampen the backs of his thighs.

"Sorry about this, Chuck," she replies, "but I have to know what happened today."

"You haven't checked in upstairs yet?"

"I wanted to be prepared."

In the end, it is Piefaced Annie's resemblance to his mother that upsets Chuck the most. He feels like a dirty little boy, standing in the dank cubicle with her. Compared to that, talking with a fugitive from Departmental justice is small potatoes. He looks up at the yellow water stains on the ceiling and tells Lila Mae, "One of the elevators in the Fanny Briggs stack went into total freefall this afternoon. The Mayor was showing off the place to some guys from the French embassy so they could see how great the city works and whatnot. He presses the call button and boom! the cab crashes down. Luckily there was no one on it."

For the first time it occurs to Lila Mae that someone might have been hurt. "That's impossible. Total freefall is a physical impossibility." She shakes her head.

"That's what happened," Chuck reaffirms. He's still looking up at the ceiling. They can hear some of their colleagues whooping outside the door. "Forty floors."

"Which one?"

"Number Eleven, I think."

She remembers Number Eleven distinctly. A little shy, but that's normal in a new cab. "The entire stack is outfitted with the new Arbo antilocks," Lila Mae argues. "Plus the standard reg gear. I inspected them myself."

"Did you see them," Chuck asks tentatively, "or did you intuit them?"

Lila Mae ignores the slur. "I did my job," she says.

"Maybe you missed something."

"I did my job," Lila Mae says. She hears her voice rising: keep cool. "What did Chancre say?"

"Had the Mayor in his office ever since it happened," Chuck says, attempting to be helpful. "So I don't know what the official

35

story is, but you get the gist from his speech. He's making it into a political thing because you're an Intuitionist. And colored, but he's being clever about it."

"I heard that bit."

"Internal Affairs is looking for you."

"What are the guys saying?"

"What you would expect," Chuck tells her. Piefaced Annie groans and he shivers.

"Total freefall? You're sure?" There's no way. The cables, for one thing.

"Yes, I'm sure," he says. "Lila Mae, I think you should really go upstairs and talk to the IAB guys. Even if you did miss something—however much you don't want to admit that possibility—the sooner you go and talk to them, the better it's going to go. They're fair. You know that."

"That would be standard procedure," Lila Mae muses. "But this isn't a standard accident."

"You should really go upstairs, I'm telling you. There's nothing else you can do in a situation like this."

"Chuck, look at me." She's decided. "You haven't seen me, okay?"

"This is ridiculous."

"Tell me you haven't seen me."

"I haven't seen you."

One of the side effects of people intent on erasing you from their lives is that sometimes they erase you when it might not be beneficial. It would have been delightful for Lila Mae's fellows in the Department of Elevator Inspectors to see her leave the ladies' room, because they could have enjoyed a few furious moments of invective, of throaty howls. No one sees Lila Mae when she departs O'Connor's and it's their loss. The newsmen outside headquarters are scrabbling away across the sidewalk like dry leaves in the wind. Midtown is clearing out. No one lives in midtown.

Lila Mae has decided to go home. She needs a night to go over exactly what happened at the Fanny Briggs Memorial Building. She can pretend that she didn't hear about the accident until tomorrow morning. Plausible. And she has a good face for telling lies. She's on the subway platform when the problem of the dispatcher occurs to her. Craig told her she had to report to base. The subway arrives: she'll say she thought it was a paperwork thing that could wait until Monday. That lie could cause her some trouble with IAB, but it's not totally implausible. Even if they don't believe her, they can't discipline her unless she was negligent, and Lila Mae will not allow the possibility that she was negligent. It's impossible.

When Piefaced Annie shakes off her stupor, she will recall a strange dream about elevators and falling, and will chalk it up to falling off the toilet, which will happen in about an hour.

*　　*　　*

From *Theoretical Elevators*, Volume One, by James Fulton:

We do not know what is next. If we were to take a barbarian and place him, loincloth and all, before one of our magnificent cities, what would he feel? He would feel fear, doubly: the fear of his powerlessness before our architectural excess and our fear, the thing that drives our architectural excess. The dread of imperfection. We do not need cities and buildings; it is the fear of the dark which compels us to erect them instinctively, like insects. Perspective is the foot-soldier of relativity. Just as the barbarian would gaze upon our cities and buildings with fear and incomprehension, so would we gaze upon future cities and future buildings. Is the next building ovoid, pyramidic? Is the next elevator a bubble or is it shaped like a sea shell, journeying both outward and into itself . . .

37

Take capacity. The standard residential elevator is designed to accommodate 12 passengers, all of whom we assume to be of average weight and form. This is the Occupant's Fallacy. The number 12 does not consider the morbidly obese, or the thin man's convention and necessity of speedy conveyance at the thin man's convention. We conform to objects, we capitulate to them. We need to reverse this order. It is failure that guides evolution; perfection provides no incentive for improvement, and nothing is perfect. Nothing we create works the way it should. The car overheats on the highway, the electric can opener cannot open the can. We must tend to our objects and treat them as newborn babes. Our elevators are weak. They tend to get colds easily, they are forgetful. Our elevators ought to be variable in size and height, retractable altogether, impervious to scratches, self-cleaning, possessing a mouth. The thin man's convention can happen at any time; indeed, they happen all the time . . .

*　　*　　*

What else can she say? His statement is friendly, steeped in chummy argot, the intonation jovial, and the man's face so banal and uncomplicated, so like this country, that Lila Mae almost thinks she knows him. When the man says, "You're the little lady," all she thinks to say is, "I guess I am."

Pause. Jim nods knowingly.

"What the hell are you doing in my apartment?" Lila Mae demands.

"What do you think we're doing?" John responds. "We're going over your place looking for evidence."

Pause. Jim, again, nods knowingly. Actually, it's more of an involuntary response to getting caught in the act, despite the reassurances of John's cool act.

"Internal Affairs doesn't have that kind of authority," Lila Mae says curtly, "whether I checked in after my shift or not. Get the hell out of my apartment." There have never been this many people in her apartment before.

Jim and John take a step closer to Lila Mae. A decent lunge and they would have her.

"So we're Internal Affairs?" Jim asks. The burgundy residue of Aunt Sally's preserves glistens on his right forefinger.

"Yes—we're the watchdogs of the Elevator Inspector Industry," John seconds.

"Department," Jim says. He licks the remaining preserves off his finger.

"We're the watchdogs of the Elevator Inspectors Department," John says.

"The Department of Elevator Inspectors," Jim corrects.

John takes advantage of Jim's distraction to flip his magnifying glass into the air and catch it. Scare her. He makes a sudden fake forward, grinning, but Lila Mae stifles her flight-response. Damned if she's going to look weak. Her visitors' absurd wordplay annoys her, perhaps even more than their trespass into her home, her one safe place. She has spent a lot of time trying to find the correct arrangement of things. She never has guests, sure, but there is always the off chance. Sure. "Let me see some identification," Lila Mae demands. "Now."

"Let's show her wink-wink identification," Jim intones.

"That'll be all, gentlemen," a voice behind Lila Mae says. The voice is as smooth as a beach stone. It belongs to a short man in a perfect blue blazer. Pince-nez in this day and age, that's what the man polishes with a handkerchief as he enters Lila Mae's apartment, polishing far too diligently for there to actually be any grit on the lenses. He moves with the rapid movements of a pigeon, and his left arm resembles a wing, pressed close to the body as it is, nooking a leather satchel. He places his hand on Lila Mae's shoulder and it is then that she truly gets scared. She cannot feel

39

his skin but she knows it is cold. "There's no reason for you to be harassing this young lady," he says.

Jim and John look at each other. Throughout the history of their partnership, it's Jim who takes his cues from his comrade, things as subtle as the tilting of a nostril or the vague tremble in the left knee. Jim is not reading any signals from John, and that's a first. They've never been interrupted before. It's so embarrassing.

The stranger, this latest stranger inquires, "Do you know who I am?" as he squeezes Lila Mae's shoulder.

John sighs and answers, "I know your identity, Mr. Reed, and a few biographical details, but can I say I really know you?"

Jim is about to add his usual improv backup to his partner, a dialogic placeholder such as, "Does anyone really know anyone?" or "In the Biblical sense?" but Mr. Reed flicks a hand, dismissing him. Such rubbish. Mr. Reed looks at Lila Mae for the first time. "Miss Watson, did you invite these men into your home?"

Everything is different now, it seems to Lila Mae. Nothing in her apartment appears to have been moved, and yet everything is different. That's how she feels. She doesn't feel as if she lives here anymore. Lila Mae looks down at Mr. Reed, for he is a short man, shorter than Lila Mae, and she says, "No, I did not." She doesn't live here.

"If I may be so bold . . ." Mr. Reed begins. His eyes are wide and far apart. Like a pigeon's. Lila Mae nods. Mr. Reed looks back to Jim and John and says, "Gentlemen, I must insist that you leave this place immediately."

John shakes his left kneecap in his trousers and Jim places the jar of preserves on the kitchen counter, screwing the top back as he does so. Even though he's been found out, habit tells him not to leave a trace. "Immediately," John mimics, trying to save face through his characteristic deadpan sass, which is now halfhearted and at best a face-saving gesture.

"Immediately," Jim says.

Jim and John head for the dim hallway outside Lila Mae's

apartment. They keep a safe distance from Lila Mae and the diminutive Mr. Reed. John takes the doorknob into his hand and says, "You want this open or closed?"

Mr. Reed looks at Lila Mae. "Open," she says.

Jim and John don't speak until they reach the landing of the floor below, and Lila Mae can't make out what they say. She hears words, though, and the sound is a loud buzzing in her ears incommensurate with the actual volume. She feels dizzy but hides it well. She doesn't know Mr. Reed from Adam. So far he's just another white man with an attitude, never mind his keen sense of timing. "Mr. Reed, is it then?" she asks.

"Mr. Reed, yes," Mr. Reed says. "I'm Orville Lever's secretary. He sent me to fetch you."

"I don't need fetching. Though I suppose I should thank you for helping me out there." Lila Mae walks over to the sullen kitchenette and returns the jar of preserves to the icebox. Then she thinks better of it and drops it in the trash.

"It was my pleasure, Miss Watson. If I may?"

"Have a seat," Lila Mae offers. She has little choice.

"I'm not sure if you fully realize the difficult position you're in, Miss Watson. Today's accident has some very disturbing repercussions."

"Which is why the Intuitionist candidate for Guild Chair has seen fit to send someone over to look after me. I don't think I need looking after."

"May I ask you a question? Why didn't you report back to the Department after your shift?"

"I was tired."

"It is standard operating procedure after an accident to report to your superiors, is it not?"

"I didn't know there was an accident until I saw the late edition on the train home."

"I think we should be going, Miss Watson. I wouldn't advise staying here tonight."

41

"This is my home."

"And if I hadn't stopped in?"

"I would have taken care of them."

"My car is waiting downstairs. You inspected the Fanny Briggs building, did you not?"

"You know I did."

"Then what went wrong?"

Nothing went wrong.

"You are aware, Miss Watson, that those men weren't from Internal Affairs, yes?"

"Yes."

"Then who were they?"

Nothing.

"Has it occurred to you yet that you were set up?"

The accident is impossible. It wasn't an accident.

Even if Jim and John had found Lila Mae's safe behind the painting, the contents wouldn't have interested them, except to flesh out John's coveted psychological profile of this night's subject. A soccer trophy from high school (everyone on the team got one, even Lila Mae, who sat on the bench all season and only joined the squad at her mother's urging she "be social"). Her high school graduation ring (poor craftsmanship). A love letter from a dull boy, her diploma from the Institute for Vertical Transport, and her prizewinning paper on theoretical elevators. Not much, really.

* * *

Her father dropped her off in front of the place where she was to live and left the engine running. Lila Mae removed the two suitcases from the back of the pickup truck. The suitcases were new, with a formidable casing of green plastic. Scratchproof, supposedly. Her father had only been able to afford them because they were, manufacturer's oaths aside, scratched—gouged actually, as if an animal had taken them in its fangs to teach them about hubris.

42

Marvin Watson was proud of his daughter. She was doing what he had never been able to do: she was studying to be an elevator inspector. His pride was limned with shame over these circumstances. He had long dreamed of the day when he would drive his only daughter, his baby and blood, off to school; and here it was. But he did not leave the pickup and did not look up at the building in which she was to live. He cranked down the window to kiss her goodbye. The old truck hiccuped if it idled for too long, setting everything to a furious tremble, and Lila Mae's lips did not even graze her father's cheek when she leaned over to kiss him goodbye. Her father drove off and never saw the room in which she would live for three years, a converted janitor's closet above the newly renovated gymnasium. They had just renamed the gymnasium after the dashing young heir to a driving-sheave fortune, a gentleman from the country's South who had donated a large sum of money to be spent at the Institute's discretion. Lila Mae lived in the janitor's closet because the Institute for Vertical Transport did not have living space for colored students.

The Institute's campus had formerly been a health spa for rich neurasthenic women from the Northeast's larger cities, which is why the students were never too far from statues of Grecian nymphs, nub-nosed spirits whose long manes eased liquidly into their sagging tunics. The spa failed after newer spas opened in the weatherless regions of the Southwest. Weatherlessness is much more amenable to those in search of succor for bodily complaint, evoking timelessness and immortality, and soon the rich neurasthenic women from the Northeast's larger cities boarded planes to be free of the seasons and the proximity of their braying families, the cause of their disrepair. The elevator magnates who bought the land and refurbished the spa's physical plant into something more suitable for a place of learning were disheartened by the rich suburb the surrounding neighborhood eventually became, and pondered, on winter nights when their wives and children were asleep and the only company was a bottle of aged Irish spirits, how life would have been different if they traded in real estate, and not mechanical conveyance. Verticality is such a risky enterprise.

Lila Mae did not mix much with the other students, who were in turn thankful that she had spared them the burden of false conciliation. As she had when she was in elementary school, she sat in the final row of her classes and did not speak unless there was no other option. She retired early in the evening, shuttering her eyes to the urgent grumblings of the gym's boiler room, whose howls filled the empty building at night like the protestations of wraiths. She rose early in the morning, when the first sunlight crept over the statues of Grecian nymphs before it advanced to the metropolis a few miles to the west. The admission of colored students to the Institute for Vertical Transport was staggered to prevent overlap and any possible fulminations or insurrections that might arise from that overlap. The previous tenant of the janitor's closet had had a sweet tooth. Every cleaning produced yet another crumpled wrapper of Bogart's Chewing Gum. Occasionally professors called Lila Mae by his name, even though it would have been difficult to say there was any resemblance. Lila Mae never pointed out the mistake to her professors, who were a cranky bunch, mostly former field men who had rejected retirement to teach at the most prestigious elevator inspecting school in the country. A black gown is remarkably effective in conferring prestige on even the most rough-hewn of men.

She learned plenty her first semester at the Institute for Vertical Transport. She learned about the animals in the Roman coliseums hoisted to their cheering deaths on rope-tackle elevators powered by slaves, learned about Villayer's "flying chair," a simple pulley, shaft and lead counterweight concoction described in a love letter from Napoleon I to his wife, the Archduchess Marie Louise. About steam, and the first steam elevators. She read about Elisha Graves Otis, the cities he enabled through his glorious invention, and the holy war between the newly deputized elevator inspectors and the elevator companies' maintenance contractors. The rise of safety regulation, safety device innovations, the search for a national standard. She was learning about Empiricism but didn't know it yet.

She remembers when she first saw the light. She was usually so tired by nightfall that she rarely noticed anything except that her room was either too hot or too cold, that the walk down to the public ladies bathroom on the floor below was full of shadows, and that janitors evidently did not need more than a single naked bulb to perform their duties in maintenance closets. The poor illumination gave her headaches when she tried to read. One night she couldn't sleep. Literally—she had to study. All semester, she'd neglected her class on the changing concepts of governmental attitudes toward elevator inspection (the evolution of the machines interested her more, to tell the truth, her first few months there) and now she had to cram for the following morning's exam. Her body didn't like coffee and tea and she rarely stayed up late, so Lila Mae took to pinching her wrist when her head began to dip. Upon rising from one of her unscheduled naps, she noticed a light in Fulton Hall. On the top floor, where the small library was. There shouldn't have been anyone in there, the library closed at dusk—elevator inspectors, even acolytes, generally being morning people. She wondered if the administration had extended the library's hours during exam period; Lila Mae had discovered she was often ignorant of much routine information her fellow students possessed. But the lower floors of Fulton Hall were dark. She decided the light had been left on accidentally and returned to the arid court transcripts of *The United States vs. The Arbo Elevator Company*.

Spring arrived, and a new semester. The work was more difficult than before—she'd discovered Volume One of *Theoretical Elevators* and was having trouble sleeping. One day in February she saw the light again in Fulton Hall. The light wasn't on every night, there was no set schedule she could define, but it was on too frequently for it to be accidental. She couldn't help but notice. Fulton Hall had formerly been the spa's pep center, a wide stone building in the center of campus. Walkways of pink tile radiated from the structure to all the important buildings for the treatment of psychosomatic maladies. Mud Therapy, Colonic Irrigation, Bleeding Chambers. Now the buildings housed Engineering, Advanced Concepts, the Hall of Safety. A pink path also led to the gym, which had also been a gym during the time of the spa, and filled with medicine balls. The path led, more or less, directly from the lit window in Fulton Hall to the janitor's closet where Lila Mae lived.

Occasionally she would see a figure moving through the stacks. She decided it was an old man: He walked with a cane. Sometimes instead of turning on the lights, he used a lantern, and he walked even more slowly then, as if inordinately afraid of dropping it. She saw him about a dozen times in all, and always felt as if they were the last people on earth. It was the same feeling she gets when she's in a shaft, standing on the car. There's an old inspector's maxim: "An elevator is a grave." Such loss and devastation in there. That's why the inside walls of the car are never sheer: they're broken up into panels, equipped with a dorsal rail. Otherwise it would be a box. A coffin. On the nights the figure haunted Fulton Hall, he was Lila Mae's elevator. The thing she stood upon in the darkness of the shaft, just him, just her, and the darkness. In the elevator well, slits of light seep from the door seams on each floor at regular intervals, and do not comfort. The slits of light speak of more light that is out of reach: There will be no redemption.

If she had known the identity of the man on the last night she saw him, would it have changed her response? On that last night he saw her and waved at her, slowly, communicating all he knew and what she already understood about the darkness. Would it have changed her response to his wave (nothing, not even a nod, the polite thing to do) if she had known the man was James Fulton and that the following morning a hungover janitor would discover his body on the library floor, dead of a stroke, the lantern wick still glowing dully? Probably not. That's the kind of person Lila Mae is.

*   *   *

Anyway, slept. In the biggest bed she has ever slept in, swimmable, Lila Mae buoyant despite her negligible body fat (a skinny one, she is). The bed possesses an undertow conducive to dreaming, but she doesn't remember her dreams when she wakes. On waking, her half-dreaming consciousness segues into a recollection of her visit to the Fanny Briggs building. It was simple: that's what Lila Mae is thinking about in her room at 117 Second Avenue.

The lobby of the Fanny Briggs Memorial Building was almost finished when she arrived. As if to distract from the minuscule and cramped philosophy of what would transpire on the floors above, the city offered visitors the spacial bounty of the lobby. The ersatz marble was firm underfoot like real marble, sheer, and produced trembling echoes effortlessly. The circle of Doric columns braced the weight above without complaint. The mural, however, was not complete. It started out jauntily enough to Lila Mae's left. Cheerless Indians holding up a deerskin in front of a fire. The original tenants, sure. A galleon negotiating the tricky channels around the island. Two beaming Indians trading beads to a gang of white men—the infamous sale of the Island. Big moment, have to include that, the first of many dubious transactions in the city's history. (They didn't have elevators yet. That's why the scenes look so flat to Lila Mae: the city is dimensionless.) The mural jumped to the Revolution then, she noticed, skipped over a lot of stuff. The painter seemed to be making it up as he went along, like the men who shaped the city. The Revolution scene was a nice setpiece—the colonists pulling down the statue of King

George III. They melted it down for ammunition, if she remembers correctly. It's always nice when a good mob comes together. The painting ended there. (Someone knocks at the door of her room in 117 Second Avenue, but she doesn't open her eyes.) Judging from the amount of wall space that remained to Lila Mae's right, the mural would have to get even more brief in its chronicle of the city's greatest hits. Either the painter had misjudged how much space he had or the intervening years weren't that compelling to him. Just the broad strokes, please.

The Deputy Undersecretary of Municipal Construction waddled over from the far wall. He said, "You come to see the elevators?" He had the fatty arrogance of all nepotism hires. Somebody's nephew, somebody's sister's boy.

She nodded.

"Is this going to take long? I'm supposed to go on break now." On break from what? Only security guards and janitors ever experience buildings like this. Like fraught ships gnashed between the ice, waiting for that warming current still far off, detained in some other part of the world. The rats hadn't even moved into the building, the roaches still deliberating. A month from now, at this time of day, the lobby will be befouled with citizens. To see a building at this stage, Lila Mae thought, is an honor. The deputy undersecretary was bored and fiddled in his pockets. The muralist's scaffolding tottered above Lila Mae like a rickety gallows.

"Just show me to them," Lila Mae said. It will be easy.

Before Lila Mae can re-create her inspection further, the porter opens the door to her room, despite her silence. He holds the silver platter with hands snug in white gloves. He smiles. She pulls the thick red blankets up to her slight chin.

"I'm sorry to disturb you," he says, "but it seemed a shame to let this nice breakfast go to waste."

"Thank you," Lila Mae says. She sits up against the oak headboard. The headboard's detailed engraving of United's first lift motor digs into her left shoulder. The man sets the platter across her waist. Eggs, ham, juice. Normally when offered so much food early in the morning (a rare occurrence, to be sure) Lila Mae pecks, and politely moves the food around on the plate to maximize the illusion of being eaten. This morning she is grateful.

The porter's mouth is quick to smile. He is a tall and broad fellow, and would almost be menacingly handsome if not for the smile. Lila Mae sees he is a strong man, although his strength is wasted on his petite duties; the white uniform fits him well, but he seems trapped by its starched and creased confines. But we take what jobs we can get, Lila Mae thinks. Whatever we can scrabble for. She doesn't take to it, being waited on by colored people. This is wrong.

He is at the window. "Shall I open the curtains?" he asks.

Lila Mae nods. It's later in the morning than she thought. The light congeals in globs on the leaves of the old trees in the courtyard. The back walls of the adjoining buildings are decrepit compared to the facades they present to the street, but serve their purpose: to fortify against those who might take the treasures of the courtyard. The garden of old money.

Lila Mae is about to dig into her breakfast when she notices that her green suitcase is ajar across the room, next to an imposing-looking bureau. And empty.

"Don't worry," the porter reassures, observing her stare. "It wasn't me. Mrs. Gravely unpacked your things last night. Mr. Reed thought it would make you more comfortable." His eyebrows bow. "What is it?" he asks.

"Nothing," she says. "I'm just tired."

"You don't look tired at all," the porter says. "You're a vision. Like you're up and ready to go."

Hmm. Lila Mae shakes her head and says, "Thanks."

"I mean it," he says through a grin. "This isn't my regular job—my uncle is sick, that's why I'm here. I'm filling in for him.

49

But if I'd known his job had this many extras, I would have come around here before." He extends his hand. "My name is Natchez," he says.

"Lila Mae."

Hmm.

* * *

"Are you with us, Miss Watson?"

"Yes, sir. I was just thinking that—"

"You are aware this is a timed exam?"

"Yes, sir."

"Then we'll begin. 1846."

"Sir William Armstrong designs and manufactures a hydraulic crane. Erected at Newcastle, the crane utilized water pressure from London's mains. Armstrong eventually used the same principles in his weighted accelerator."

"The main function of the pole shader?"

"Is to prevent heating outside the prescribed parameters."

"A citizen has what chance of being in an elevator misfortune?"

"Injury or fatality?"

"Both."

"One in three hundred million and one in six hundred fifty million, respectively."

"Nonmetallic material may be used in T-rails provided what?"

"The rated speed for the car does not exceed zero point seven six meters per second."

"The three types of safety gears?"

"Instantaneous, Instantaneous with buffered effect, and Progressive. Instantaneous type exerts a rapidly increasing pressure on the guide rails during the stopping period. The stopping time and distance are short. These gears can be employed in cars rated for speeds not in excess of zero point seven six meters per second.

Instantaneous type with buffered effect incorporates an elastic system of either energy accumulation or energy dissipation. It generally consists of a system of oil buffers on the lower car frame and safety planks on the guard rails. Effective for rated speeds of up to two point five meters per second. Progressive type applies limited, increasing pressure on the guard rails and is primarily used in Europe on cars with rated speeds of one meter per second or less."

"That was a very full answer."

"Thank you, sir."

"The standard accident curve possesses what shape?"

"The failure rate for elevators is expressed by RT equals one minus FT, where R is reliability, T is time and F is failure. The equation is characterized by a 'bathtub'-shaped curve with three distinct phases. The initial or 'early failure' phase begins with a relatively high incident of accidents—mostly due to installation errors—and then drops off sharply. This is the first wall of the 'bathtub.' The next phase, called the 'random failure' phase, is a plateau and extends for the majority of the elevator's service life. This flat plane is the bottom of the 'bathtub.' The accidents in this phase are unpredictable and generally result from passenger mis-use or poor maintenance. It is also in this phase that the rare 'catastrophic accident' occurs. The curve ascends quickly again in the final, or 'wear-out' phase, when the elevator is past its period of prime use. The opposite wall of the bathtub. Most of these accidents can be prevented, again, by diligent inspection and careful maintenance during this crucial time. May I take a drink of water?"

"Yes. The Four Questions?"

"As put forth by Mettleheim: How did this happen? How could this happen? Is it exceptional? How will it be avoided in the future?"

"The verdict in *The United States vs. Mario's?*"

"Ruled that restaurant dumbwaiters are hand elevators and

subject to scrutiny by municipal elevator inspectors, despite the fact that they do not carry human freight."

"And the fallout?"

"Critics charged that the elevator inspector 'cabal' was attempting to unduly extend the scope of its jurisdiction."

"The Sixteen?"

"Elevator, freight: an elevator used for carrying freight on which only the operator and the persons necessary for unloading and loading are permitted. Elevator, gravity: an elevator utilizing gravity to move the car. Elevator, hand: an elevator utilizing manual energy. Elevator, inclined: an elevator traveling at an angle of inclination of seventy degrees or less from the horizontal. Elevator, multideck: an elevator having two or more compartments located immediately above the other. Elevator, observation: designed to permit exterior viewing by passengers. Elevator, passenger: an elevator used primarily to carry persons other than the operator. Elevator, power: utilizing power other than gravitational or manual. Elevator, electric: a power elevator utilizing an electric driving-machine. Elevator, hydraulic: a power elevator where the energy is applied, by means of a liquid under pressure, in a cylinder. Elevator, direct-plunger hydraulic: a hydraulic elevator having a plunger or cylinder attached directly to the car frame or platform. Elevator, electro-hydraulic: a direct-plunger elevator where liquid is pumped by an electric motor. Elevator, maintained-pressure hydraulic: a direct-plunger elevator where liquid under pressure is available at all times for transfer into the cylinder. Elevator, roped-hydraulic: a hydraulic elevator having its piston connected to the car with wire ropes. Elevator, private residence: a power passenger elevator installed in a private residence or in a multiple dwelling as a means of access to a private residence. Elevator, sidewalk: a freight elevator for carrying material exclusive of automobiles and operating between a landing in a sidewalk or other area exterior to a building and floors below the sidewalk or grade level. That's the Sixteen."

"You're doing very well, Miss Watson."

"Thank you, sir."

"We're almost done here. Answer me this: Do you know how many colored elevator inspectors there are in this country?"

"Twelve."

"And do you know how many are employed as such? Are not working as shoeshine boys? Or maids?"

"I don't know. Less than twelve."

"So you don't know everything. That will be all, Miss Watson. You'll receive your grade next week."

* * *

The falling elevator's wake is sparks, thousands of them, raking the darkness all the way down.

* * *

The address is 117 Second Avenue but everyone knows it as Intuitionist House. Edward Dipth-Watney, two-time winner of the Werner von Siemens Award for Outstanding Work in Elevator Innovation (first for his Flyboy limit switch, the second time for the "smart" overspeed governor), purchased the townhouse two decades ago, when the movement was still the soiled stepchild. The elevator community regarded Edward Dipth-Watney as a man of quixotic temperament; while not entirely swayed by Intuitionism, he felt that anything that caused such bellowing and recrimination merited a place to germinate and unfold itself, and hopefully cause more bellowing and recrimination. He was also a well-known model train enthusiast.

Edward Dipth-Watney's achievements were, and still are, appreciated; his name will maunder about the indexes of elevator inspector textbooks until the end of time. One snapshot: Arbo Elevator Co., the fortunate licensees of Dipth-Watney's Flyboy limit switch, dipping the prototype in gold and bestowing it upon its inventor as a Christmas gift one cold year. Edward Dipth-Watney was not interested in the gilded privileges of fame, however. The longevity of Fulton's science was uncertain; nonetheless, Dipth-Watney reasoned, if God had given him a gift, the least he could do was to help others find theirs. It was this same faith in God's will that prevented Edward Dipth-Watney from witnessing the results of his efforts on behalf of the international Intuitionist brotherhood. He believed the cyst on his neck to be another of His gifts, a reminder against vanity. He was incorrect.

In the years following its benefactor's death, the House thrived into the international headquarters of Intuitionism, continuing to stubbornly prosper even after Institute administrations reversed themselves, offered classes on the new science and even bestowed large (although not well-situated) offices upon its intrepid instructors. Very little actual research goes on at the House, but burning midnight oil was never the building's intended purpose. Inspectors and theoreticians of elevators are still social creatures despite the toll their profession exacts on their souls. Every Tuesday, James Fulton (and later, Orville Lever) stood in the downstairs drawing room and lectured on the intricacies of his science. Lectured on the implications of European maintenance deviations on Intuitionism, expounded on the gloom of the shaft and how it does not merely echo the gloom inside every living creature, but duplicates it perfectly. Afterward there were mint juleps for everyone, and still later, after Fulton had retired to his Tudor-style house on the Institute for Vertical Transport's north campus, Swedish films featuring large-breasted volleyball players. Fulton was unaware of this dubious activity; the House chauffeur regularly packed the Tuesday night lectures with traveling salesmen who were in search of a good time and willing to pay for it. Fulton, if he ever wondered about it, probably took his lay audience as evidence of the universal applicability of his theories.

Ever since Lever replaced Fulton as the man of the House, the importance of 117 Second Avenue has trebled in the hearts and minds of the global Intuitionist tribe. It is now his campaign headquarters and home to a formidable optimism new to these generally sullen detective-philosophers of vertical transport. The new rumors have invigorated; the conventional wisdom whispers that Lever has a genuine chance of winning the election for Guild Chair. Their time has come, as they knew it would. Lever's Tuesday night lectures no longer linger haughtily over the errata of nuts-and-bolts Empiricism, but excoriate. The House walls vibrate with the sibilants of campaign rhetoric. If he wins, the House will change forever.

For now the regular life of the House continues as it has for years, so as not to jinx the gathering magic of the time. From the continent come foreign scholars of the art, and after lecturing at the Institute they retire to the House and the second-floor guest rooms. (Lila Mae would be astonished to hear the names of the luminaries who have slept in the bed she lies in right now. Her fingers are laced beneath her skull and she stares at the ceiling.) Grand parties celebrating the publication of the latest Intuitionist tract are held here, and it is custom for the guests to comment with trickling awe on the sublime properties of Mrs. Gravely's apple brown Betty. The local membership (those who have sworn oaths to Intuitionism, savvy Empiricists hedging their bets, and apolitical inspectors who just want to get away from the wife) still convene for poker games and, on special nights, to taste unblended scotches of the finest quality. Correlative to the House's widening influence, the Swedish films have swelled in attendance now that the chauffeur, emboldened by how much his supplemental income has increased his estimation in his in-laws' eyes, started inviting House members to join the tieclip, toaster and Bible salesmen at his after-hours confabs in the garage, said members whom he can single out with ruthless acuity, something in their eyes.

Ask her and Lila Mae will not admit that her heart skipped a beat when Mr. Reed suggested it might be wise for her to spend a night or two at the House, but it's true. A secret part of her wanted to stay in her home so that other unwanted guests might drop in and give her an outlet for her anger. It was rare that she felt this way, relishing violence. She is mistress to her personality and well accustomed to reminding her more atavistic inclinations that the world is the world and the odd punch or eye-gouge will not make it any other way. Very disturbing, however, this late business. It's one thing to understand the muck of things, accept it, live in it, and quite another to have that muck change so suddenly and dramatically, to stumble down to a newer, deeper shelf. That's how Lila Mae sees it. Things are happening too fast for her to convince herself that she does not need time to think, to get to the bottom of things. Even if that involves taking assistance from this man Reed—and it is the acceptance, and not the aid itself, which galls her and makes her pride curdle. It means she owes him. This specimen.

Her room at the House is twice as large as her one at the Bertram Arms, and twice that again when the curtains are wide, as they are now, and all that forbidden light takes the room. She gets sky in her room at the Bertram Arms, but she doesn't get light. There's a difference. She doesn't know what to do with her breakfast platter—does she leave it outside the door, as they do in hotel scenes at the picture show, or does she leave it at the side of the bed, act naturally? Time to get up at any rate. There's not a single piece of dust on the large oval mirror hanging on the opposite wall of the room. Rubs her belly: she should eat like this more often. Misses her suit: she doesn't spend her little money on things that she doesn't need, but she needs the cut of her suit to see herself. The bold angularity of it, the keen lapels—its buttons are the screws keeping her shut. The tailor seemed to know what she needed, understood the theater Lila Mae needs to leave the house whole and be among other people. An old man.

Mrs. Gravely (whoever that is, the cook, a bitter old bitch, Lila

Mae can see her, gray-haired and bitter for sure) has hung her suits in the closet, along with two white cotton shirts Lila Mae has never extended the courtesy of a hanger to. Even her clothes are getting the royal treatment in Intuitionist House. Lila Mae packed the extra suit even though she does not intend to stay another night. She doesn't know why. Her suit does not betray the scent of mothballs, which lingers in the closet, medicinal fog.

Dressed, she's in front of the mirror. Armed. She puts her face on. In her case, not a matter of cosmetics, but will. How to make such a sad face hard? It took practice. Not in front of a mirror or in front of strangers, gauging her success by their expressions of horror, disgust, etc. She did it by lying in her bed, feeling and testing which muscles in her face pained under application of concerted tension. To choose the most extreme pain would be to make a fright mask. A caricature of strength. She achieved calibration one night while testing a small muscle attached to her upper lip, hitting upon a register of pain a few inches below the high-tide mark of real pain. This register of discomfort became the standard for all the muscles in her face, above the eyebrows, under the jaw, across the nostrils. She didn't check with the small mirror in the janitor's closet, didn't need to. She knew she'd hit it.

Her face is on. She's ready to see Mr. Reed, whom she spies through the window. He sits on a stone bench in the garden, polishing his pince-nez, which are never dirty.

*   *   *

See, the Empiricists stoop to check for tell-tale striations on the lift winch and seize upon oxidation scars on the compensating rope sheave, all that muscle work, and think the Intuitionists get off easy. Lazy slobs.

Some nicknames Empiricists have for their renegade colleagues: swamis, voodoo men, juju heads, witch doctors, Harry Houdinis. All terms belonging to the nomenclature of dark exotica, the sinister foreign. Except for Houdini, who nonetheless had something swarthy about him.

Some counter-nicknames from the Intuitionists: flat-earthers, ol' nuts and bolts, stress freaks ("checking for signs of stress" being a commonly uttered phrase when the Empirically trained are out running the streets), Babbits, collators (this last word preferably hissed for optimum disdain).

No one can quite explain why the Intuitionists have a 10 percent higher accuracy rate than the Empiricists.

* * *

Everything in the garden is dying, that's what time of year it is. The leaves blaze and desiccate in their dying before twisting to the ground as ash. Lila Mae crunches toward Mr. Reed in one of the city's secret gardens. The taciturn sentries (Victorian row houses, stodgy brownstones) have their backs turned to her. This interloper has dispensation, business with authority, and there are hungry thousands on the street beyond demanding closer scrutiny. Keep them out. Keep the dying garden safe.

"Mrs. Gravely doesn't allow smoking in the house," Mr. Reed says, affectless. "I smoke out here." He brushes some leaves off the bench and motions for Lila Mae to sit. He is not the same man as last night. For a few seconds, anyway. Then the lines of consternation in his brow relax: he puts his game face on, parrying Lila Mae mask for mask. "I trust the accommodations were up to your standards?" Mr. Reed inquires.

Messing with her, a jibe at the clenched room she lives in? Keep cool: "I slept fine," Lila Mae says.

"And the breakfast? How was the breakfast?"

"It was good."

"The gentleman who brought it to your room—he was polite?" Mr. Reed is looking very intently at the ground. He's thinking out loud, Lila Mae thinks.

58

"Yes."

"Our usual man called in sick this morning," Mr. Reed whispers, trancelike. "He sent over his nephew. We've never used him before."

Lila Mae doesn't say anything. She can smell more rain coming. A few yards away, the ubiquitous dead leaves clot the surface of a stone fountain still retaining a puddle from the rain a few days ago. The fountain cherub dances on one foot (dances to what? to next year's spring, to having a master to dance for?), its tiny mouth cupping the sodden autumn air. What Lila Mae knows about Mr. Reed: graduated at the top of his class at the Midwestern Institute for Vertical Transport, quickly hustled up the ladder in one of the larger Departments on the other coast. All the signs of becoming an industry bigshot. Then Fulton unleashed Volume One and the man was smitten. Lila Mae can relate: the first volume of *Theoretical Elevators* was a conversion experience for her, too, after a pithy index entry in her Intro textbook ("Fulton's recent vulgarities notwithstanding . . .") dispatched her into uncharted backwaters of the library stacks. No wonder the Institute exiled Intuitionist classes into the dingy recesses of the course catalog, no wonder the tiny classrooms were always so full, the instructors broken and cursed under the burden of such knowledge. Fulton's words discovered and altered Lila Mae early in her studies; she can only reckon what kind of spiritual catastrophe the book would have caused in a man like Mr. Reed, who had dutifully served Empiricism for so long. Must have felt the world had betrayed him.

What else Lila Mae remembers from the *Lift* magazine profile last summer: Like most of the early converts to Intuitionism, Mr. Reed quit the elevator inspecting game proper to preach the new gospel. What was the point, really, those first pioneers reasoned, when Fulton had pissed on every tenet of their former faith? Here's where Mr. Reed distinguished himself: not as a thinker but as a mule. He did the grunt work. He toiled at integrating the

59

alien science, this tumor, into the larger elevator community, convincing petulant Institute deans to teach this heresy (the very thought of it!), brokered the admission of taciturn and unapologetic Intuitionist inspectors into big-city elevator inspector Departments. There's the story of how he cadged Midwestern into constructing an entire Intuitionist Wing after a tortuous thirty-six-hour negotiation, winning his prize after talks degraded to a coin toss. And a fix at that—it was a trick double-heads coin he'd got out of a candy machine down the hall. A tricky old bird. That's how Mr. Reed appears to Lila Mae now that he has his face on, after recovering from Lila Mae's unexpected intrusion into the garden: a vulture. Not the odd pigeon he was at Lila Mae's apartment, but a calculating scavenger. A soldier.

Of course Orville Lever pressed this soldier into service as his campaign manager. Mr. Reed is not too academic for the field men or so full of well romanticism that the brains can't relate. Lever's a likable chap, but everyone knows Mr. Reed is the brains behind the operation, anyone can see that, the only man capable of pulling off the election for the Intuitionists. Lila Mae doesn't know why he's bothered to intercede in her Fanny Briggs mess, but knows she'll find out soon. The grim mist of master-plan comes out of his pores and pollutes the air in the garden.

After a time, Mr. Reed turns to Lila Mae and says, "It's too bad Orry is out of town talking to the good people at Arbo. It would be nice if you two met."

"I shook his hand once," Lila Mae tells him. "At a rally." Orry. Orville.

"You should come to our open nights, Miss Watson. Have you ever considered becoming a member?"

"I just assumed," Lila Mae replies.

"You should know what we're like by now, Miss Watson," Mr. Reed says with a bit of exhaustion. "As a group, that is. You're one of us." He removes his hand from the newspaper he's been pressing down on. "You should take a look at this," he says, handing the paper to her.

It doesn't take Lila Mae long to digest the tabloid article, from the heights of the loud ELEVATOR CRASH! headline to the dregs of the final quote from Chancre. Nothing she didn't expect. "Slanted," Lila Mae announces.

"Did you see Chancre's last statement? I'll try my memory . . . 'My opponent and his cronies have been trying all sorts of tactics since the start of the campaign, but I think this incident says more about their tomfoolery than any of their dirty tricks.' "

"He's frothing," Lila Mae says. " 'Dirty tricks.' "

"He has a point," Mr. Reed tells her, his mouth tight. "He's talking about the black box."

And that smell of rain is stronger now. The infamous design problem from her school days: What does the perfect elevator look like, the one that will deliver us from the cities we suffer now, these stunted shacks? We don't know because we can't see inside it, it's something we cannot imagine, like the shape of angels' teeth. It's a black box.

"Two weeks ago," Mr. Reed begins, rubbing his pink hands on his lap, "Lever received a packet in the mail. It contained torn-out journal entries dating back a few years, and they were notes on a black box."

"Everyone's working on black boxes," Lila Mae counters. "That's where all of American and Arbo's research and development money goes. There's nothing new about that." If Otis's first elevation delivered us from medieval five- and six-story construction, the next elevator, it is believed, will grant us the sky, un-reckoned towers: the second elevation. Of course they're working on the black box; it's the future.

"It was Fulton's handwriting. They were obviously ripped out of his final journals, the ones we've never been able to find. Obviously we were very interested. We made a few inquiries and discovered that a reporter from *Lift* had received portions of it, too. Chancre as well."

Lila Mae shakes her head. "There have always been rumors that Fulton was working on a black box," she says dismissively. "But most of the evidence shows that Fulton was devoting his energies to Intuitionist theory, not engineering. He hadn't been involved with mechanism since he became Dean."

"The evidence you've seen," Mr. Reed says. "He was doing a bit of both, from what we know now. You have to understand that in his last year, he barely spoke to anyone at all, except his maid, and when he did come out of the house his behavior was, to say the least, erratic. The diary shows that he was working on an elevator, and that he was constructing it on Intuitionist principles. From what we can tell from his notes, he finished it. There's a blueprint out there somewhere."

Lila Mae tries to get her head around that last bit. At least Mr. Reed is taking it slowly, trying to walk her through it. But still. "I don't see how that's possible," Lila Mae murmurs, twisting a button on her suit. "I mean from an engineering standpoint. At its core, Intuitionism is about communicating with the elevator on a nonmaterial basis. 'Separate the elevator from elevatorness,' right? Seems hard to build something of air out of steel."

Mr. Reed withdraws a cigarette from a silver case. "They're not as incompatible as you might think," he says. "That's what Volume One hinted at and Volume Two tried to express in its ellipses—a renegotiation of our relationship to objects. To start at the beginning."

"I don't get you," Lila Mae admits. Reluctantly.

"If we have decided that elevator studies—nuts and bolts Empiricism—imagined elevators from a human, and therefore inherently alien point of view, wouldn't the next logical step, after we've adopted the Intuitionist perspective, be to build an elevator the right way? With what we've learned?"

"Construct an elevator from the elevator's point of view."

"Wouldn't that be the perfect elevator? Wouldn't that be the black box?" Mr. Reed's left eyelid trembles.

"Unbelievable," Lila Mae says. She thinks of her room at the Bertram Arms. It's a miracle she lives there, how accustomed she is to this small world. How small her expectations are. Which part of Fulton's writing affected her most? The first line that comes to her head is an incandescent flare: *There is another world beyond this one.* Lila Mae asks, "What does this have to do with the accident yesterday?"

Mr. Reed takes a long, contemplative sip from the air. "Think about it," he says. "The most famous elevator theoretician of the century has constructed the black box, and he's done it on Intuitionist principles. What does that do to Empiricism?"

Lila Mae nods and Mr. Reed continues: "Now Chancre's up for reelection. There have always been rumors about Fulton's black box and suddenly comes this new variable—it does exist, and it's Intuitionist. Not only do you lose the election, but everything else, too. Your faith. You have to embrace the enemy you've fought tooth and nail for twenty years."

"You have to find the box," Lila Mae says.

"You have to find out if it's true or not, and you have to find out quickly."

"And set me up as a preemptive strike," Lila Mae realizes.

Pompey.

"It didn't have to be you," Mr. Reed tells her. "It could have been anyone. If Chancre can't find the box, he can at least stall until after the election, fight the rumors by orchestrating a high-profile failure for the Intuitionists. And their liberal policies."

Liberal meaning her. "But I haven't heard any rumors."

"It's been pretty inner-circle, Miss Watson. Until Monday, when the new issue of *Lift* comes out. It's the cover story. Forced Chancre's hand." Mr. Reed taps his cigarette case on his thigh and stares at the cherub in the fountain. It hasn't moved. It never does. "An elevator doesn't go into freefall. Not without help. He's

63

scared. Yesterday proves it. And as for us," he looks back at Lila Mae, "let's just say we're anxious to get our hands on the box and let it speak for itself."

"Who were the men at my apartment?"

"Are you surprised at Chancre's tactics? That he's a thug? He plays golf every Tuesday with Johnny Shush. They were probably some of Shush's men. The mob does more than just control the city's elevator maintenance contracts, you know. They have a lot of muscle." He looks up at the sky for a long moment. "It looks like it's going to rain, but it's not. Not today."

He's getting that airy look in his eyes again. "So where is it?" Lila Mae prods.

"We'll find it soon," Mr. Reed replies. "We think we know who sent out the journals. I think we'll have it soon."

This slow debate about the rain: it's not about rain at all, but the fragility of what we know. We're all just guessing. The second elevation, she thinks. The new cities are coming. "Thanks again for yesterday," Lila Mae says. "And for the room."

"A safe house," Mr. Reed says. He attempts to smile. "You'd be surprised how many people have taken an interest in your career, Miss Watson. The first colored woman to become an elevator inspector. That's quite an accomplishment. We're glad to have you in our camp." He pats her thigh. "All this business should be sorted out on Monday. Mr. Jameson, our House counsel, will talk to Internal Affairs and they'll back off. We take care of our own."

She looks down at the tabloid headline. "What about the accident?"

"You will be absolved. Did you do your job?"

"Yes."

"Then the fault lies with the Empiricists and Mr. Chancre, who have betrayed the public trust. Mr. Jameson will take care of it. If Chancre wins the election, he'll have no reason to press the issue. And if he loses, he won't be able to because Lever will squash it.

64

Once we show Chancre a united front on Monday, his goons will stop harassing you. He'll know we're on to him." Mr. Reed again attempts to smile and is more successful this time. "You'll be back in your apartment Monday night."

"I don't want to," Lila Mae says.

"No?"

"I want to find the black box."

*   *   *

So complete is Number Eleven's ruin that there's nothing left but the sound of the crash, rising in the shaft, a fall in opposite: a soul.

Part **TWO**

Ben Urich on a Saturday night: ambling quickly down the street, a blur in his favorite powder blue seersucker. He's flipping a dime as he walks—heads, he always bets on heads and is correct about half the time. Whistling a doo-wop confection that's always on the radio in the coffee shop where he eats his breakfast, where he folds his newspaper into tight squares to better peruse the sports pages.

It's late but not too late. He notices that the big shows are starting to let out, vomiting dandy citizens and intrepid tourists onto the sidewalk from brightly lit lobbies. It's not too late, he looks at his watch, and celebrations coalesce in his mind, festivities to be groped and devoured once he picks up an advance copy of his cover story at the office. O'Connor's? He'll have to spend half an hour explaining what the story's about before the inebriated inspectors start buying him drinks, not to mention the fact that the Saturday shift is a generally surly bunch, swollen with career ne'er-do-wells, men of little ambition who sweat out their days looking at the calendar for their retirement date. Tough crowd. Plus, the place isn't that cheerful. Is downright depressing. Plus, he has no idea how amenable they'll be to the prospect of an Intuitionist black box. Especially after a few hours of the bottom shelf. The Flamingo is starting to jump at this time of night, and that colored band they got on Saturdays is just what he wants in mood music. Sex music. The music, a few boilermakers, and a present from Lady Luck at the bar: easily impressed bottle blondes who won't ask many questions, legal secretaries in torpedo bras, the odd beautician. Heads. This is my city, my night.

She was talkative enough after she'd had enough Violet Marys. Suspicious at first when he pressed her too early for details about her job at United Elevator Co.—him being a notorious muckraker at the biggest trade journal there is, *Lift* magazine. He put on his 100-watt smile and waved his index finger at the waiter when the drinks ran dry. Keep 'em coming. He told her he didn't mean to make her uncomfortable, he was just asking about her work, it sounded so interesting. She blushed and drained her Violet Mary. The sanctity of the journalist's creed, the indefatigable war against industry corruption, throw in a toothy anecdote about his suffragette mother: these matters and more Ben Urich discoursed upon, to the effervescent delight of his companion, Miss Betty Williams. He was only laying the groundwork this night; the cover story would clinch the deal. Ensured of his integrity, there was no reason Miss Betty Williams couldn't pinch a file or two from the United archives. For background purposes. The customary assurances that under no circumstances would he quote from the documents. Inviolability of sources. He was merely trying to serve the public to the best of his ability, he informed her, adhere to the values instilled in him by his mother at an early age, while she painted placards arguing for a woman's right to vote. He noticed that her eyes flashed a bit when he dropped newsroom lingo, and commenced to disperse words like *copy* and *lede* into his lullaby, to a commensurate increase in eye-flashes. He'd drop a copy of his *Lift* cover story by her office and the next day or the next after

70

that press his new acquisition for a choice file or two. Ben Urich kissed Betty Williams's swaying cheek as he packed her off in a taxi. Fairly swooning.

Heads. It wasn't all smoke, however. Ben Urich takes his job as self-appointed watchdog of the country's vertical transport industry seriously, and he feels he deserves credit for his work. Like exposing the Fairweather Scandal, which resulted in the resignations of seven elevator inspectors and five clerks in the Buildings Department and caused the formation of the first city-Guild joint commission on irregularities in municipal elevator inspection. His series on the alleged ("alleged," whirling the journalist's baton) mob control of elevator maintenance in the city may not have brought any indictments, but still stands as the first public report on the industry's biggest dirty secret. Well, one of them: now that Fulton's black box is out there somewhere, the whole future of vertical transport is up for grabs. Ben Urich's future, too. He's paid his dues. Can scrounge up a legit reporting gig before long, after all the fallout. One of the city's bigger dailies, maybe even a glossy. Heads.

There's not much for a night watchman to do at the *Lift* building at this hour but scrabble at his university-by-mail course. So it comes to pass this night that Billy the night watchman is parsing Victorian English when Ben Urich taps on the front door.

"Hey, *Jane Eyre*," Ben Urich says brightly when Billy unlocks the door. "Good book."

"Good enough," Billy mumbles. Billy's a round gentleman. The loop of keys chime in his moist hand. "I woulda thought you'd be out on the town on a night like this."

"I'm not working," Ben Urich informs Billy, intrepid sentry of empty office buildings. "Did the printer drop by those advance copies of the new issue? I wanted to pick up a copy."

"Got 'em right here," the night watchman and nocturnal freshman says, withdrawing the bundle from behind the desk. He scissors the rope and pulls off the top copy from the stack.

In the brief seconds it takes for Billy to hand him the magazine, Ben Urich already knows something is wrong. The flash of red. The mock-up he approved the other day featured a close-up on an engineer's blueprint: the plans for Fulton's black box. Not the actual plans, of course, but *Lift* assumes a capable imagination in its readers. The flash of red is all wrong.

Events proceed in this negative vein. His name does not appear on the cover at all, and the illustration depicts Santa Claus in all his winter-solstice girth shimmying down an elevator cable. He wears a standard tool belt. The headline reads, GETTING READY FOR THE HOLIDAYS: 10 X-MAS MAINTENANCE TIPS. The least of Ben Urich's objections is that Christmas is still months away, and it is criminal for the preeminent trade journal to participate in the advertising and retail worlds' extension of the holiday season.

They pulled it. They pulled his story.

"Something wrong, Ben?"

Before anger, pragmatism, as it always is with Ben Urich. With some cutting, it could go in one of the smaller elevator newsletters who don't pay as well and have a smaller circulation. And less prestige. Could he get it into one of the general-readership mags? Have to provide more background for the lay reader, dwell more on the Intuitionist-Empiricist debate. Explain Intuitionism, a subject he knows enough about to get by without looking like an idiot, but would have a hard time articulating for the average joe. No, he's fucked. *Lift*, or no one.

"Say something, Ben. You want a little nip? I got a bottle."

"Is Carson upstairs?" Ben demands, twisting the copy of *Lift* into a club.

"Nobody's up there, not tonight," Billy responds.

Ben's out the door. It was getting hot in the lobby. He thinks back on his editor's behavior over the last few days. Carson seemed all for it, said this was the biggest story he'd seen since the sad debut of Arbo's Mighty-Springs, the Edsel of helical buffers. Just to make sure, Ben Urich checks the table of contents.

Test-driving the new European cabs, a report on the 15th International Conference of Elevator Contractors, and that damned fluff about the holiday season, but nothing on the black box. His name wasn't on the contents page. Ben Urich pulls his dime out of his pocket but he doesn't flip it. He drops it in a public phone and inserts his finger into the rotary dial. Carson's home phone is?

"Excuse me, sir, do you know what time it is?"

Ben Urich waves his hand over his shoulder.

"Do you know what time it is?" the voice asks again.

"No, I don't," Ben Urich says.

He has time to dial one number and watch the plastic ring slide halfway back before he feels two hands grip his shoulders. He's spun around. There are two stocky men before him. One has firm hands on Ben Urich's shoulders in authoritative pincers. The man's cheek is swollen into an angry red ball. The other man has a soft, kind face and asks Ben, "Do you know what Johnny Shush does to people who anger or otherwise tee him off?"

The events of this night are definitely proceeding in their negative tendency. Indeed the velocity has increased. These men and their boss are why his exposé did not run. "Yes, I do," Ben says. Best to play along and escape this night with his hide intact. He knows the drill.

"Jim?" the talking man says.

The man with his hands clamped on Ben Urich slaps him across the face, bends his body in half, lifts him like a baby and throws Ben into the backseat of a maroon Cadillac. The talking man is behind the wheel, the other man at Ben's side. He holds Ben's wrist in a snug and unquestionable grip.

The driver starts up the automobile. Ben Urich is getting his bearings. He's surprised this hasn't happened sooner. His hard-hitting reportage, his ruthless quest for the truth. An unknown person or persons once mailed him a dead rat wrapped in taffeta, but that could have been any number of people, for any number of things. He's surprised this hasn't happened sooner.

The driver says, "We're taking you for a little ride right now. Just a little cruise." He extricates the car from its improbably tight berth between a dirty red van and an ominous Ford sedan. They traverse two city blocks without words. Ben Urich, for his part, would plead for his life if he could dislodge the stone from his throat.

The driver says brightly, "Would you mind terribly if we asked you not to pursue your current story?"

Ben Urich manages to say, "It's done. Finished," and the man in the seat next to him breaks his finger.

Ben Urich's index finger is a key player, versatile, dependable for mundane tasks and in the clinch, where it truly distinguishes itself. Never hesitant to mine a dry nostril after barnacles, yet a sensitive enough instrument for navigating house keys into cantankerous locks. Ben uses his index finger to summon waiters hither to collect the check, and to tap surfaces (tabletops, seats, his right thigh) when he's nervous or just killing time. Far worse than the roseate flare he feels when the silent man bends his finger an ill-advised ninety degrees past where it would normally wander during normal use is the sound of the resultant break. Twiggy. The sound is far, far worse than the pain. Initially. It says to him, this is how fragile your body is. Not to mention pressing the call buttons of elevators: his index finger is the most naturally of all the hand's digits conscripted into call-button service.

They allow Ben Urich's scream to diminuate into an uneven, back-and-forth whimper. The silent man even loosens his grip on Ben's hand, to remind his captive of freedom, the ease of mobility from which he has just been exiled. "My name is John," the man at the wheel informs Ben. "That's Jim next to you. Jim's just been to the dentist and won't be adding much to our conversation. Words, anyway. Occasionally he will underscore what I say with a well-timed gesture. I don't know where half of these people learned how to drive, but there are some truly bad drivers out on the road tonight."

Ben can't move his index finger. When he tries, his other fingers merely flop around in awkward sympathy. Accountable for an essential central quadrant of his typewriter, too, his index finger is. Ben notices that the car is headed downtown, stretching through the membrane of post-theater traffic. The traffic lights are unforgiving at this time of night, mysterious and capricious, as if appalled by this latest indignity of citizens and their vehicles. Traffic lights, the quintessential civil servants. At the next stop light, Ben's left hand crawls up the window and bleats against it. The car idling next to the Cadillac carries an aloof couple in black evening wear. Back out to the suburbs for these two, away from metropolitan disquiet. The woman looks over at Ben and the crab-wriggling of his hand. She frowns and turns back to her husband. The light changes and John commands the car forward.

"See," John drawls, "no one really cares about their neighbor. We could be taking you out to dump you in a landfill for all they know, and they just keep on driving. They're more concerned about their lackluster driving skills than their fellow man." Ben looks up groggily at the rearview mirror. The driver has been staring into his eyes. "Tell me, Mr. Urich, how many times have you lied to us tonight?"

"I haven't lied, Jesus, please let me out," Ben croaks.

John does not seem impressed. His dark eyes flicker out to the pavement before them, then return to Ben. "That's another lie," he says. "Since you're obviously of a mendicant bent, I'll tell you. Four times. And for each lie, my partner Jim is going to break a finger by exerting pressure on—well, I'm not sure exactly what the bone is called proper, it's been a while since I flipped through *Gray's*—but suffice it to say that Jim is going to exert pressure where it shouldn't be exerted."

Jim bends Ben's middle finger until it touches the back of his hand, and there is another twiggy sound.

John starts again, "You lied when you said you wouldn't get upset if I told you not to pursue a certain line of inquiry. I can see by the shiny areas on your suit around the elbows and knees that you are not a man who lives and dies by the petty dictates of the social sphere. Most people, they go out, they want to look their best. Like the folks in that car back there—they've had a little dinner, seen a show, and they look nice. But that doesn't mean a whit to a man like you, a man of such keen moral sense. It offends you that two thugs—for that's what we are when you really get down to it, no matter how I try to convince myself otherwise—that two thugs would tell you to back off of what you see as a moral imperative. So you lied. That was one finger." John swivels his head back and forth. "Hold on a second," he asks. The dark blue sedan in front of him is sending mixed messages tinged with an unsubtle flash of aggression. "Did you see that? This guy just cut me off. If he wanted to turn, he could have at least signaled, you know what I'm saying?"

"Please, I swear I'll back off the story," Ben begs. "I swear."

"Yeah, well," John says. "You lied again when you said you knew what Johnny Shush did to people who cross him. Because if you really did know—didn't just cook something up from what you picked up in the tabloids or god forbid the movies—you would have never ever, ever, ever done anything to make Johnny angry. You would have known better. We wouldn't be here right now. Driving in midtown at this time of night? Forget about it. So that was another lie, and another finger. Two more lies to go. You lied when you said you didn't lie, so that's another finger, but I'm going to ask Jim to hold off on the breaking-finger business for now because that snapping sound really distracts me and it's hard enough to drive with these maniacs in this city without me being distracted. Is that okay with you, Jim? Just nod because I know it hurts to talk, what with your tooth and all."

Jim nods, grateful that his friend and partner understands him so well.

"There's one more lie, and it's the first one you told us. When I asked you for the time, you said you didn't know. But I know it was another one of your mendacities because I can see your watch right there, right below where Jim is holding your wrist. And that's the worst lie of all, because when a stranger asks you the time, you should never lie. It's just not neighborly."

* * *

Lila Mae reclines on the bed, drawing plans for war. After their talk, Mr. Reed excused himself to attend to pressing business— related or not related to the matter concerning Lila Mae, she doesn't know—and left her to the garden. A slow hour passed, distracted by intermittent drops of moisture from above, as if the sky were conducting a feasibility study on the implications of rain. Of committing to a course of action. Lila Mae left the garden and resumed her scheming in her room. At eight o'clock, Mrs. Gravely served her a dinner of no small culinary accomplishment. Mrs. Gravely was not as Lila Mae imagined. She was a small, energetic woman whose gray hair coiled tightly on her head like a knob. She smiled politely as she placed the tray across Lila Mae's knees and even paused, before departing, to beat fluff into the pillows. She didn't say anything. As Lila Mae ate (slowly, as her mother had taught her), she wondered why the handsome man from the morning had not brought it to her.

She recognizes his knock a few hours later: light, regularly spaced, forceful. Her day's worth of plans recede and Lila Mae sits up in the bed. Tells him to come in.

"I just came up to see if you needed anything," Natchez says. His thumb is locked into the corner of his pocket, his fingers splayed across a hip.

"No, thank you," Lila Mae responds. Then, thinking better, adds, "You're on all night? I mean, you sleep here?"

He shakes his head, amused. "No, ma'am," he says, "I'm off in

77

a few minutes. I just wanted to see if you needed anything before I leave. Mrs. Gravely's asleep, so you're on your own once I'm gone."

"I'm fine. Thank you again."

His body tilts to leave, but Lila Mae stops him with, "Is that where you're from? Natchez?"

"That's where my mama's from," he replies. He leans against the door. "She didn't like it enough to stay there, but she liked it enough to name me after it. She still wants to hear people say it."

"I'm from down South, too."

"Where?"

"A dirty town."

"You're not much for talking, are you?"

"I talk."

Natchez shakes his head again and grins. "Okay, then," he says. "You one of those visiting professors they always have staying here? You giving a speech?"

"No, I'm an elevator inspector." Lila Mae's voice automatically rises at those last two words, up to the tone she uses when she's on a case.

"I didn't know they let us do that," Natchez tells her. "Even up here."

"They don't but I'm doing it anyway."

"Is that good work—working on elevators? That's a city job, right?"

"It's not bad," Lila Mae says, stealing a quick look at his hands. His fingers are wide. Arrogant, they seem to her. "They go up and they go down. You just have to understand why they do that." She watches his eyes. "What do you do when you're not here? This isn't your regular job, right?"

"I'm just filling in. I do this and that," he says. "Whatever comes my way. This city is tough, I'll tell you that."

"It's a tough city," Lila Mae repeats. She's just reached the end of her conversational props.

Natchez doesn't mind. "I'll see you tomorrow then," he says. "My uncle, he's still sick."

"What's wrong with him?"

"He says he can't feel his leg." Natchez frowns. "He says it feels like it's been cut off."

"That's terrible."

"It happens to him from time to time."

"Thanks for checking in on me."

"You sleep tight, Lila Mae. Sleep tight."

*　　*　　*

The children masticate rock candy in greasy teeth and wait for their saliva to thicken into sugar. In the heat everything is sticky. Their tongues are green and red, from the candy.

At the Exhibition of the Industry of All Nations, the flags from every civilized country dangle in the limp air like the rags of stable hands. The sun stokes, gleams on the monstrous edifice of the Crystal Palace, which is a replica of its namesake in London: iron and wood and glass, radial ribs strengthened by slender cross-ribs. A Royal bauble. Before they invented verticality, that was all there was to aspire to, glass and steel confection delivered by spyglass from overseas.

To the west of the Crystal Palace is the fetid Croton reservoir; east is Sixth Avenue, a gargoyle of carriages and hooves. The Crystal Palace will fall five years later in 1858, devoured by fire in fifteen minutes, and become Times Square, in due course. But today, a thousand windows snare the light and the glass is streaked with the brackish film of condensed sweat. It is a greenhouse, and what treasures bloom there! In one room is arrayed raw materials on velvet, behind glass: minerals, ores in all shapes, coal, copper, stone, marble, crystal, diverse wonders all. In one gallery a locomotive squats on iron haunches atop a black pedestal: the machine is this dynamic age distilled, these vehicular times. They come from all over the world. Hamburg presents many articles in horn, some pretty furniture, a large collection of sticks, embroideries, and Turkey showcases fine silks, raw materials, stuff of the earth, carpets and rugs much remarked upon. A million people under that glass during the course of the Exhibition. They dally and gasp at the exquisite watches from Switzerland, very diminutive, true craft, barely an inch in circumference and wound and ticking audibly, most beautifully set with lovely enameled exteriors. Grain and chocolate and guns, muskets and French pistols (the famous duels) and a stuffed Apache. Crimson fruit from Amazon vines and brown slivers of llama meat, dried and cured.

On the second floor are the reaping machines and threshers, still and elegant, like lithe animals stooping to lick moisture. The Bowie knives weep in the sunlight; they say Americans are never seen without one. (A quick look around disproves this Continental humbug). A monkey in a sable cape on a leather leash can tell the future. One display features a horse that's only a foot high and a two-headed infant in a jar, for the children's delight. The ladies and gentlemen step aside and wave their handkerchiefs in deep respect as he walks by: the Chinese Mandarin and two retainers. (Newspapers later report that he was just an opium smuggler pulling a gag.)

The sound of the organ on the second floor, against which two hundred instruments and six hundred voices would be nothing, so loud on this first day, July 14, 1853, falls away—the heat is even taking its toll on the organ, one man remarks. No, the organ has ceased because the man with the lungs of a bear, the Vice President of the United States, is about to address the assembled: "Our exhibition cannot fail to soften, if not eradicate altogether, the prejudices and animosities which have so long retarded the happiness of nations. We are living in a period of most wonderful transition, which tends rapidly to accomplish that great end to which all history points—the realization of the unity of mankind.

The distances which separated the different nations are rapidly vanishing with the achievements of modern invention. We can traverse them with incredible speed. The publicity of the present day causes that no sooner is a discovery or an invention made than it is already improved upon and surpassed by competing efforts. The products of all the quarters of the globe are placed at our disposal today and we have only to choose which is the best and cheapest for our purposes, and the powers of production are entrusted to the stimulus of competition and captial. Ladies and gentlemen, the Exhibition of 1853 is to give us a true test and a living picture of development at which the whole of mankind has arrived and a new starting point from which all the nations will be able to direct their further exertions." The monkey in the sable cape picks a pocket.

That first night the man attempts to kill himself and does not succeed. It is merely one act of many in the Great Hall, one rough stone among all the gathered jewels of the world. Elisha Graves Otis stands on the elevator platform. No one has seen his act before, and after all they have seen this day, there is little enthusiasm in the Crystal Palace for the unassuming gentleman. Despite his promises of the future. He is a slender middle-aged man in a herringbone frock coat; his right hand strokes a white vest. If the assembled stop to see the act, it is most probably because of exhaustion, the toll of a lifetime's worth of exotic sights crammed into one glorious day and the swamp heat in the Palace, only now receding with the evening. And there's nothing new about freight elevators except, perhaps, to some of the country yokels, but not to city folk.

The platform rises thirty feet into the air, grasping for the glass dome above that is black with night. They are drawn from the Persian tapestries and the Egyptian scarabs, summoned from the Ethiopian pots to Mr. Otis, the assembled in the Great Hall come and stare at the platform and the man and the ratcheted rails. They want the future after all. "Please watch carefully," Mr. Otis says. He holds a saw in the air, a gold crescent in the lamplight, and begins to sever the rope holding him in the air. As the fame of his act grows over the next few weeks and months, the Crystal Palace will never again be as quiet as it is now. The first time is the best time. It is quiet. The rope dances in the air as the final strands give. The platform falls eternally for a foot or two before the old wagon spring underneath the platform releases and catches in the ratchets of the guard rails. The people in the Exhibition still have a roar in them, even after all they have seen this day. A Safety Elevator. Verticality is not far off now, and true cities. The first elevation has begun. Mr. Elisha Otis removes his top hat with a practiced flourish and says, "All safe, gentlemen, all safe."

*　　*　　*

The chauffeur does not speak, he drives, spinning the steering wheel with the palms of his hands. Minute grace of a painter: he makes short, careful strokes, never too extravagant or too miserly. He has a small red cut on his nape where the barber nicked him. As the black Buick squeezes through the bars of the city toward the Institute for Vertical Transport, Lila Mae thinks back to what Mr. Reed said. He said, "Perhaps you are the perfect person to talk to her. She won't talk to us."

Lila Mae Watson is colored, Marie Claire Rogers is colored.

The file she holds contains paper of different shapes, grades and thickness. Some of the words are handwritten, some have been imprinted by a typewriter. The one on top is Marie Claire Rogers's application for employment as a maid with the Smart Cleaning Corporation. She was forty-five years of age when she applied, had two children, had been widowed. The application lists where she had worked previously; apparently she'd spent most of her life picking up after other people and was very experienced in this line of work. Tending to messes. One of her former employers endorses her talents in a letter of reference, describing her as "obedient," "quiet," and "docile." Another document, paperclipped to the application and eaved with the Smart Cleaning corporate logo, relates Mrs. Rogers's six-months assignment to the McCaffrey household. Her term there passed without incident; Mrs. Rogers's work was characterized by Mr. and Mrs. James McCaffrey as "efficient and careful." The McCaffreys moved to cheerier climes, according to the Smart Cleaning Corporation's records, and Mrs. Rogers was reassigned to one of their regular clients, the Institute for Vertical Transport.

Lila Mae recognizes James Fulton's signature at the foot of an employee evaluation form, dated a year after her reassignment to the faculty housing of the Institute. Ink identical to that of his signature is observable in small boxes above, where the ink has been used to form x's in a column of boxes that indicate "excellent." Except for one box in the "fair" column, regarding a question about punctuality. The date on the form tells Lila Mae that Fulton had just resigned from the Guild Chair (to murmurs of varied volume from the larger elevator inspector industry) to become the Dean of the Institute. The final stage of his career. He'd stolen all the plums; there was nowhere else to go.

The Institute letterhead is more distinguished and staid than the ersatz antiquation of Smart Cleaning company stationery. Rarefied austerity appropriate to a place of higher learning. The document Lila Mae holds is addressed to the Institute's Board of Directors, and the emotional tenor of the words, the unmodulated panic, provides an intriguing contrast to the serenity of the Institute crest atop the page. The letter urges "swift action" regarding Fulton's "eccentric" behavior ("eccentric" being a word, Lila Mae notes dryly, that white people use to describe crazy white people of stature), detailed below. Lila Mae has heard most of the stories before—the quick rages, the sudden crying fit in the middle of groundbreaking ceremonies for the new Engineering Wing—but most of the outrageous acts she reads about now are new to her.

White people cover their own. Fulton's behavior does not make her reconsider the father of her faith; Lila Mae does not expect human beings to conduct themselves in any other way but how they truly are. Which is weak.

The next document she finds is no real revelation, either. Fulton has acceded to the Board of Directors, the anonymous secretary reports (with much more enthusiasm than was present in his first document), and decided to resign. He has accepted our offer of allowing him to retain his faculty housing, as well as the proviso that a caretaker move in with him. This particular piece of paper (which shakes with the Buick's velocity; not everything is within the chauffeur's control) goes on to describe Fulton's rejection of all the caretakers the Institute proposed (or "nannies," as he referred to the pageant of efficient taskmasters who essayed his front door). The woman he wanted was the housekeeper, Marie Claire Rogers. No one else. The secretary is happy to report that Mrs. Rogers agreed, and will move into the old servant's quarters on the first floor the second week of the next month. Congratulations, gentlemen, Lila Mae says to herself.

Lila Mae and the House chauffeur, Sven, are well into uncharted suburbia, which has been overgrown with kingsize discount emporiums and family restaurants catering to the primary color crowd since the last time she was out here. It is easier to breathe than in the city, there's less to see. She looks back down at the next piece of paper, an old *Lift* magazine article Lila Mae read when it first appeared. The sheets are limp and glossy, thin as a breeze. The trial is over. The judge has decided. Marie Claire Rogers must relinquish any of Fulton's papers in her possession to the Institute for Vertical Transport. According to the *Lift* reporter (whose choice of adjectives reveals him to be an Institute ally), when Fulton knew he did not have long to live, he bartered his personal papers for assurances that Mrs. Marie Claire Rogers could live in his campus house for as long as she saw fit. Needless to say, the Institute had already believed that they would get

Fulton's papers once he died, having already constructed the necessary reliquary nooks; this unexpected stipulation was just a gnat's annoyance. Or so they thought at first. Once Fulton's spirit departed, Mrs. Rogers tendered the papers in question. But not all. Obviously some notebooks were missing, ones from the final two years of Fulton's life. Academia, posterity, the implacable engine of history would not be denied. But Mrs. Rogers was quite adamant about holding on to the journals, and assailed her landlords with invective not often heard in Yankee climes, by white ears, relenting in her insufferable behavior only when ordered to do so by the court of the Honorable James Madison (no relation). The article ends there, but Lila Mae adds a postscript to herself, about the nature of evidence. It was obvious from the dates on the journals that some were still missing, but no one could prove that they were not, as Mrs. Rogers maintained, destroyed by Fulton in a wee-hour fit of hopelessness, or even stolen—the maid claimed that on the day of Fulton's funeral, the house had been broken into. Rumors have flourished in worse soil than this.

The car is near the Institute. She knows this without looking up because the sounds of the city have finally fallen away, as if Lila Mae and her driver had discovered the one true valley. The gnashing and grinding of the city, the keen laughter that follows a fresh kill. Perfect place for a spa out here, to urge one's self back into health, gather arms for the social world. The final contents of the file are the handwritten notes of one Martin Sullivan, an Intuitionist acolyte at the Institute. *Subject slams door in my face, insults my mother, Subject catches me sneaking in through the kitchen window and stabs me in the hand with a meat thermometer, Subject sees me hiding behind tree and begins to approach menacingly—I decide to leave the perimeter.* Martin Sullivan goes on to catalog the contents of a garbage pail collected as evidence one week earlier. *Primarily food-related waste,* Sullivan notes, *with approximately 10 percent paper refuse. Two false starts of what appears to be a personal letter to someone named "Aunt Ida," and so on. One item looked promising—a copy of* Kwicky's Weekly Crossword, *with two-thirds of the puzzles attempted to varying degrees of completeness and accuracy. But despite my best efforts, I could not find any hidden messages or other concealed meanings in the puzzles.*

That's it. She's the next one up, the next hassle for an old woman.

It has been a long time since she has been here. So long that her initial reaction is not of routine but of first impressions: she remembers entering the wide black gates of the Institute for the first time, her father's hands on the wheel. She wonders again if news of the accident has reached her parents, if the reports contained her name. (Another thought: there is a file on her accumulating somewhere now, like the one she holds in her lap, an accretion of falsehoods.) She is not like the others who have come to interrogate and nag Marie Claire Rogers. Lila Mae has come to clear her name. At any cost.

Mr. Reed told her, "She refuses to talk to us. Perhaps you're the perfect one to talk to her. You're both colored."

* * *

From *Theoretical Elevators:* Volume Two, by James Fulton.

To believe in silence. As we did when we lived in bubbles. Sentient insofar as we knew it was warm: Silence provided that warmth. The womb. Ants have it easy for speaking in chemicals. Food. Flight. Follow. Nouns and verbs only, and never in concert. There are no mistakes for there is no sentence save the one nature imposes (mortality). You are standing on a train platform. A fear of missing the train, a slavery to time, has provided ten minutes before the train leaves. There is so much you have never said to your companion and so little time to articulate it. The years have accreted around the simple words and there would have been ample time to speak them had not the years intervened and secreted them. The conductor paces up and down the platform and wonders why you do not speak. You are a blight on his platform and timetable. Speak, find the words, the train is warming towards departure. You cannot find the words, the words will not allow you to find them in time for the departure. Nothing is allowed to pass between you and your companion. It is late, a seat awaits. That the words are simple and true is only half the battle. The train is leaving. The train is always leaving and you have not found your words.

Remember the train, and that thing between you and your words. An elevator is a train. The perfect train terminates at Heaven. The perfect elevator waits while its human freight tries to grab through the muck and find the words. In the black box, this messy business of human communication is reduced to excreted chemicals, understood by the soul's receptors and translated into true speech.

*   *   *

No caramel soda, no prune juice, and definitely no coffee: Pompey won't drink anything darker than his skin, for fear of becoming darker than he already is. As if his skin were a stain that could worsen, steep and saturate into Hell's Black. They sent Pompey to sabotage the elevator stack in the Fanny Briggs building, Lila Mae is sure of that. It would have appeased their skewed sense of harmony to pit their two coloreds against each other. Dogs in a fighting pit. Pompey would have jumped at the chance, white foamy saliva smeared across his cheeks. Didn't he say something to that effect when they were in O'Connor's, just after the crash, when Lila Mae crouched against the wall like a thief? *She's finally got what's been coming to her.* Something like that. Pompey in his too-small beige suit, bowler hat tilted, mischievous in the machine room.

She's waiting in the car for Marie Claire Rogers to show up. The faculty houses lean behind a regiment of oak at the bottom of the hill. Always the incongruity: the preoccupied theoreticians and the bare-knuckled former inspectors united in academia, living behind indistinguishable Tudor facades. Through the car window Lila Mae can see the gymnasium where she used to live, see the small gutted hole that was her window onto campus. She draws a line across the air to the upper floors of Fulton Hall, the library where the man died. The man whose house she sits in front of now, with a man who does not speak in the driver's seat. Sven breathes heavily through his mouth like a horse.

The tap at the window startles her. "If you're going to be here all day, you might as well come in," the subject says, her words threading through the inch of open window to Lila Mae's right. Marie Claire Rogers adds, "Just you. Not him."

She is a short woman, a hut on strong stumpy legs, and looks younger than Lila Mae expected. Not as used-up and exhausted as her profession should have made her. On this overcast day she is a solid living presence, a bull in a bright red sundress that squeezes up around her neck in white ruffles. Dry browned flowers clench in a fist on her straw hat. She does not wait for Lila Mae's response, starting up the stone walkway to Fulton's house, her house, in small, measured steps. Lila Mae tells the driver not to wait for her, she'll make her own way back to Intuitionist House. Not a personality given easily to nostalgia, Lila Mae has nonetheless decided to walk around the campus after interviewing Mrs. Rogers. See if anyone is living in her old room. Perhaps it is the past days' dislocation.

Lila Mae opens the door to the foyer and sees the red blur to her left. Mrs. Rogers says, "I saw you and him parked in front when I come around the corner." She plucks a long hat pin from her head and sets her straw hat next to her on the couch. "I waited twenty minutes and you weren't moving. I'm not going to be kept out my own house."

"I'm sorry to trouble you," Lila Mae replies. "I just wanted to ask you a question or two. If you have the time."

Mrs. Rogers shakes her head wearily. "I wouldn't let you in," she says flatly, "but you're not like them other men been coming around here, in their city suits all full of themselves. Like they have to be nice to you because you have something they want, even though they think they better than you." She stares into her visitor's eyes. "But I give them so much trouble I guess they figure in their heads they send you and I'll talk to you."

"Something like that."

"And I'll just say what I've been keeping because we belong to the same club." Mrs. Rogers's hands scrape across her lap as if to brush something away. "Why don't you sit yourself down," she says, standing, "while I make some tea."

The house is not what Lila Mae had expected, but then Fulton's been dead for six years. It is Mrs. Rogers's house now, by contractual agreement. There was no mention of it in the file, but there must be rumors that Fulton and Rogers were lovers. Why else go to so much trouble for a servant. Did she start redecorating when he was alive, by creeping degrees? Fifteen ceramic horses stand on the mantle above the fireplace, in poses ranging from mid-gallop to pensive graze. She can hear Mrs. Rogers clinking and fussing down the hall. Boiling water. What did Fulton say as she remade his house. Too far gone to notice the world around him, or too intent on his black box to care about the shells of things. The appearance of matter.

Mrs. Rogers returns with tea and brown wafers. The tea smells and tastes of cloves. The chair Lila Mae sits in is old and firm. Intractable. Mrs. Rogers asks, sipping tea and eyeing Lila Mae over the lip of her cup, "Why don't you get on with it, then?"

"I just came here to ask you about Mr. Fulton."

"That's what the rest of them men said. What people you with? You with the Institute or that Department in the city? Or some new people come to harass me?"

"My name is Lila Mae Watson," she says. "I'm an Intuitionist. Now I work with the Department of Elevator Inspectors. In the city."

"Um-hmm," Mrs. Rogers says. Without emotion. "Ask what you going to ask." She nibbles a biscuit with tiny teeth.

"It was just you living here with Fulton?" Rogers may not make it easy, but she will find out what she wants to know, Lila Mae decides. She will.

"Somebody had to," Mrs. Rogers answers wearily. "He couldn't get along without having someone around to keep him out of craziness. Keep him from himself. First they brought in all these nice old ladies from Europe or some such." She waves out the window as if that place were just beyond the trees. "But James just ran them right out the house as soon as they walked in. Said they scared him, them being from Sweden and Russia and so on. Then one day he said that he'd only have me under his roof with him."

"And you accepted."

"All my kids married and gone off," Mrs. Rogers replies, her head tilting just a bit toward a picture on the table next to her. Lila Mae hadn't noticed it: faces and bodies she can't discern, posed in the traditional arrangement of family photos. "What am I going to do," Mrs. Rogers continued, "stay in that city with all that foolishness that goes on these days? There ain't much to do out here, but you don't have to think about some kid knocking you over the head for your money."

"You were friends then, you and Fulton."

"I worked for him and we became friends. He was good to me. Did you know they wanted me to spy on him? Once he started writing those books of his about feeling the elevator and hugging the elevator and business—"

"Theoretical Elevators," Lila Mae offers.

"That's them. Once he started up with that, those old crackers on the hill didn't know what to do with him. Acting like he got bit by a mad dog and carrying on like that, then he starts writing those books. I think that's what got to them the most—the books. They didn't know what to make of them, coming over here at all hours—I don't know if they was trying to make him stop or just keep it to himself. One day he's off giving a speech and one of them comes in here, some dried-up old white boy, comes into my kitchen and tells me 'they'd appreciate it if I kept them informed' about James's comings and goings and what he does in his room at night. Like I was going to be a spy in my own house, because that's what this place became as soon as I moved in here. My house. I told them to get the hell out of my kitchen, and said if they came around my house again I was going to tell Fulton. And you know he'd throw a fit." Mrs. Rogers places her teacup on the end table and stares at Lila Mae, switches gears: "What's taking you so long?" she says forcefully. "Ain't you going to ask me where I'm hiding the rest of Fulton's stuff? That's what everybody wants to know. 'Can we just talk to you for a minute,' 'Do you have a minute?' No, I don't have a minute, not for them."

"We're just trying to make sure," Lila Mae says. She's losing control of the situation, letting this bitter old bird get the best of her.

"How'd you get mixed up with these people anyway?" Mrs. Rogers asks. "You all dressed like them, but you must still have some sense."

"I came to school here," Lila Mae responds. Keep the conversation on Rogers, not herself. That's not why she's here. "A few years back."

"Is that all there is to it? Just that?"

"Like I said, I'm an Intuitionist. I'm a student of Fulton's teachings, and if there's some more out there somewhere, I'd like to find them."

"You went to school here?"

91

"A few years back."

"I think I remember you," Mrs. Rogers says flatly, nodding her head. "There never been too many of us around here, who weren't scrubbing floors or picking up, that is. Yes. I remember you. I remember you because you were the only colored gal around here who didn't work here. I used to see you walking all fast everywhere, like you had someplace to go and didn't have no time to get there. You were always walking fast by yourself."

"I made it through."

"I guess you did." Mrs. Rogers's brown eyes are locked fast on Lila Mae's. "Was it worth it? All the stuff they put on you?"

"I have my badge. I earned my badge." Lila Mae realizes with no small measure of embarrassment that her hand is in her pocket, tracing the crest on her gold badge. She reaches for a biscuit on the tray.

"That's not what I'm asking, is it?" Mrs. Rogers says. Satisfied with the awkward expression on Lila Mae's face, a crumpled ball of paper is what it looks like, Mrs. Rogers leans back on the couch and smiles. "Forgive me," she says slowly, "I'm just an old lady going on and on on a Sunday afternoon. You came here to ask me something. You want to know if I'm holding something back. Something of Fulton's the world and all those people up on the hill up there can't live without."

"Why did you hold on to his papers? You had an agreement, right?"

"That was what James wanted." The smile on her face is distant and strange, as if pleased by far-off music. "He told me because he knew he was going to die soon, the way people just know they're going to go soon, he told me that when they came around poking after his things I was to give them whatever he had in his study, but anything in his bedroom was off-limits. That's what he told me, and I could tell he meant it. He kept some of his work in the bedroom and he kept some in his study and those are two different places. That's what he wanted, and that's what I was

92

going to do by him, no matter what those old crackers and their lawyers were saying."

"But eventually you gave in to them."

"You know what I think? I think Fulton was going to burn those papers up in the fireplace, only he didn't know he was going to go on so soon. But they brought me up in front of that judge and they make me swear on the Bible. What else am I going to do? I ask you—what else am I going to do? I had to swear on the Bible. I know James would be upset with me, but what else was I going to do? I can't start over again, and James wanted me to have this place."

"And you gave them everything?"

"I gave them everything and they still didn't believe me. Somebody broke in here the day we buried James. Knocked everything over looking for something. I told them someone had broken in here and maybe they took something, but they still didn't believe me." A tiny mechanism in the old woman's body clicks into place, suddenly activated. By what, Lila Mae doesn't know: but she understands that her interview is coming to a close. Mrs. Rogers barks, "I look outside my window the other day, and you know what I see? I see a man picking through my trash can. I know the man who comes for the trash, and this wasn't no trashman. Then he takes off running. What do you have to say to that?"

"I don't know."

"You know how many people come around here lately asking the same question? Sometimes they fat and sometimes they tall and sometimes they even show some respect. They say they're from these people or they belong to that group and so on. And do you know what I say to them? I slam my door shut. Looking at me with that look. I seen all kinds of white people in my life, and I'll tell you something. They all alike. Every last one of them. Act like I'm not even in the room. To hear them say such things, the things they say, right in front of my face, like I'm not even in the room. Such horrible things. And they all the same, except for James. I

93

got nothing to say to a one of them. No more. After what they did to me and mine my whole life."

Flying teacups, throw one of the ceramic horses at Lila Mae. In another minute if she doesn't get out of there.

"And they send you. Got some little nigger gal on the payroll. This is a new world. They think they can send you over here and I'll talk to you. Like we know each other. Wearing a man's suit like you a man. Let me ask you something. Why are you here? On a Sunday?"

"Because it's important," Lila Mae responds. Defiant. Believes in her mission.

"To who?" Mrs. Rogers demands. "To you or them?"

And Lila Mae doesn't say anything and Mrs. Rogers says, "That'll do for now." The last thing the old woman says, when Lila Mae is halfway down the walk: "He's not the man you think he is. Remember that: he's not the man you think he is."

* * *

There were no windows and they took his watch so he had no idea how long he had been down there. Long enough to have been nicknamed the Screaming Man, long enough for him to have earned the sobriquet a dozen times over. He screamed the first time when the large man without eyes broke the first of his fingers. He screamed a couple times after that, and things just flowed from there.

The large man did have eyes, but they receded so far into his skull that the Screaming Man might have been peering into an abyss. When they arrived at this place, the two men hoisted his quivering form down damp stone steps, through hallways gouged out of reticent earth, down to this room. They chained him to the cot that stank of piss and vomit and other murky fluids the human body can be counted on to expel from time to time. Pus. The mattress bore tattoos, dark amorphous stains that corresponded to

94

where different body parts fell on the mattress, a brown cloud around the right knee, some murk congealed near the groin. He screamed when he saw the mattress, and screamed more as they chained him to the bed and he saw his limbs and parts positioned over previous guests' secretions. Dazed and agonized as he was, he understood that the small room was underground and that no real people would hear his screams. For the men who held him were not real people. They were monsters and they were going to kill him.

It cannot be said that the Screaming Man was unaware of his crime. He knew he was trespassing even as he did so. He trespassed for many reasons, for reasons going back several years, for reasons that bided their spiteful time until the moment of their vindication. The moment of the web. He did not break the laws of the country but the laws of a powerful man who commands a legion of block-browed enforcers who have pledged their fealty in blood. He had stopped screaming for several hours and had even entertained dreams of release, small dramas of contrition and forgiveness (we just wanted to send you a message), when the short man with nimble fingers entered the room and commenced to torture him. "Just pruning the overgrowth," the short man said as he cut the Screaming Man. Said Screaming Man, who truly and thoroughly earned his nickname at that point, and for several hours afterward.

The blood from his wounds (plural) sprayed the cinderblock wall and dried and eventually became indistinguishable from the dried blood from the others before him. It was not the spray patterns of his blood, intriguing and lively as they were, that distinguished him from his predecessors but the unaccountable originality of his screaming. His screaming, so steady and dependable for a time (crescendoing and receding, then redoubling in intensity at perfect intervals, as if pain were a virtuoso and his screams the very libretto of hell), slowly trickled away until it seemed to the men standing watch outside his door that the moment might come when the Screaming Man was not screaming. Had, in fact, stopped screaming. But then the Screaming Man would start screaming again after a time, and the man who had wagered on the Screaming Man's relapse would wearily hold out his palm to his more optimistic comrade, who dutifully tendered his gambling losses and pondered silently to himself why some people succumb to shock and others do not.

They all screamed, of course, those sentenced to that room by Johnny Shush's capricious morality. But what intrigued the men who watched over the Screaming Man, as well as those who tortured him, was the cast and caliber, the inexhaustible clarity, of his screaming. Its sheer novelty, unheralded in a man of such unassuming mien. They had never heard pain sing like that before, in all the permutations of torture ever enacted on the small room's humble stage. And some truly extravagant stuff had gone on in there over the years. One prosaic gent outside the room, went by the name of Frankie Ears on account of the vestigial, flaplike things on the sides of his face, said that it sounded like the Screaming Man was losing his job, his wife and his dog all at the same time, this image apparently being the worst thing Frankie Ears could conjure up. But no. The Screaming Man's scream was the sound a soul would make, if you could hear the sound a soul makes when it is shed of skin and exposed to the air, the harrowing mortal sphere. Lose five fingers—they won't grow back, but you still got five more, right? They had cut off half his fingers (and nailed them to the clubhouse bulletin board beneath the newspaper headline announcing the Justice Department's latest failed indictment against the irrepressible Johnny Shush) but they hadn't cut off the other half yet. There's still hope, the men in the small room never give up hope that they can talk their way out of the mess no matter how hard they hurt, the extremity of their disfigurement. (Hope, it has been observed, is the most terrible of all torture implements.) The Screaming Man, however, screamed as if he were losing not just his life but peaceful eternity, the silent hereafter where the dead repose on daisy beds, brows untrammeled by care. The men who stood watch downstairs, normally of imperturbable heart, experienced a new unease. Some, to themselves, plotted a career change, contemplating this or that cousin who had just opened up a restaurant or Ford dealership. They had never heard screaming such as this before. Pure. Lucent. Without corruption. As if he were a prophet, and the language of his prophecy shrieks and yelps that those he was meant to save could not understand, but only surmise that his message was important and make their own personal preparations for the Reckoning. Thank God for rest breaks, duty shifts, one guard said to himself.

Johnny Shush never went into the basement. He said it depressed him. When Johnny Shush arrived and the guards brought the Screaming Man up to the first floor so that Johnny Shush could deliver his usual "You done me wrong, now you gotta pay" speech to the still remarkably not-hoarse Screaming Man, it so happened that Lazy Joe Markham was bringing that colored gal downstairs. The colored gal looked at the Screaming Man, and the Screaming Man looked at the colored gal and did what came naturally. He screamed.

* * *

The dark blue Buick still perches at the curb, despite Lila Mae's instructions that the chauffeur depart without her. She would make her own exit from her alma mater. The infamous Intuitionist loyalty. As she walks down the path from Fulton's front door, Lila Mae can see the driver's hands limp on the wheel, lollygagging like beached jellyfish. The engine barks and gargles as soon as she sits down on the smooth leather of the backseat. As she sits, she lifts the cloth of her trousers' knees. To ease friction.

The old woman and her musty house, where schools of dust whirl and blink in the sunlight, minute sea creatures. Lila Mae does not dread briefing Mr. Reed on the outcome of her mission—it is herself she has failed. Mrs. Rogers's will is as blank and brute as hers. Perhaps someone did break into the Fulton home and steal the last journals after all, and it is this person who has mailed the packages of Fulton's journal. So distracted is she over the afternoon's turn of events that it is some time after they have cleared the filigreed gates of the Institute for Vertical Transport when Lila Mae notices that the driver no longer has the red scar on his neck, that his neck is a pink concrete column. That there are no buttons to unlock the door in the backseat, or handles to roll down the window. That this is not the car she arrived in, that this is not her driver (although both men share an affinity for silence), that they are not turning back toward the city but somewhere else altogether.

* * *

The ferry across Earth to Heaven. It seems silly to her now that she didn't see it before: an Intuitionist black box. Toward the end of her sophomore seminar on Theoretical Elevators, Professor McKean had the class describe the elevators they would build if free from all constraints. Some of the students took constraint to mean the exigencies of innovation, and hustled to rescue their favorite creations of yore, merely adding, say, a modern selector to the keenly antiquated hulk of a Sprague-Pratt. Others made improvements (or so it seemed to them) upon prevailing design concepts of the day, like the sandy-haired youth from Chicago who submitted a blueprint that owed much to recent developments in Austria. Lila Mae, who at that point in her career was still hung up on linearity, cobbled together an up-to-date model from the best the big firms had to offer (a broken-arm door closer from Arbo, a corrosion-proof sheave from United), envisioning a future cooperative and patentless. (Smiles ruefully at the recollection of it now.) One young gentleman with grave eyes tendered a blueprint that consisted only of an empty shaft and "an eerie dripping sound." No one was very happy with the high marks Morton received for such frivolity.

Lila Mae found Professor McKean hard to figure: he'd been in the war. His left arm was gone at the elbow and he pinned back his coat sleeve with the small, bright medal he'd earned for courage in battle. No one asked him for details, there were rumors of course, but no one asked him and he did not speak of it. McKean was tall and gaunt, with gray hair still grazed down to a military buzz. Gray hair even though he was still quite young. Lila Mae is still not sure how he felt about Intuitionism. She knew it was the first time he had taught the course, and yet his tone was so flat and arid that he could have been teaching the new science for decades, to dispatched thousands. For all his enthusiasm, he might be enumerating how many shirts he was dropping off with the Chinese laundry. No passion—but then, Lila Mae thinks, Intuitionism isn't about passion. True faith is too serious to have room for the distraction of passion.

The seminar was held in a basement room beneath the Edoux Auditorium. The steam pipes hissed petulantly, or else the radiator gonged; at any rate one had to enunciate and raise one's voice to be heard despite the modest dimensions of the room. The acoustics did not bother Lila Mae, who rarely spoke. She did not feel she understood enough about Intuitionism to talk about it, no matter the extent of her sincerity. As if to speak out of turn would be the apotheosis of vulgarity, the most unseemly corruption.

The six other students did not share her prudence, and their ignorant mutterings melted into the sonic adipose of the steam heat. Three of them were, like Lila Mae, avid converts to Fulton's mythology, another two well-meaning liberals who were intrigued enough to spend a year of their vertical education on the subject. The final member of their voyage was one Frederick Gorse, and he sat at the far edge of the boat, equally queasy with a diffuse disgust and the choppy waters of their discourse. Gorse, a plump and soft specimen (he reminded Lila Mae of an old, confident pig who understands his meat is too rotten for the slaughterhouse), was an intractable Empiricist who had only signed up for the seminar to understand, and thus better arm himself against, the apostate rabble who were making so much noise in the community. He had the Guild Chair in his eye, anyone could see that, and if his frequent ejaculations of "Poppycock!" and "Humbug!" were any indication, one day he'd be a toothy foe for Intuitionism. Upon first acquaintance Gorse already seemed an ancient nemesis. Professor McKean kept Gorse in check, Lila Mae realized later, by letting him speak; outnumbered among the converted, and arguing for the very doctrine against which the other students had united in revolt, Gorse was such an efficient teaching aid that McKean could have made a convincing case for including him in the Department's annual budget.

Lila Mae should have seen the black box and the new cities of the second elevation because Fulton's first writings were technical, arcane investigations of the mechanism. *Toward a System of Vertical Transport* is still a basic text for Empiricist thought. No one knows enough about his history to place his design genius in relief; Fulton just appeared at the Pierpont School of Engineering one day, eighteen years old, slow of speech, tentative, and proceeded to astound. The black box explains all. It was Fulton's odd perceptions that made him a technical wiz, his way of finding the unobvious solution that is also the perfect solution. It also allowed him, Lila Mae sees, to pierce the veil of this world and discover the elevator world. Because that's what *Theoretical Elevators* did, it described a world, and a world needs inhabitants to make it real. The black box is the elevator-citizen for the elevator world.

One day toward the end of the seminar, when spring had begun to stir above their underground bunker, Professor McKean brought up the Dilemma of the Phantom Passenger. (Obviously, they were still knee-deep in Volume One of *Theoretical Elevators*.) His one hand in a fist on the scratchproof surface of the conference table, Professor McKean asked if someone would care to explain the implications of last night's assigned reading.

Morton, the creator of the dripping-sound elevator, stated, "The Dilemma of the Phantom Passenger asks what happens when the passenger who has engaged the call button departs, whether he changed his mind and took the stairs or caught an up-tending car when he wanted to go down because he did not feel like waiting. It asks what happens to the elevator he summoned."

Professor McKean said, "That's right. Fulton asks this question and leaves it to the reader, abruptly proceeding on to the psychology of the Door Close button. How do you think Fulton would answer his question?"

"Obviously," Gorse said, "the elevator arrives, the doors open for the standard loading time, and then the doors close. That's it."

Johnson, the burly freshman who always sat next to Lila Mae, ignored Gorse and offered in his stumbling voice, "I think that Fulton would say that the elevator arrives but the doors do not open. If there's no need for the doors to open, then the vertical imperative does not apply."

Professor McKean nodded. "Any other theories?"

Bernard, who could usually be relied upon to provide a sensible response, said, "For one thing, the vertical imperative applies to the elevator's will, and doesn't apply to passengers. I think what Fulton was referring to in this section was the 'index of being'—where the elevator is when it is not in service. If, as the index of being tells us, the elevator does not exist when there is no freight, human or otherwise, then I think in this case the doors open and the elevator exists, but only for the loading time. Once the doors close, the elevator returns to nonbeing—'the eternal quiescence'—until called into service again." Bernard sat back in his metal chair, satisfied.

Professor McKean said simply, "That's good. Anyone else?"

Lila Mae waited for someone to give her an answer. No one did. Lila Mae cleared her throat and said in a thin voice, "Fulton is trying to trick the reader. An elevator doesn't exist without its freight. If there's no one to get on, the elevator remains in quiescence. The elevator and the passenger need each other."

Professor McKean nodded quickly and then inquired of his pupil, "And if we set up a film camera in the hallway to see what would happen, what would we see when we developed the film, Watson?"

Lila Mae met his eyes. "By leaving the camera there, you've created what Fulton calls 'the expectation of freight.' The camera is a passenger who declines to get on the elevator, not a phantom passenger. The film would record that the doors open, the elevator waits, and then the doors close."

"Very good," Professor McKean approved.

Gorse, who had been fidgeting and fussing in his seat for the last few minutes, was unable to contain his contempt. Spat, "Just because you can't see it doesn't mean it's not there!" and slammed a fat fist onto the table. The fundamental battle.

Professor McKean frowned. He pushed his chair from the conference table until it hit the wall with a dull bang. With his right hand, he unpinned his war medal from his sleeve. His jacket sleeve, unhinged, swayed back and forth pendulously. "Gorse," Professor McKean said, "Is my arm here or not here?"

"It's . . . not there," Gorse responded timidly.

"What's in this sleeve?"

"Nothing," Gorse answered.

"That's the funny thing," Professor McKean said, smiling now. "My arm is gone, but sometimes it's there." He looked down at his empty sleeve. He flicked at the sleeve with his remaining hand and they watched the fabric sway.

*　　*　　*

One time during an idle hour in the Pit, she asked Martin Gruber how Johnny Shush got his name. Martin Gruber is one of the Old

Dogs, a season or two away from retirement, cushy consulting jobs. He has weathered corruption probes, bullying by numerous city administrations, and the rise of the electric elevator. But he misplaced his usual volubility at her question. He looked around to see who might be listening and instructed, "No one speaks of it. Kapeesh?" As in: *shush.*

Shush, whispered the black mouths of the empty warehouses, the broken windows so secure in their shattering that they no longer remember glass. She did not know the neighborhood they drove through to get to this place, this underground room. Prefabricated houses swaddled in aluminum siding thinned and disappeared, the traffic lights disappeared, there were no more people, and the warehouses began, carcasses of prosperity. As the sedan rolled by the warehouses, rumbling over old trolley tracks, it was possible at certain points for her to see sky through the windows and up through the collapsed roofs. Decay heightening the visible. She was too curious to be scared. She did not bother to speak once she recognized the driver: Lazy Joe Markham, one of the Finnegan Five.

It was an old story. Once the government broke the elevator manufacturers' maintenance monopoly (we install them, and we'll keep them running for a monthly fee), all sorts of sharpies moved into this newly vacated entrepreneurial nook. The mob bullied owners to use their men as elevator maintenance contractors. They never did much for the elevators' ailments, but developed the peculiar hobby of dropping takeout Chinese containers and wax-paper sandwich wrapping down the shafts, apparently enthralled by the way the refuse twisted and tumbled as it traveled down into the darkness to molder among the buffers at the bottom. The mob had a stranglehold. Shush owned the West Side, from the crown of the Island down to the docks.

A few years ago, one of Shush's men was caught by the cops torching a pool hall (nothing to do with elevators, some unrelated business of concern to organized crime). The cops flipped him, and he turned state's evidence. The nervous stoolie captured the Finnegan Five on magnetic tape sharing war stories about the delightfully gusty entrails of a new luxury high-rise. Lila Mae couldn't recall if the Finnegan Five did any hard time; more importantly, they did not rat on Johnny Shush. This one, Lazy Joe Markham, apparently had been rewarded with his silence by getting a chauffeur job.

Mr. Reed telling her, Chancre and Johnny Shush play golf together.

When they finally arrived at one warehouse, identical in dilapidation to its cohorts in the lost industrial section, Markham took her down some old stone steps, where she passed a bloodied man being carried up the stairs by other men. He was screaming.

According to her internal clock (reliable, wound as she is), she has been here for two hours now. In the room is a square wooden table with a jagged black burn in its center. Two seats face each other across the table, and she sits in the one that fixes her back to the door. In accordance with interrogation-room policies upheld in dingy Mafia hideouts and police stations all over the country. The floor of the room is clean, not that she needed confirmation of the mob's influence over the city's custodial unions. The door is solid and gray, studded with rivets along the edges. An industrial door for little her.

Lazy Joe Markham frisked her when he brought her into this room, lightly and decently sliding his hairy hands along her body, catching for a second at the unexpected place where her waist erupts into jagged hip bone, recovering, sliding down her trousers. He was not fresh. He was not rewarded for his search. Him and the two men who searched her apartment: meticulous and thorough, as Johnny Shush is known to be.

She has time. She may be concerned at this point. She thinks, I have to be at work tomorrow. After not checking in after the accident, if she does not appear at the Pit at nine o'clock, she knows she is officially suspicious. If Mr. Reed is right, and she will be cleared of culpability in the accident, then she must continue along the routine: submit to an Internal Affairs inquiry. Keeping her overnight will damage her case. Wishful thinking: that all they want to do is detain her. She dismissed Mr. Reed's driver, and Marie Claire Rogers wouldn't know her hostage car from the one that brought her to the Institute. No one knows.

She wants the man to stop screaming.

*   *   *

Chuck, poor Chuck, he really wants it, working late on a Sunday night alone in the office, nary a critter underfoot except for his scurrying ambition. Has a bottle of soda pop to his left, a pile of notebooks to his right. In front of him, his words, pulled from himself with a struggle, they cling to his person like leeches. The words pile up the more he works on it. Right now they only make sense to him. *Time will vindicate this time:* something his wife, Marcy, will hear sometimes in the middle of the night, out of her husband's sleeping lips. It's hard to work at home, is why he's here. Marcy's aimless chores (rubbing rags against surfaces, holding glasses up to the kitchen light, all to some insufferable hummed ditty) distract him. He needs to work on his monograph, so he comes to the Pit. "Understanding Patterns of Escalator Use in Department Stores Simultaneously Equipped With Elevators"—the heft of the thing, he can barely stand it sometimes, being of delicate sensibilities.

Saturday afternoons find Chuck on stakeout. For the last six months of his life, every Saturday he goes to Freely's and watches the estuary roll through the front doors, rumble and mix into First Floor, Ladies' Cosmetics, The Men's Store, Jewelry. In the gallery of deluxe pleasures (perfume bottles ridged with jet-plane speed lines, curvilinear pink and aqua automatic toasters) where all the options are set from above, by men in secret rooms on the top floor, there is still one elemental choice left to be made. Elevator or escalator. Chuck vehemently disagrees with esteemed Cuvier, who thinks the choice is random, a simple matter of proximity. As they ricochet from bauble to bauble, snared by this sparkle, seduced by that luster, the shoppers opt for the vertical conveyance at hand, whatever is convenient. Which doesn't suit Chuck. He relies on primary sources. Ten Cents One Ascension. When the Otis Elevator Co. unveiled the world's first escalator at the 1900 Paris Exposition, the sign at the foot of the golden gate read, TEN CENTS ONE ASCENSION. Could it be any clearer than that? This need to rise is biological, transcending the vague physics of department store architecture. We choose the escalator, we choose the elevator, and these choices say much about who we are, says Chuck. (There is more than a smidgen of spite in this formulation, unseen by driven Chuck: he's trying to justify his specialty.) Do you wish to ascend at an angle, surveying the world you are leaving below and behind, a spirit arms wide, a sky king; or do you prefer the box, the coffin, that excises the journey Heavenward, presto, your arrival a magician's banal theatrics? Whenever Chuck touches the black rubber of the escalator guard rail (such a mysterious substance! what alchemy!), he understands he has made a choice. The right one.

He works late in the office, as he is now, contorting and torturing his data to support his thesis.

His bladder, always his bladder. He eases his fingers from the typewriter keys. His desk lamp provides an intrepid cone of light, all darkness outside the circle. Chuck cannot see the huge map of the city that drapes one wall of the Pit, punctured here and there with motley colored pins marking the Department's holy war against defective, cagey and otherwise recalcitrant vertical conveyance in this bitter metropolis. Cannot see the silent locus of office interaction, the water cooler, its cool fortitude. He walks past the rows of black binders filled with the city's hieroglyphic elevator regulations, the codebooks of their mission through disorder, and he stubs his toe more than once, beset by unseen enemies. Out in the hallway his passage is easier (paradoxically, his bladder pains more the closer he gets to the bathroom, always), because Chief Inspector Hardwick is in his office. Whiteness throbs behind the opaque glass and he hears grunting. Hardwick shouldn't be here this late, but then liquor stores aren't open on Sunday and perhaps he needed to retrieve a bottle of whiskey from his office stash. This is a tense moment for Chuck. He needs to wee-wee, but his natural affability and late-night yearning for company tells him to say hello. Hardwick is monosyllabic and their greeting shouldn't last for too long. Chuck makes a promise of flowers, a box of candy and no more soda to his bladder, and knocks on the door. He takes the grunt as a welcome and steps inside.

The man is not Hardwick. The man is squat, fat, and has a few greasy strands of black hair stroked across his denuded pate. Even from the doorway Chuck can see ashing on his shoulders sloughed off from his remaining hair. The man doesn't seem to mind Chuck's appraisal. He's eating a large submarine sandwich like a watermelon, chewing outward to his mitts. And has a generous stack of folders that apparently have been keeping him busy.

"You must be Charles Gould," he says through ground salami. "It says in your file you like to come in on Sundays."

"What are you doing in Hardwick's office?" Chuck asks in return.

Wearily, the man withdraws a leather billfold from his jacket and flips it open. "Bart Arbergast, Internal Affairs," he says. "I'm working on the Fanny Briggs case."

Chuck hasn't heard from Lila Mae since their encounter in O'Connor's bathroom (when you gotta go, you gotta go, insists his bladder), and he recalls the angry scuttlebutt of his comrades: That uppity bitch was bound to mess up sooner or later; they've handed the election over to Chancre now. Chuck tried to call her yesterday, but when the operator put the call through to the public phone in the hallway outside her room, no one answered, not even one of her strange neighbors. No Caribbean lilt to tell him Miss Watson does not answer her door. "I'm sorry to disturb you, then," Chuck tells the IA man, his hand on the doorknob.

"Not so fast," Arbergast says, sucking up a sliver of onion into his mouth like a cat devouring a mouse. "You're a friend of this Watson character, yes?"

"Friends can be hard to come by in this Department."

"I understand what you're trying to say," Arbergast nods. "Gould—that's a Jewish name, right?"

"Yes. What of it?"

"And you're an escalator head, huh?"

"Yes, that's my area of expertise. I think it's important to have a specialty. Something you're good at. That way—"

"Just like those damn escalators—you just go on and on." Arbergast sticks a fingernail into his gums. "To be honest, I don't care much for you tread jockeys. Why don't you just start your own guild instead of trying to weasel in with the elevator boys? It complicates things, all this interdepartmental paperwork you guys cause."

"If the higher-ups would recognize that escalators are just as important for speedy conveyance as elevators, there wouldn't be such headaches all the time."

Arbergast inspects the soft brown matter beneath his fingernail and eats it. "At least you guys stay out of trouble," Arbergast says. "Mostly. I was just looking at your file. Seems you had a little incident at Freely's a few months back. Something about harassing the clientele?"

"That was blown all out of proportion," Chuck says quickly. "I was merely trying to ask the woman what made her walk out of her way toward the elevator bank when there was an escalator right there, and she told the store dick that I was bothering her. Tell me if you think this makes sense: there's big queue for the eleva-tors—she could see that clearly from her vantage point—and yet she rejects the escalator, which was nearly empty. She—"

"Roland's bones! You escalator boys got a snappy answer for everything, don't you?"

Tiny red freckles of exasperation emerge in Chuck's cheeks. "Is this an official interrogation, or can I leave?"

"You can leave anytime you want," Arbergast grants, rubbing his lips with his sleeve. "But if you want to help your friend, you might think about helping me out with some things that are both-ering me." He waves his sandwich nowhither. "Want to have a seat?"

A few yards away, down the hall: forgiving porcelain. Chuck pulls a chair from the wall and sets it opposite Arbergast. The things he does for friendship.

Arbergast looks over his notes. "Last Friday," he begins, "there's an accident at the Fanny Briggs building. Eighteen-deep elevator stack. State of the art. City's pumped millions into the building, it's the Mayor's big baby. This Lila Mae Watson of yours inspects it, gives it a clean bill of health. Are you with me?"

"You haven't told me anything new yet."

"It's lip like that gives you guys your reputation. So why give the assignment to Watson? She's got a clean record. Impeccable, in fact. But it's a pretty plum, Fanny Briggs. Something Chancre would probably give to one of his toadies for good service. Why her, is what I'm asking."

"Like you said, she does good work," Chuck says, crossing his legs. "She deserved it."

"Deserves got nothing to do with it," Arbergast grunts. "One of the stack crashes, coincidentally just as the Mayor is about to take a test drive. That makes it a high-profile mess-up. If you wanted someone to take a fall, you couldn'a planned it better."

"Perhaps," Chuck concedes. This IAB guy is starting to seem

more interesting than he did a few minutes ago. He notices shallow depressions around the man's temples where forceps pulled him from his mother's legs.

"Take the elevator itself," Arbergast continues. "Top of the line, like I said. Forensics hasn't turned in a report on what they scraped off the bottom of the well, but I can tell you a thing or two. The cable snapped. That's new Arbo alloy cable. You could lug a freighter with that stuff, but it comes in two somehow. The cab itself had those new Arbo antilocks on them. I was there when Arbo performed the final trials on those babies, and they're sweet. Officially rated for two-five meters per second, but they can take twice that. They didn't fire. That's just for starters. This elevator went into total freefall, which hasn't happened in five years, and that was in the Ukraine and who knows what kind of backward standards they got there. They probably got their cabs hooked up to mules out there, for all I know. It hasn't happened in this country since before you were born."

"So you're obviously thinking sabotage, then."

"You said it." Arbergast pops the last nub of his sandwich into his mouth. "Somebody was monkeying around in there. And this Watson is the last person we know for sure who came into contact with them."

"There's a problem with your thinking, Inspector," Chuck says. He presses down absently on his crotch: let's wrap this up. "Why would Lila Mae—Inspector Watson—give the stack a clean bill if she was going to sabotage it?"

"I don't know. Throw us off. Give herself an alibi."

"That just doesn't hold water, I'm afraid." Hold water. "You're going to have to find someone else to pin this on."

"What you have to understand, son, is that I'm going to pin this on whoever fits." Arbergast crosses his arms across his newly replenished belly. "That's my prerogative as a member of Internal Affairs. I got no one else. Tell me this, tread jockey: where is she?"

110

"I don't know," Chuck answers.

"She should have checked in after her shift. Motor Pool says she returned her vehicle after her shift on Friday but didn't punch out."

"That's not so rare. I myself don't always punch out. Sometimes you're just tired."

Arbergast nods quickly. "Assuming she didn't hear about the accident on the radio, of course. But why not come in the next day? Surely she would have heard about it by the next afternoon. It was in all the papers."

"She's not required to. Her next shift is tomorrow, and that, according to regulations, is when she has to come in."

"She's not even curious?" Smiling now. "Just a little? It's her career."

"You have to understand something about Lila Mae. She's different than you and me."

"She's colored."

"That's not what I'm referring to, Inspector. With how she sees things. It's not easy for her to work here. Just look at the paper, how Chancre named her to the press. If it was one of his boys, he never would have told those jackals who'd inspected Fanny Briggs."

"He seized an opportunity for his campaign," Arbergast dismisses. He lets out a burp so lively it is almost visual. "That's politics. You know that. I'm going to tell you something. I don't care for Chancre much. He's ruthless. He's a bully. And I don't care much for the Intuitionists and their hocus-pocus. I care about what happened at Fanny Briggs last Friday at approximately 3:35 P.M. I don't care if the Mayor was showing around the King of Siam. I just want to know what happened to that elevator. Somebody fixed it good. And what I know now is that Lila Mae was the last one up there. She must know something. More than what she put in her report. Personally, I don't like Watson as the perp here, but she's all I got and I'm going to go with what I got. So why don't you do your friend a favor and have her talk to me as soon as she punches in tomorrow. Or she's going to be in more trouble than she already is." Arbergast stands up, last month's issue of *Lift* magazine in his mitt. "Now I got to check out the head. You've kept me here long enough."

Arbergast takes his time in the bathroom, but after Chuck has finally appeased his bladder (for now), he puts a call through to Lila Mae's building. He has never seen Lila Mae's building, but he can picture the phone ringing on and on in the empty hallway.

*   *   *

She hears keen laughter in the hall outside her room, gut chortle she has heard many times before in the office. She hears the steel door scrape open behind her. Chancre says to the men outside the door, "A Chinaman and nun, oh that's rich, my boys, that's rich," and he's inside the room. (Cell, she prefers.)

Enter Chancre in his Sunday suit, a white number favored by Southern gentlemen. He sits in the seat opposite Lila Mae, swabs his greasy neck with a blue polka-dot handkerchief. "Not many windows in here, huh?" he says, looking with distaste at the dingy room. There is no maître d', cigarette girls with incandescent smiles and fishnet stockings.

She says nothing.

"Heard you had yourself a little visit to that colored lady of Fulton's today," Chancre says. He inspects the damp lines of grit he's just rubbed into his hankie. "Your old stomping grounds, right? I still go back to old Bridgehook whenever I can. Chairman of my thirty-fifth reunion. Can you beat that?"

There is not much to hear from the other side of the table.

"That's right, you don't talk much. I've heard that you don't like to talk much. It's all right. Must be hard for you in the Department. They can be a rough bunch of guys sometimes—I should know, because I made them that way." His wet lips part:

112

faintly yellow teeth. "But you've distinguished yourself. Don't think I haven't noticed your good work. Bobby's always given you high evaluations. Are you happy there, working for the Department, Miss Watson?"

"I like my job," Lila Mae responds. Her voice is thin. He is fat and pink. On the United Elevator Co. advertisements, they airbrush away the pocks in his cheeks, the red slivers in his nose. In person he is too flesh, a handful of raw meat. Dogs have been known to follow him, optimistic.

"I'm glad to hear it," Chancre says brightly. "You have a great future ahead of you, I can see that. If only you don't misstep. And it's easy to take a wrong step."

"This your way of trying to win my vote?" Lila Mae asks. "A one-on-one campaign speech?" Where will Chancre be without his elevator industry endorsement money, his grilled porterhouse steaks soft in blood, tumblers of whiskey. Where will he be when the black box emerges from the silt, breaks the surface, and utters Fulton's final curse against him and his ilk?

Chancre smiles and sits back in his chair. It complains of his bulk and Lila Mae would love to see it crash down, dash Chancre to the floor. Chancre says, "I don't need your vote. Not at this point. There's no way Lever is going to cinch this election. I've seen to it."

"And what happens when *Lift* comes out tomorrow and your constituency reads about the black box?"

He smiles again. "*Lift* isn't running anything about Fulton. They've changed their editorial stance on the issue, you might say."

Lila Mae doesn't respond to that. She hears screaming from the next room, a door slamming shut and Shush's cronies laughing out in the hall. Keep her here, let the accident scandal grow, hurt Lever even more. He is a thorough man, she thinks.

"What did you talk about with the maid?" Chancre redirects. This next bit is something new for the usually taciturn Miss

113

Watson: sarcasm. She says, "The new helicals coming out next month from United." Not much, really, but sass does not come easily to her.

"I know you don't have it on you because they searched you. Do Reed and Lever already have it?"

"So who did you get to monkey with the Fanny Briggs stack? Pompey?"

"I suppose if you had it," Chancre considers to himself, "Reed wouldn't have sent you out to the Institute."

"Total freefall—that's overdoing it a bit, isn't it? That's not a natural accident. Even IAB will figure that out."

Chancre shakes his head. He says with amusement, "I don't know what line that Reed has been feeding you to get you in on his scheme, but we didn't do anything to the elevators in the Fanny Briggs building. I don't have to. The Chair is mine—right now we're just taking care of details."

Lila Mae smirks. "Just as you didn't have Shush's men search my place." Look at him. Chancre bullied his way up the ranks of the Department, expert in the currency of deal, the Old Dog of Old Dogs. Slapping the backs of his comrades in good fun, guffawing, chasing whores with the Mayor when he was still Assistant District Attorney and as hungry as Chancre. She remembers he defeated the previous Guild Chair, "Boss" Holt, by default when the old bastard withdrew the night before the election. Chuck's collection of lore describes certain pictures: Holt in an assignation with a long-limbed chorus girl. A setup.

"Reed really has you turned around, doesn't he?" Chancre says. He folds his handkerchief in half, and half again. "A frame job, then? Why would we wait until after this accident of yours before searching your house? If we had, according to your theory, sabotaged Fanny Briggs, why would we wait until you'd been tipped off we were out to get you? Now, let's say by some strange turn of events you were in possession of the blueprints. You would have handed them over to Reed and Lever like a good little girl, and there would have been no need to go to your house." The handkerchief is in his pocket, right where he wants it. "You didn't even enter into things until the accident on Friday, and even then, you weren't a concern until you went over to that swami shack you guys call a clubhouse and they sent you to talk to Fulton's woman." Chuckling now. "You Intuitionists really are crazy. Maybe instead of 'separating the elevator from elevatorness' you should separate paranoia from fact."

She sits back and makes a fist in her lap, under the table, where the smug old cracker can't see it. Why is he feeding her this line? The elaborate abduction scene, the trip through the industrial graveyard, making her sit in the dungeon to accelerate her fear. "You certainly made the most of the accident in your press conference," she says. Watch his eyes through all this pa-laver.

"There's an election on, isn't there? I'm supposed to make the most of it." Chancre drops his politician game and looks deep into Lila Mae's eyes, switching tactics as if he knows what Lila Mae is thinking. "Look, Lila Mae Watson: those friends of yours have got you into a heap of trouble. Two weeks from now, where will you be? In my Department, that's where. The boys give you grief, I know that. But you've been spared. You should have seen what they did to Pompey to break him in. Now he's my boy. I'm not like the rest of the fellas, though. I'm all for your people. You might not think so, but I am. I'm all for colored progress, but gradual. You can't do everything overnight—that would be chaos." His fingers fiddle the air between him and Lila Mae. "I want to make you an example. Of what your people can achieve. That's what makes you run, right? To prove something?"

Lila Mae says, "In exchange for what?"

Chancre pauses a moment, savoring, responds: "Do your job. Serve the Department. Reed's got you running around looking for

Fulton's little box—well, if you happen to find it, you give it to us. What good is it going to do them in the long run? They may sway some of the undecideds, but the Empiricists have always been the party of the Elevator Inspectors Guild, and always will be. You believe what they tell you and think that Lever and them are 'friends of the colored people' or some such, but they're the same as anyone else. They want to get what they can out of the system. Just like me. And just like you." He shouts, "Joe—open it up, will you? We're done here."

Back to Lila Mae: "We're done here, right?"

"I can go?"

"We'll even give you a ride. Aren't a lot of buses around here."

She hears the door open behind her. Chancre stands. "So we understand each other, right?"

Lila Mae says, "And if I don't go along?"

Chancre stretches and sighs. "I thought I was clear. I pride myself on making myself understood. Especially around election time. I want you to find Fulton's box and give it to me. Because no one cares about a nigger. Because if you don't, the next time you come down here, you won't meet with me. You'll talk to one of Shush's boys, and they are never misunderstood."

* * *

Lila Mae has forgotten this incident. But no matter. It still happened. It happened like this:

It was a night in late August, a night that rekindled in rattling windows and tree branch palsy that lost recollection of autumn, misplaced for the succession of bright summer distractions, trapped heat in small rooms and sweaty underarms. But it was always there waiting. Autumn always comes, and that first night late in summer is a reminder, a small hello, dear, that it is coming. That night toward the end of her sixth summer was the night of the annual visitation.

116

She couldn't sleep for the wind's tiresome argument with the house. A minor player in that argument, almost a bystander, was the scraping of dry leaves across the field behind the house—it was to Lila Mae that it spoke, recommending a glass of water for her parched throat. It was silent downstairs, and late; this realization pit itself against her mother's quite firm instructions that she be in bed by nightfall. And stay there. Here it was, a good ways into nightfall, and she was indeed in bed as instructed. And thirsty. Her parents must be asleep—she hadn't heard a sound since that last sound, that loud hinge-squeaking of her parents' bedroom door as they retired for the night. At the usual time, when they always went to bed. She had contemplated this larceny many times before and always persuaded herself against it: to steal a glass of water. The possibility of a spanking hand invariably convinced her against that course of action, so rebellious, going for a glass of water when she should be in bed. But not tonight. Tonight fall had happened by, and that meant another summer had passed. More or less—there would still be a hot day or two, but hot days under the brown pall of autumn. Another summer had passed. She could count summers and that meant she was older, or so her persuasions whispered. Old enough, her dry throat urged, to hazard discovery while on a late-night adventure for a glass of water. She pulled back the quilt with a dangerous flourish. So be it: a glass of water.

The door opened without a sound. She knew it would—she'd gotten that far, at least, on her previous, scrubbed missions. She looked down the hallway to her parents' room and saw no line of light beneath the door. They were asleep. She paused, knowing that her parents were everywhere, like air, and perhaps possessing bat-powers of hearing. She'd learned about bats and how they hang upside down on clothespin claws when they sleep, and how they have big ears because they have no eyes. She did not hear the springs in her parents' bed sing as they did when her father heaved himself out of bed to investigate, for example, a little girl's illegal trespass beyond her door. Creak—the floorboards creaked. With that first blush of courage she stepped into the hall and the floorboards creaked. So loud they'll be out spanking her any second. But no. Still no sound from their room. If she stepped very slowly with just her little toes first, the floor did not give up creaks. She was brave after four steps, quickening her feet's pressure on the gullible floorboards after four successful steps, and on the fifth they creaked. She could feel the dirt beneath her toes even though she'd watched her mother sweep that very afternoon, with her sure, strong strokes. There was invisible dirt and she felt it. She did not hear the bed springs sing. When she got to the head of the stairs, she remembered that the stairs were very loud if you stepped on them, but not loud at all if you stepped close to the wall, away from the center where there was less support. Needless to say, she was very thirsty when she finally made it down the stairs, for it took a long time for her to traverse the peril of the stairs. She remembered half a prayer and said that half a prayer to herself all the way down; she could not be bothered to remember that other half of the prayer because she only faked it in church, mouthing the words, only occasionally speaking them so her parents would not spank her. She did not hear any sound from the room upstairs, so maybe half a prayer is enough sometimes. Or has no effect one way or another. She wondered what she had been afraid of all the other times before when she had been thirsty at night and wanted to come downstairs but didn't. Felt that same wonder as she padded across the parlor rug and slowly opened the door to the kitchen. After feeling her way around the kitchen table and its sharp corners, she reached into the sink for a glass, and that was when her father struck a match, loud and rough, on a leg of the kitchen table and lit the kitchen table candle. She almost wet her nightclothes. Thought, they really are everywhere. She pulled her arm back quickly and stood before her father's hands.

He'd been sitting in the dark with a glass of his whiskey. The dark grease from his day's work on his automobile was smeared up his large arms to his elbows. She saw that he was half slumped over the table and making words with his mouth but not making sounds. He looked at her through heavy eyes. Her father pushed the wooden chair away from the table and tapped his lap. He told her to come here. She sat on his lap, hesitating for a second because she thought the machine grease on his pants might stain her nightclothes and she would get in trouble with her mother, but her father said to come so she sat on his broad lap. He tapped the paper on the table and asked her, "They teaching you how to read, girl?"

She nodded, looking at the yellow paper on the table before her. It had drawings on it, and words.

Her father said, "Tell me what that says, then," tapping the paper again and leaving a portion of black fingerprint on the page.

She peered down at the paper, which was yellow in the candle's light. Above and below the drawings the words sat in small lumps and taunted her. She thought she would get in trouble. There were a lot of words she had never seen before so she looked for a few reassuring words she did know and found them scattered around. *At. The.* She struggled. She didn't know where to start because the words she had learned aready were far apart, not grouped together so that she could pick a spot and begin there. Starting one place was the same as starting any other place. So she picked one of the drawings at the top of the page, the one that looked like her mother's loom, and drew the tiny letters together, taking them one at a time and drawing them together. Where the white space was, that was the end of the word. The wind still aggravated the windows in their frames, and the leaves chortled. She said haltingly, "On . . . yon . . . ho-host-ing . . ."

Her father said, she felt the words in his chest against her back, "Union Hoisting Engine." Her father read, " 'Arbo's Patent

Double Gear Hoisting Engine, adapted in connection with Safety Platform for Storage Warehouses, Packing Houses, Shipping Docks, Mines and etc. Motion of Platform at will of attendant up to a hundred feet per minute.' That means it's strong and fast," he added. Her father pointed to another drawing that looked like two small water barrels connected by a wooden frame. Her father read, " 'Lifting Power-Gear Combination. For Universal Hoisting Machine, as illustrated below, showing the 'Belt Attachment' by which the machine is instantly stopped in case the Gearing reaches an unsafe motion from any cause, as in the breaking of a Belt while the machine is in use.' That means if anything goes wrong, that will hold the elevator up. So it won't break." He continued through the Arbo Elevator Co.'s old catalog, reading out to her the names of machines, the Universal Hoisting Machine, the Metropolitan Hoisting Engine, the Relief Hoisting Engine, the Automatic Safety Drum, the Lifting Power-Screw Combination— this last one almost looking like a fat metal bat to her, hanging on the ceiling like it did in the drawing. Her father read every word on the page to her and when he was done he told her, "You better listen to your teacher. You better listen to your teacher and learn what she tells you."

He shook her off his lap and drank his whiskey. "What'd you come down here for?" he asked her, talking loud now, not like when he was reading and he whispered.

"A glass of water."

"Then get it and get your ass in bed," he told her.

She was in the parlor with her glass of water when she heard him blow out the candle in the kitchen. Like he was autumn.

* * *

Everything is a mess. Her bureau rifled, oddly sad stockings hang limp out a drawer. Papers in no stack, their perpendicular corners mapping the better part of 360 degrees across the rug. Her potted plant depotted, an akimbo regret of roots and soil. Her plastic pear, Lila Mae's one salvo toward knicknackery, dud on the floor. Some of her books are downright gone, Ettinger's *Hoists and Pulleys* an agony of broken spine, *The Counterweight and Its Effects* hiding under the radiator among cobwebs. Cushions overturned and exposing cleaner faces. Window shades askew, indolently slouching in their frames. A mess. Untidy.

Lila Mae closes the door of her apartment. This is not Shush's style, unless they wanted to underscore her discussion with Chancre. As if her drive out to the warehouse weren't enough. (Markham had the gall to tip his chauffeur's cap to her when he dropped her off here.) The two men who were here the other night were religious in their neatness. They'd obviously been here a while before she came upon them, Lila Mae thinks, and had left no mark. Respectful guests. These new men did not need to make a secret of their work, didn't care. They thought she had it, or had a clue, a scratchmark on a pad, that might lead them to it. The black box.

She hadn't wanted to go back to Intuitionist House. She wanted to see her apartment, sit on her couch where she has boiled away so many hours, until they lifted away in a fog. Where she feels as much peace as she ever feels in this city. Chancre's words rippling out, perturbations, even to here. She thinks, he's trying to get under her skin but does not understand that Reed and Lever do not have her loyalty. Her loyalty is to Fulton, to his words, and she is involved now because she has been wronged. They have sullied her name. He will not confuse her.

Will she sleep here tonight. Will the man Natchez still be at the Intuitionist House, and will she hear his comforting rap at her door.

She hasn't eaten since breakfast and here it is after midnight and most of her neighbors' windows are dark. Her block is a working block, where the lids rest firm on the metal trash cans in front of the buildings, because that is how they do things in this country they have sailed to, to scrabble up. Things are different here than on the dear islands they have departed. Packing, cramming a life into a few tattered bags as an offering for a better life. They go to sleep early because hard work is how you get ahead in this country. So they have been told.

The door to her icebox is ajar, the snout of a milk bottle peeks out, its issue a dry white cloud on the floor. She picks up a can of tinned meat from the kitchen tile. She digs out some of the gray material onto a piece of bread and mashes the meat into a lumpy layer with the underside of her spoon. The meat and the bread are of the same consistency. The hunger dizziness in her head drains away down some inner sluice. She eats and thinks: to visit her house on Friday and then trash it today is redundant except to prime her fear. Reel in their threats from abstraction. She looks over her room, at the things they have touched: there is no indication as to when they were here. They could have wrecked her room late Friday night after she left, or any time on Saturday, before they were sure she did not possess it. Chancre's invidious spell: we did not sabotage the Fanny Briggs stack, we have not been to your apartment. Who else, then? A shard of gristle digs into her gums. What's left of the animal when you have ground it up: a few stubborn pieces. She will not be so easily dislodged. He cannot make her distrust Reed because she has never trusted Reed.

The painting has not been moved. She removes it from the wall, twists the combination into the lock and opens the safe. Everything is there. She thinks, these white men see her as a threat but refuse to make her a threat, cunning, duplicitous. They see her as a mule, ferrying information back and forth, not clever or curious enough to explore the contents. Brute. Black.

She goes into her bedroom and replaces the mattress on the box spring. She is soon asleep in her clothes. The sheet is dislodged from one corner, and its loose and untucked edge cuts beneath her neck, a soft guillotine.

*   *   *

She grabs the griffin's head and rams it against the plate. The griffin was, Lila Mae guesses, a gift from Griffin Elevator Co., the now-defunct British firm. Siding with the Intuitionists is never terribly wise.

After a time, the heavy door of Intuitionist House opens and she sees Natchez. His broad face is glad after an initial moment of surprise. He says, "You're back, Lila Mae," and shifts the paneled door wide.

"Did you miss me?" Lila Mae asks, before she can check herself. Check that impulse.

Natchez sweeps his arm into the foyer. "Mr. Reed was running around like a chicken with his head cut off yesterday." He surveys, assesses: "But you seem to be in one piece."

She sees herself in the long mirror on the other edge of the hall. She is in one piece. For now.

"May I?" Natchez asks and Lila Mae reluctantly gives him her trenchcoat. He has to do his job. His employers are always watching. Everywhere the pair are under cruel gazes from the smoky portraits of men she recognizes from textbooks, paintings that entomb their subjects with the final slash of brown paint. Any dispensation she has been granted is provisional: she is not wanted here. "They're in the parlor," Natchez says. If he considers his position and place, his face does not betray it.

They walk toward the parlor, Natchez trailing a step behind her. She wants him parallel, equal. "Your uncle is still sick?" she asks.

"It takes some time when he gets his spells," Natchez answers. "He'll be up again soon."

The parlor door is ajar. She can see one long bookcase; she can

123

hear, "I stand before you a fellow disciple, here to talk to you about the pernicious visible." She turns to say goodbye to Natchez, but he is no longer there. She knocks lightly and strides inside, her step suddenly strong.

Mr. Reed and Orville Lever rise from their brown leather armchairs when she enters. Polite for a lady. The fireplace between them is orange and live, to warm their cold blood. It is not cold outside. Mr. Reed places his folder at his feet and says, "Orry, this is Miss Lila Mae Watson." His expression is hard for Lila Mae to read, stone.

Lever extends his hand. "Mr. Reed has told me so much about you, Miss Watson, about all you've done for us." Lever is a perennial sapling despite his gray hair and loose neck-flesh. There is room at his cuffs, his collar, and his pants drape deflated off small knees. She cannot remember if he looked this wasted the last time she saw him, but that was before the campaign. Lila Mae thinks she would probably look worse than this if she had to talk all day, she who abhors speaking. He wears a nailhead suit in a Saville Row cut, in contrast to Chancre's street thug look: their contest is between the academy and the pool hall, chess and boxing. The Intuitionists have chosen an appropriate champion.

"Orry," Mr. Reed says, "why don't you run along upstairs and continue rehearsing by yourself? That's probably a more constructive use of your time than worrying yourself over these matters."

Lever nods and gathers his speech. "Yes, yes," he agrees sleepily, "You're right. I'll be upstairs if you need me." He turns to the elevator inspector. He is one of those translucent white people, every vein swims up to the surface of his skin. "Miss Watson, it was a pleasure. I hope we'll meet again soon."

Once the door is shut, Reed directs Lila Mae to Lever's seat and she sinks into it. It seems to close around her body. He says, "Where have you been, Miss Watson? We were worried when you didn't return yesterday with Sven." His tone is even, emotionless.

"I decided to make my own way home," Lila Mae answers. She has no doubts about the efficacy of her game face, the cadences she reserves for white men like Mr. Reed. "I haven't been back to the Institute for a long time."

"I thought something had happened to you."

"Mrs. Rogers wasn't much help, I'm afraid."

Mr. Reed nods quickly. His mind is turning on itself. "Sven says she let you in. You're the first person she's said more than two words to since we received the packet. What did she tell you?"

"She says she doesn't know anything about the blueprint," Lila Mae tells him. "She was adamant about that. That she's already given up all she had."

"Do you believe her?"

"It's hard to say. I don't think she trusts anyone."

Mr. Reed sets his head back against the chair and crosses his legs, considering this. "The postmark. The postmark on the package was from the Institute's post office. I was sure . . ." He drifts off for a moment. "Do you think she may be holding out for an offer of monetary compensation?"

Lila Mae shakes her head. "I don't think that's it," she says. "I saw her face. I don't think she'll talk to me again."

Mr. Reed doesn't say anything. He gets up and walks over to the writing table. He hovers there, then remembers something and tries to look nonchalant as he locks a drawer. Lila Mae can't see it but she can hear it. So what do you have in there Mr. Reed? He removes a magazine from a pile of papers and gives it to Lila Mae. She looks at the cover of *Lift*, the silly illustration of Santa Claus, and searches through the contents page. She is aware that Mr. Reed is watching her, and makes a show of searching for the article on Fulton even though Chancre informed her that it would not appear. She looks up finally and asks, "Where is it?"

"Exactly the question I asked when I picked it up off our

doorstep this morning. I put a call through to the editor-in-chief, a fellow I know. The switchboard informed me that he had called in sick. Then I asked to speak to the reporter, Ben Urich, and the operator told me he hadn't shown up for work today."

"Are you saying that Chancre got to them?"

He looks at her. Does he suspect? His eyes are holes. He says, "That would be the logical conclusion. Our opponent has a long reach." Mr. Reed sits back in the chair. "I thought you were going to return here after the Institute," he says.

"I decided to spend the night in my own bed," Lila Mae responds.

"Didn't we agree that that wasn't wise, Miss Watson? Given the current climate?" He's drawing an invisible glyph on the arm of the chair with a bony finger.

Didn't we agree. As if she were a child. "I wanted to sleep in my own bed." She says, "Do we have any other leads?"

"I have an idea or two about who our mysterious person may be," Mr. Reed tells her. "But I'm not prepared to discuss it. My theories are, at the moment, only half formed. In any case, I imagine that preparations for the Follies will keep our adversaries busy until after Wednesday. Do you plan to attend?"

"The Follies?"

"You're not performing, are you?"

She'd forgotten about the Funicular Follies. "I've never been," she informs him.

"I try to avoid them myself. Such a garish display. But with the election next week, it's important for Lever to put in an appearance. In these crucial final days."

"Of course," Lila Mae says. It will not be wise for her to attend, since it's a Department function and she is currently a suspect quantity in the office.

Is her concern in her face? Mr. Reed says, "You decided not to report to work today, I assume."

"Evidently."

"That won't look good with Internal Affairs. That was a mistake."

"I'll handle it. Once we have the box, it won't matter, correct?" Place it back in his lap.

"Of course," Mr. Reed says to her. "But I don't know how Chancre will play it with the tabloids."

"I'll handle it," she says. "What's next, then?"

Mr. Reed stands. "If you really want to help . . . if you're not going to take my advice and talk to IAB, it's best if you just stay out of sight. I'll have more information in a few days and we can talk about it then."

She nods. Reluctantly. She is not sure if Mr. Reed trusts her any more than she trusts him. Possible he went to her apartment last night to look for her and saw the mess? Perhaps he is trying to get her out of the way, now that she has served her role as their colored liaison to Mrs. Rogers. The one who knew her language.

He says, "Your room is still available upstairs. I think it is our best option at this point."

Our. Keep her on ice, away from enemies and undue influence in this crucial time. "I agree," she says.

Mr. Reed looks down at papers and poises his pen. She has been dismissed. Lila Mae walks stiffly out of the parlor. Every room she enters lately is a cell, she thinks as she steps up the stairs to her guest quarters. Each room is an elevator cab without buttons, controlled by a malefic machine room. Going down, no one else gets on, she cannot step off. There is a tap on her shoulders at the top of the stairs. It is Natchez, who asks, "Can I visit you tonight? There's something I need to talk to you about."

* * *

She knew he was nervous about asking her, judging from the protracted ellipsis between "Would you like to see that new picture at the Royale" and "with me," a gap that the song on the

127

radio took astute advantage of, wedging in a bridge and chorus. She said yes. They'd gone to the movies together plenty of times before. Movies good and bad, over the course of many years. Lila Mae's parents liked Grady Jr., and Grady Jr.'s parents adored Lila Mae. Grady Jr., in fact, often stopped by the house just to talk with Marvin Watson. About fishing, or the eternal question of when exactly the county would get around to paving the roads of colored town. Usually they talked on the porch, as Marvin Watson did with his friends, which was how he regarded Grady Jr. Lila Mae and Grady Jr. were friends, and he had just asked her out on a date. After she said yes, she paid for her chocolate shake as she always did when they stopped in at the drugstore. And he paid for his vanilla shake, and they went their separate ways for the afternoon.

She knew things were different from the way he smiled at her when she opened the front door to the night air. Lila Mae and Grady Jr. had grown up together, skinned knees in tandem, learned to crawl through mutual toddler encouragement. It was a tricky crescent of a smile, and Lila Mae had never observed it in his repertoire before, in all the years they had known each other. Never seen it before in her whole life, one might say. He asked, "Are you ready?" and soon Lila Mae was in the passenger seat of his father's red and rusting pickup truck. He'd been born chubby; the subplot of his maturation had been a long skirmish toward natural proportions. Before Lila Mae could sit down in the car, she had to remove Grady Sr.'s toolbox from the seat, and on the rutted trek to the movie theater, a screwdriver and hammer clinked against each other at every pock in the road. And there were many pocks in the road. The moon had just cleared the treeline.

She knew there was not much time left for the movies, or much else. Grady Jr. was heading up to the capitol in the fall to go to college. Lila Mae had not seen much of him that summer; he spent most of the summer working at the quarry to save up for books and anything else he might need up North. Summers had not been the same for a long time, Lila Mae reckoned. There was no school, but nothing else to take its place. The streets were shrinking, and she felt about the places they led to the same way she felt about her hair when she saw it on the bathroom floor after her mother cut it off. She sensed that the change she felt within her was sister to the change within Grady Jr. They always did everything together. He didn't speak much as they drove to the Royale.

They walked around the side of the Royale to the stairs that led to the entrance reserved for colored patrons. Walked up the stairs to the balcony seating reserved for colored patrons, up to nigger heaven, and when Lila Mae reached in her pocket to pay Skinny, Grady Jr. preempted her and paid for the both of them. Grady Jr., who had kept a rigid accounting of every cent Lila Mae had ever owed him, and would demand the two or three cents she owed him for candy or a comic book, whatever she had borrowed, each time he saw her. He was a curious boy. He wanted to be a dentist, a pragmatic choice. Teacher, doctor, preacher, undertaker. What a colored boy can aspire to in a world like this. Colored people always got bad teeth, always got a soul needed tending. Always dying. His father did carpentry, whatever he could pick up. His mother worked in town cleaning for the judge's family. Scrubbing stone steps. Grady Sr. had names for each of his tools that he would never utter in the presence of another living person. A dentist. But first he had to go to college, which was not a problem because he was a nice boy, and industrious, and the colored college in the capitol was eager for boys like him. The future of the race. It was the third moon of the summer, and it hung above the treeline as if the night were a farm and it a farmer, and he would take his time as he tracked through the crops, knowing and understanding it was his and only his and he knew all its secrets.

129

She had not seen the movie before and had seen the movie before. That's how Lila Mae perceived the movies. Sometimes they had different titles, but the actors were usually the same, and if they were not the same, they looked the same. At one point Lila Mae noticed that she and Grady Jr. were sharing the same armrest. She was sure that she had laid claim to it when the lights dimmed, and had not noticed when this situation came to be. Now she was acutely aware of the situation. How had he snuck his arm up there? She did not move her arm. She noticed that his arm began to press against her, a firm warmth. The pressure against her arm, and the warmth, would retreat and then insist again as it rediscovered its boldness and purpose. On the screen, a white lady with long dark hair wept as she realized that social forces would keep her from her love. Eventually, Lila Mae removed her arm and placed it across her lap. A few minutes later, Grady Jr. sighed.

As for Lila Mae, she had her own plans for the future and had started to make inquiries.

"That was some movie," Grady Jr. said, as they started for home.

"It sure was," Lila Mae seconded.

As they cleared the town limits, Grady Jr. said, "That was some movie. It was pretty short."

"It seemed like a regular movie," Lila Mae said.

"No-uh," Grady Jr. said. "I looked at the clock when we were leaving the movie. It wasn't even an hour and a half long. It was short." There were no more streetlights, and few houses to offer light from their windows.

"Maybe it was," Lila Mae replied.

Grady Jr. cleared his throat and stared at the road. "This morning when I ran into your father, I told him that I'd have you back on the front porch by eleven, but it's not even close to that, and we're already on the way to your house."

He had turned off the county road, into the patchy trail that wound to Miller's Hollow. She had passed the overgrown entrance countless times, and sometimes her mother or her father would make a joke that she didn't understand. She knew one or two jokes herself, though: that half of colored town wouldn't be walking and breathing if not for Miller's Hollow, and more than one marriage ceremony had been performed, under duress, a month or two after the betrothed had spent some time at Miller's Hollow. There was another way to the Hollow, a path through the woods that the children played in. Whenever the clearing's daylight was visible through the trees, the children stopped and doubled back into the woods. While they were not prohibited from going there, the children understood that it was not their place. It would have been a nice place to play and stumble; kites would have soared in the lively wind that poured up out of the quarry. But the children understood, and found other places to play.

Lila Mae felt let down when she and Grady cleared the woods. It wasn't a hollow at all, she saw, but a wide clearing that terminated at the sullen lip of the quarry. The excitement over such an illicit adventure evaporated quickly. The hollow wasn't thrilling or scary or even dull; it was just a place where no trees grew, and brown grass dried out in the sun.

"That was some movie," Grady Jr. said again. He cleared his throat again.

"Yes it was," Lila Mae said. That was the last either of them said for a time. She was aware of his breathing, and the new loudness of everything in the car, every minute shifting. The car's engine ticked off seconds as it cooled, insects clicked and night birds exchanged confidences. She could see the white stone of the other side of the quarry over the curved red hood of the car. It looked like the moon. She'd left the earth some moment when she had blinked and now she and Grady Jr. were on the moon, and that's why it felt so cold, because the moon is cold. And still.

Grady placed a trembling hand on her shoulder and it stopped trembling once he put it there, once he had a place to place it. She felt she was supposed to look at him, and did so. His lips first bumped into her nose, then her cheek, and then he recovered and placed his lips on her lips. His lips were dry and sharp. Once his lips were in place, he did not move them, and the two of them, Lila Mae and Grady Jr., sat there for a time, their lips touching. Then he pulled his lips away and stared out the windshield and placed his hands firmly on the steering wheel. Lila Mae adjusted her feet around the toolbox.

Grady said, "It must be eleven o'clock by now."

Lila Mae said, "It must be."

They looked over at her house when the pickup truck pulled up in front. They could see her father draw back the curtain in the porch window and wave.

Grady said, "I'm sorry. I didn't mean to make you mad."

Lila Mae said, "I have to go inside," and all night she cursed herself because she knew that she and Grady Jr. would never go to the movies again. She wasn't mad at all, but she didn't say that. He should know how she is after all this time. She wasn't mad at all, she wanted him to kiss her more. But Lila Mae didn't say that.

*   *   *

She has removed her jacket and tie and opened the top button of her shirt. Natchez did not specify a time. It's inching on midnight. She disassembles elevators in her mind and imagines that there is a discrepancy between the mass of the elevator before disassembly and after. That this mass returns when the elevator is reassembled. Fulton did not write that, she extrapolated it from the second volume of *Theoretical Elevators*. She is an Intuitionist but is not a fan of the new additions to Fulton's work that come from overseas, are debated in the rooms below her by Intuitionism's epigonic practitioners. They muddle through and sometimes the journals are not all empty, but she prefers her own extrapolations. She thinks her creations adhere to the spiritual side of Fulton's words, while the rest of the movement gets dizzy in the more recondite apocrypha. An unforeseen loss in mass. A mystery.

When he enters he holds a piece of chocolate cake before him as he creeps through the doorway. "I thought you might like some of Mrs. Gravely's cake," he says. He is still in his servant's uniform, a tight white trapezoid around his torso. He sits on the bed next to her. "It was a big hit at dinner," he adds, "which you weren't at."

"I wasn't hungry," Lila Mae says over the fork.

"You have a lot on your mind?" he asks.

"You could say that."

"You don't mind that I came up here?"

"No, I'm glad." Half gone already, the cake.

Natchez looks over to reassure himself that he closed the door and says, "I don't know what Mr. Reed down there told you about your house, but it wasn't like he said it was."

She sets the plate down on the nightstand. "What are you talking about?"

Natchez takes a deep breath and looks at the door again. It's still shut, Lila Mae thinks. He says, "Yesterday when you didn't come back with Sven, he threw a fit. He was mad—I didn't think that little white man had it in him, but there he was, yelling at Mr. Lever and Sven and saying all sorts of stuff. He said Sven should have waited for you. Then he said you must have made a deal with Chancre—I think that's his name—and that you had double-crossed him. I was outside in the hallway. Then he got on the phone and told some men to go and find it. He gave them your address."

The cake in her stomach curdles. "He said this?"

"I figured he was talking about the black box," Natchez says. He sits up straight. "When he said 'it.' "

All wrong. "What do you know about the black box?" she demands.

Natchez smiles. "I know a lot about it," he says. "Fulton was my uncle."

* * *

The boy dreams of places that are not like this, where there is no mud and there is pavement, where there are not wood walls that don't keep the cold out but buildings that erupt from the ground like ancient gods awakening. The night in the places he dreams of is not abundant and terrifying, making him tiny, because the buildings are so tall that there is no night and no stars, just darkness. He is never out in the open where people can see him because the people are locked up in their holes, stacked up one on top the other like in a beehive. They do not speak. Nobody knows anybody's business. Nobody knows where you came from.

There is another world beyond this one.

He understands that she loves him deeply and painfully. She is his mother. But he does not look like her except around the eyes. Their eyes want to hide from their faces, the mother and the son. When they walk into town she makes him walk closely behind her, she clutches him behind her back, as if to shield him from the eyes of the white people. As if she thought they would see him and take him away from her. She does it less now that he is older and taller, but it seems to him it was always unnecessary. The white people do not see colored people, even in broad daylight, in the middle of town. He is as light as white folk when he has not been in the sun much, perhaps that is why she was afraid, but he stays in the sun as much as he can and usually has a slight nut color to his skin. The sun never makes his skin as dark as the skin of his mother and sister. If he stays out of the sun, as in winter when the light is dead and stingy, the darkness in his skin sleeps.

134

He understands that his sister loves him even though they don't have the same father, and when she gets mad at him she reminds him of this, and this is supposed to hurt him. But it doesn't hurt him because he has never met his father so he might as well not exist. And if he doesn't exist then there's no point in feeling anything at all about him. You make do, like when there's no food in the house. You make do. Besides, her father only shows up once in a while, and no good ever comes of it.

He has always been terrified of the woods. Outside, surrounding the house, advancing on the house. Except he's the only one who knows the trees and sticker-bushes are advancing on the house, coming to get him. The moon lets him know. The moon's light picks up the movement of the branches and places it on the wall of his room, and he watches the shadows shake and threaten him. The moon has been warning him since before he could speak that his time with his mother and sister is short: he must leave this place or something bad will happen to him. He does not belong here and the woods are casting him out. The woods say what other people's tongues will not say.

His sister says she knew he was coming that night when their mother came home torn. She says she knew by their mother's silence and crying after that night that something new was coming into their house, and it turned out to be him. Their mother did not go into town to work and the neighbors brought them food and took his sister into their houses some nights when their mother got loud, or was crying and would not leave her bed. Then he came and their mother got better as soon as she saw him and started to go into town again to work. To work for someone else. His sister cleaned him when he was dirty even though she was not that much bigger than him.

Some colored babies are light when they're newborn but he didn't get colored as he got older. His hair was very curly when he was born but it got less curly as he got older. His sister teased him that he had white folks' hair, but one time their mother heard her say this and she yelled at his sister to never do that again. And she didn't. She said she was sorry, later that night when they went to bed. Said it to God in her prayers, I'm sorry for what I said. The boy forgave his sister because it did not occur to him that he had been insulted until his mother got mad. His sister told the truth.

He has a few books he has stolen and they contain devices. He does not understand all the words so he makes up meanings for the words he does not know, using the words around those unknown words. Later he discovers his definitions are right. He has never had trouble understanding the devices. They mean: up.

His mother does not like him to go to town by himself but that's where all the roads lead. And so. The colored people know who he is and do not mistake him for something else. One day he is in town at the store and he holds penny-candy in his hand. There is an old colored man he has never seen before, holding two oranges. The old man is in front of him in line and the boy is happy to wait. This peculiar thing happens: the old colored man steps aside to let him buy his candy. He thinks the man is going off to get something else but after he pays for his candy the man has not added anything to his oranges. He waits behind the boy. It takes him a long time to figure out what happened. Long after he has finished the sweet candy. What he figures out is sour.

* * *

"It could be him," Lila Mae concedes. In the picture, two colored women and one white man stand under slanting sunlight on the porch of an old wooden house. The warped front steps grin. She reconsiders: he is not a man yet, he hides his hands in his trouser pockets boyishly. His black hair is hacked into a bowl cut, jagged and raw above his eyes. In the next picture, and the next, Lila Mae cannot see his eyes at all. He has found his trademark brown trilby, and the brim's veil of shadow hides his mother's eyes. He is

136

surrounded by white men in their first suits, which are loose and shy at the wrists, just short of dignified, almost there. A cocky gang, mouths full of newly acquired cant: the graduation picture of his class at the Pierpont School of Engineering. His mother's arm disappears behind his slim neck in the family photograph (flaky white creases where it has been folded and refolded), he stands shoulder-to-shoulder with his school chums in the graduation picture. He is welcome in both, no intruder, accepted by his companions. But in the school picture she cannot see his eyes.

"It is him," she says. She extracts the next photograph from Natchez's stack, hands firm. It is the Pit before the reign of cluttered walls and tacks, bureaucratic appurtenance. He stands with his fellow warriors, the first champions of the Department of Elevator Inspectors, the men who will rescue this newly vertical city from toddler pratfall. Their haircuts are Safeties, but it is not clear how he favors his hair, the trilby hides his eyes. When he held the Guild Chair, the office walls were not, as they are now, festooned with orchestrated candids of Chancre and municipal burghers, Chancre herding his porcine family in their Sunday best. In this photograph the walls are bare. No other traces of a life before this. He looks away from the camera to the stack of reports on his wide oak desk, concerned. The alumni bulletin announcing his ascension to Dean of the Institute for Vertical Transport features the head shot that she has seen many times, on dust jackets, haunting the marginalia of textbooks. He stares down into the camera now, proud or fearless or empty, offering his black eyes as matching pits for the pit-eye of the camera. He challenges the machine to a duel now, no more hiding: the better man wins reality. His face has overripened into a sagging middle age, but it is the same man from the first photograph.

"Why?" Lila Mae asks. "Never mind."

Natchez slides his mother's photographs into a pile in his lap. "He'd send her letters. This stuff," tapping the memorabilia, "if

137

he got mentioned in the newspaper. If he got a new job. As you can see, she kept it all. When she died I found it all in her trunk. Wrapped in this ribbon right here."

He purses his lips. Lila Mae looks at the envelopes: even then, the Department used those cream envelopes with the foul glue. The ones in office now are probably from the same shoddy gross. "When she got something in the mail from him," Natchez continues, "she'd get all mad for a few days and I learned to walk softly, because she'd whip for little stuff she wouldn't normally raise her voice about. She told me her brother ran away when he was sixteen and she never saw him after that."

Her hand grasps the photograph of him and Natchez's mother and grandmother. "All this time," she murmurs. To turn his back on these two women. "Who was his father?" she asks.

"I always knew they didn't have the same daddy, but I didn't know his was a white man. She never spoke of it. But there it is." He trails off, then offers, "Somebody in Natchez. A white man in Natchez. Gran'ma Alice used to clean their houses."

They hear someone move downstairs and they do not speak. They wait. She stares at the door, not at the man next to her. But she can feel him look at her. For the long time it takes for the sounds to move away, to another quarter of the house.

"She died last summer," Natchez resumes in a whisper. "That's when I found out who my uncle was."

She can look at him again. "And the man who works here? Your uncle with the numb leg?"

A splinter of a grin. "I gave him some money to disappear for a few days. I wanted to get inside this place."

"You want the black box."

"It's my birthright. I got claim to it as his nephew, is the way I see it. I'm his only living relative. From what I seen, he's a big man with these elevator folks. The Great James Fulton. And all this carrying on they been doing the last few days, Mr. Reed and

138

them and putting you out to talk to that woman up there. They want that machine he made. It's my birthright."

"Then that's it," Lila Mae decides. It's true, no more rumors. The box is out there. "How did you hear about it?"

"It's in his last letter to my mother," Natchez answers. "I got it back at my place with the rest of my mama's things. He sounds all crazy, going on about this and that, but then he says he's figured out the perfect elevator. That they'll all be surprised when they see it. But then he passed on years ago and it hasn't come out yet, has it? Somebody has to have it because ain't nobody using it." He gestures vaguely around the room. "I wanted to see what these people was like, so I came here. First day here, I find you."

His words recede. Who else knows that Fulton was colored. Mrs. Rogers. Did he tell her? Was she his mistress like they insinuate? What they say about colored people when we're not around. What did Fulton do when they acted white? Talk about "the colored problem" and how it is our duty to help the primitive race get in step with white civilization. Out of darkest Africa. Or did he remain silent, smile politely at their darkie jokes. Tell a few of his own. "Watch that," Natchez says, "that's my blood." She's crumpled the photograph in her fist, adding new, nongeometric creases to the ones already there.

"Can I count on you?" he asks her, next to her on the bed, close enough.

"For what?"

"They always take away from our people. I don't know if they know he was colored, but if they do you know they ain't going to tell the truth. They would never admit that. Them downstairs would never say that they worship a nigger. Make them puke all over their expensive carpets they got. They'd die before they say that." Lila Mae is looking down at the stack of photographs in his lap. Fulton a spy in white spaces, just like she is. But they are not alike. She's colored. Natchez says, "When I hear them talk about

139

his invention, they always saying it's the future. It's the future of the cities. But it's our future, not theirs. It's ours. And we need to take it back. What he made, this elevator, colored people made that. It's ours. And I'm going to show that we ain't nothing. Show them downstairs and the rest of them that we are alive."

After he leaves, Lila Mae does not sleep. Because she remembers how his hand felt when he grabbed it in his and said, "I need you if I'm going to do it."

I need you.

Part ONE

Aspirants to luxury often opt for red and gold, hues long-soaked into their mentalities as the spectra of royalty. There are no kings these days, in these cities. Just moles. Red drapes two stories tall hang from assembly-line pins, floor to ceiling, cinched at the waist by gold sashes and shod with gold tassels. Gold trim traipses the edges of the red tablecloths, a scheme repeated in miniature on the napkins nuzzling the men's crotches. In the deep red carpet beneath their feet gold creatures, refugees of no identifiable myth-system, writhe in pools of lava. Red and gold, damnation and greed. Gold the trumpets and saxophones, red the cheeks and noses of the musicians from all their plangent huffing. In case anyone finds himself lost, in case anyone wonders what this spectacle is that proceeds in Banquet Room Three of the Winthrop Hotel, a humble placard just inside the chamber offers, FUNICULAR FOLLIES. Gold script on red. The hapless wayfarer, en route to the hotel cocktail lounge, has been duly warned.

Rick Raymond and the Moon-Rays, smart in white tuxedos, summon ditties upbeat in tempo and inconsolate in lyric from the

145

instruments they have purchased on lay-away. Rick Raymond notices that the elevator inspectors do not dance. This is not a solid rule among their clan so much as the tasteless fruit of learned helplessness. They don't know where to place their feet, have untold psychic bruises still tender from adolescent embarrassments and don't, collectively, dance. It is a shame, for they love the music despite their unfortunate malady. This is the music they no longer hear on the radio; it has been crowded out into unstable frequencies by new rhythms. It is slipping away. But Rick Raymond and the Moon-Rays are pros. They've weathered much worse gigs than this. The unpleasantness at the Mortonswieg wedding, to name one recent example. With a crowd this sedentary, so intent on flagging down the help for refills, the band needn't worry about nettlesome requests. The music required for the upcoming acts is uncomplicated, the format of the festivities loose. A no-hassle night before an audience of drunks—Rick Raymond is glad, for his band is notoriously sloppy.

Rick Raymond pushes the blue ruffles of his tuxedo shirt away from his chin, where they tickle. He sings about a girl named Mary Lou and her eyes so blue. The band gets a lot of gigs on account of Rick's preternatural resemblance to a popular singer and matinee idol. He is not above stealing some of that singer's more famous moves, like he is now, cradling the microphone stand as if it were some swooning lass, petting invisible blonde hair. Your eyes so blue, he croons.

Quite the ham, Rick Raymond, but look at these pigs. This affair is a few bubbles short of champagne. The snouts of these men are up at their plates, nudging shrimp cocktails, which look like bones floating in blood. Their tuxedos have identical wide lapels, and a close inspection of all the labels on the inside pockets will attest to the handiwork of a certain Ziff Brothers, 10% DISCOUNT IF YOU BRING A FRIEND. The shrimp cocktails are reinforcements, following greasy battalions of tiny hot dogs and stunted egg rolls (the snacks perched on silver trays, wallowing in small

146

brown pools of oil, dripping amniotic fluid). These appetizers appease the stomachs of the men, which have been thrown into tart consternation by the sudden influx of free whiskey. First drinks, then appetizers and drinks, then follies and drinks, and dinner and drinks, always, on their high holy day, this most august occasion, the 15th Annual Funicular Follies. Biggest night of the year for these shamen of the vertical vehicular.

Rick Raymond sings of Peggy Sue and her love so true. Fingers root after the final residue of cocktail sauce, tongues lick fingers. And now cigars! Early this morning the elevator inspectors, pep of step, dutifully filed into the Pit to confront their scattered desks (addresses of miscreant cabs, all-points bulletins on cabled fugitives). Discovered five cigars in that paper disarray, five cigars apiece from Big Man Chancre, to be smoked at this hour, now, in this room. Holt started the cigar ritual during his administration but nobody remembers that now. Chancre has usurped his predecessor's munificence by gifting five, not that paltry four cigars. Gray blue genies escape the caves, these elevator inspector gorges, and commune by the ceiling. Confer, trading notes on the dynamics of air on this northern continent, free from any form of ventilation.

They sit at the edges of the round tables, the elevator inspectors, and smoke cigars and trade misinformation about which of their comrades will perform this evening, and no one needs to remark upon the importance of this night, the forty-second anniversary of the Department of Elevator Inspectors. Retired inspectors boast of their private sector sinecures, the beat cops update their elders on the mood of the street these days. They share irregularities, shady confidences, exploits, tales of graft, while stealing the occasional glance at the Internal Affairs table, strategically placed at the back of the hall, and only half full. The IAB boys have only been invited here tonight out of the vestiges of ancient solidarity, polite gesture. They are not wanted and know it. Mostly they come for the free food and drinks and the whores at the cocktail lounge down the hall. They crack wise and angle scuffed brogues on the empty seats at their table, taking full opportunity of their proximity to the kitchen door to raid each new arrival of the hors d'oeuvre tray. Except for one man, a carbuncular specimen who is intent, who is not drinking, who is very much on the case even though he punched out hours before.

Pretty baby, Rick Raymond concedes, you drive me crazy.

They have left the wives at home, what wives remain to these men. Elevator inspection is hard on a marriage, a family. Once in a while, with greater frequency as the night stumbles on, one of the inspectors makes a clumsy grab for one of the cigarette girls, who are as a group blonde and young and endowed by the Creator with exceptional breasts or legs, but never both. Squeal and smile at the swatting paws. Each fumble is followed by a chorus of hearty guffaws from the rest of the table. And the man joins the laughter of his comrades and shrugs off his failure while simmering inside. Because these minor escapes of ass and tit are no joke: this is real hunger. Scenarios, as they will, unfold. Her cigarette tray, the candy and mints and tobacco, the humiliating detritus of his life, is what separates them, willfully schismatic. Can she be persuaded to forgive him his paunch, his retreating hairline, slurred speech, this young girl, this forgiving young nearsighted girl lays down her cigarette tray. He whispers. She agrees silently, it is all in her eyes: her eyes are wide in knowledge of his need. Forgiving. Outside the banquet hall at the reception desk, the clerk winks man-code. The room key is red and gold in his hand.

Lila Mae picks up empty plates from the tables of her coworkers. No one recognizes her.

It's time. Rick Raymond taps the microphone and the men stir from their scuttlebutt and applaud. From more than one man's oily lips issues that whistle one only hears in crowds. Rick Raymond says into his mike, "Welcome to the Funicular Follies, inspectors!" His words are obscured by the roar. "Settle down, gentlemen, the fun's about to start. You guys having a good time tonight?" More roar, a shattered glass or two. "Well hang on to your hats, because this opening act is sure to give you even more *lift!*" The snare drum is only too eager to abet this pun. "May I present to you, fresh from a two-week sellout tour of Australia, the Great Luigi!"

There are shouts of gratitude and amazement from the assembled, heads turn to seek out Chancre at his table near the stage. It's Chancre's doing, after all, no one doubts that. The Great Luigi begins his number, something from some opera or whatnot, they can't understand the words anyway—more important than the song is the man's appearance, the signal Chancre is sending the week before the election. The famous tenor is an international sensation. He's sung for heads of state, diplomats, dictators of small countries with enormous mineral wealth, and here he is at the annual function of the Department of Elevator Inspectors. This is Johnny Shush's gift to Chancre; the mobster can't be here tonight, not with the increasing attention of the Feds to his sundry operations, but he can send an emissary from his underworld kingdom, demonstrate his influence, and by extension, Chancre's. More than one person here tries to figure out what the mob has on the Great Luigi (wears a dress?) but then doubles back: no point thinking about Johnny Shush's business. Chancre makes a great show of mouthing the words with the tenor even though it's obvious from a cursory inspection that he's never heard note one of this song before. Appearance is everything. The Great Luigi lifts his head to address a dusty chandelier: this is no grand theater. He had to prepare his number in a supply room off the kitchen, next to a stack of canned peas. The long white tails of his tuxedo drag unenthusiastically. When the last note recedes, Chancre's out of his seat rousing a standing ovation from his troops. The tenor nods curtly, clicks his heels and is out of here as fast as his spindly legs allow.

Rick Raymond leaps into the breach. "Talk about feeling small. What a talent, eh my friends? This next act will have a tough time following that up. Did someone say up? Cause that's where these girls will take you. Let's hear a loud elevator-inspector welcome for United Elevator's Safety Girls!" There is no need to ask these men for applause, for they swat their hands together in rapacious glee, and hoot and growl for good measure. This is the fifth appearance of the Safety Girls, and every one has been a triumph of lower impulse. It is not clear what the Safety Girls do in between this night and the annual elevator trade show. Perhaps they practice their kicks and steps, their inviting smiles. This attraction, too, has another meaning: Chancre endorses United in their ad campaign. Chancre could have gone with Arbo, or American, but he went with United, and they are grateful.

Rick Raymond and the Moon-Rays help out with an energetic rendition of a song from a movie musical that was popular a few years back. The twenty Safety Girls, in their short and tight crimson outfits, contribute their fit bodies and off-key voices. They've changed the lyrics. Instead of the familiar "All I want is Lady Luck," the elevator inspectors are rewarded with "All I want's to get you up."

Lila Mae thinks, her dues are paying for this.

He left her a note telling her to come, so she did. The note read, *See you at the Funicular Follies. I have a surprise for you. N.* The note is hidden in her shoe right now, slightly lumped from dried sweat.

She found the note under her door this morning after a Tuesday of anxious and aimless cogitation. No work, no house, she spent the majority of the day in the downstairs parlor, in the hollow of a large leather chair. Rereading Fulton, immersed in the grimoires. From time to time Mrs. Gravely offered her a snack, from time to time Natchez would nod or smile in the doorway and continue on to his chores. Mr. Reed and Lever were out on some business, but Natchez still went through the elaborations of secrecy. She found it endearing, boyish, and she waited for him to visit her last night. He did not. She found a note under her door this morning.

The House parlor contained in its sturdy shelves the entire corpus of Intuitionist lore, from the recent pamphlets smuggled out of distant Romania to the hopeful minutes of the Intuitionist societies in countries yet unblessed by the wonder of vertical transport. It all flowed from the books she held in her lap, Volumes One and Two of *Theoretical Elevators*, and it all meant something differently now. Fulton's nigrescence whispered from the binding of the House's signed first editions, tinting the disciples' words, reconnoting them. Only she could see it, this shadow. She had learned to read and there was no one she could tell. She understood that the library would be empty if these scholars knew Fulton was colored. No one would have worshipped him, his books probably would never have been published at all, or would exist under a different name, the name of the plagiarizing white man Fulton had been fool enough to share his theories with. She read the words in her lap, *horizontal thinking in a vertical world is the race's curse*, and hated him. She had been misled. What she had taken for pure truth had been revealed as merely filial agreement. And thus no longer pure. Blood agrees, it cannot help but agree, and how can you get any perspective on that? Blood is destiny in this land, and she did not choose Intuitionism, as she formerly believed. It chose her.

She ate by herself at the dinner hour, at the head of a long mahogany table attended by empty chairs. Natchez served her a thin brown broth, then pink lamb and a yellow paste of vegetable matter she did not recognize. Natchez did not speak beyond the parameters of his duty, communicated their understanding instead through laden glances. He acts as if this is a spy game, she thought. He did not come last night. He slipped a note under her door asking her to come to the Funicular Follies.

She did not have a plan, which is unlike her. She stared at the distinguished white awning of the Winthrop Hotel, watched the doormen in their red coats ingratiate themselves with the arrivals and departures, fingers nimble on the brims of their black caps.

She cannot afford to be seen by her colleagues, not after her three days of unexplained absence. She cased the building. From the modest forty stories and staid, circumspect ornamentation of the facade, she estimated the age of the Winthrop Hotel at thirty years, figured the elevators for reliable Arbo Regals, the late models with the oak interiors and brass handrails. Elevator operators, one sure hand on the wheel. She discovered the service entrance in the alley on the north side of the building.

A thin man with a slight, pouting face looked up from his clipboard and informed her, "You're late." He quickly hustled over to her, grabbed her arm. She allowed him to touch her, she allowed herself to be led down the hallway, past walls of the alienating gray made famous in prisons and schools across this country. They rounded a corner, and another, the man walking swiftly as if, she thought, afraid of these tight quarters, the tottering linens and stacks of dishes. They stopped at a black door whose chipped edges revealed strata of old paint of many colors and years. He said, "You'll find your uniform in here," adding after a sure appraisal, "We should have your size." Her hand darted for the doorknob and the man turned on his heel. He said, "Tell the agency that seven o'clock means seven o'clock and that if they don't get their act together," he searched for the right threat as he trotted away, "we'll be forced to take our business elsewhere."

The Winthrop Hotel did indeed have her size, previously worn by her menial double as she ripped off sheets, scrubbed toilets, avoiding eye contact with the people she served. It was the first time in months she had worn a dress. She felt exposed around her ankles, and as she shook her shoulders to force the black dress into comfort, she touched her neck to adjust her tie and found white lace instead. Her suit hung on a rack with the coats and day clothes of the rest of the help. Their clothes were sensible and betrayed the cumulative rough caresses of untold ablutions in basins and tubs, patient scrubbing. Her jacket was flat on the hanger but still seemed to retain her shape, thanks to all those sharp angles. She wasn't wearing proper shoes but did not concern herself. She thought, they won't be looking at her shoes. They won't be looking at me at all.

The big test came when she first knocked open the swinging doors of the kitchen and shuffled into the banquet room, having been directed to a platter full of miniature pizzas by the kitchen manager, who had greeted her emergence from the changing room with a terse, "Get to it." This is her first Funicular Follies. She understood that this night was for all the Department but her. She went through the effort of pulling her hair back into a knob on her scalp but in retrospect considers this unnecessary. They do not see her. The colored help brings the food and clears the tables, the white waiters refill the drinks. They ask the white waiters about the action at the cocktail bar, but do not ask the colored help for anything except for what they offer from the hors d'oeuvre tray. Food. They see colored skin and a servant's uniform. As an inspector she confronts superintendents, building managers, who do not see her until she shows her badge. In the Pit, she toils over paperwork next to these men every day. In here they do not see her. She is the colored help.

Natchez said he had a surprise. Where is his surprise?

She returns with a new fork for Martin Gruber to replace the one he tossed across the room at Sammy Ansen. (She adopted a circuitous route to avoid Pompey's table: she doesn't want to press her masquerade, but considers strychnine. He drinks copiously. He is not one of those grabbing at the white cigarette girls' gams. He knows better than that.) She has wiped off any visible remains of this new fork's recent trip through the grease and rinds of the garbage pail and envisions the extravagant bacteria metropolis that will thrive in his stomach. Invisible and insidious. Like her. She places the fork next to Gruber's plate and he doesn't even look at her, contemplating instead the beckoning recess where one particular Safety Girl's legs meet.

153

Rick Raymond says, "I think we all might need a cold shower after that one, eh boys?" The saxophone shrieks suggestively. "Maybe we should shift gears and let you boys cool off. This next act will probably do it for you. Sirs, the Funicular Follies are proud to present on the stage—the return of Mr. Gizzard and Hambone!"

The Moon-Rays start in with some quick ragtime as the two men enter from stage right. The inspectors are going mad. The skinny man wears a white T-shirt and gray trousers. Clothespins hold his suspenders to his pants. The fat man wants to be a dandy, but his green and purple suit is too small for him, exposing his thick ankles and wrists. Their elbows row back and forth in unison and their feet skip 'cross the stage to the music. Their faces are smeared black with burnt cork, and white greasepaint circles their mouths in ridiculous lips. Lila Mae is still, an empty glass in her hand. Underneath the minstrel makeup, she recognizes Big Billy Porter as the fat man and Gordon Wade as the skinny man.

When the applause stops, they quit cavorting and slap their thighs with a flourish. Big Billy Porter (Mr. Gizzard, evidently) says, "Hambone, you ole nigguh, where you git dat nice hat you got on yo head?"

Wade answers, "I got it at dat new hat stoe on Elm Street."

"Tell me, Hambone, did it cost much?"

"I don know, Mr. Gizzard—de shopkeeper wasn't dar! Say, you evah hear de one about de fine genimun?"

"What fine genimun dat be?"

"Dis fine genimun is walking home late one night when he come on dis nigguh lying down on de street."

"Do say, Hambone. He drunk?"

"He look lak you on Satday naht, all drunk all over hissef! Now dis fine genimun want to help him out, so he ax de nigguh what was lying dere, 'Do you live here?' An de drunk say, 'Yazzum, suh.' An de genimun ax de nigguh, 'Would you like me to help you upstairs?' An de nigguh say, 'Yazzum, suh,' and dey go up in

154

de building. When dey git up to de second floe he ax, 'Is this your floor?' 'Yazzum, suh,' dat nigguh say. Den de genimun start thinking, I don wanna face dat nigguh's wife—she liable to throw some hot grits on me fuh bringing her man home drunk lak dat. So he open de first door he see and shove de nigguh through it, den he go back downstairs. But lo and behole, what do he see when he git hissef outside agin?"

"I don know, Hambone—what do he see?"

"When de genimun git hissef back outside, dey anudda nigguh drunk on de street. So he ax dat drunk, 'Do you live here?' 'Yazzum, suh.' 'Would you like me to help you upstairs?' 'Yazzum, suh.' So he did take him up de stairs and put him in de same door with dat first nigguh. Den he go back downstairs. And guess what—dey anudda nigguh on de street again! So he walk over tuh him, but befoe he get dere, de nigguh stagga ovah to a policeman and cry, 'For God sake, suh, potect me from dis white man. He be doing nuttin all naht long but tekkin' me upstairs an trowing me down de elevator shaft!' "

Even though she knows what she will see, she looks over at Pompey. His mouth is cracked open with laughter. He slaps the table and shakes his head.

Billy Bob Porter–as–Mr. Gizzard says, "Hambone, dat's terrible. I's regusted!"

"Regusted? Doan you mean dis-gusted, Mr. Gizzard?"

"Dis gusted, dat gusted, I be all dat. Say, Hambone, what's say you and I tell dese good folks bout de ole man who go tuh see de doctuh?"

"Mr. Gizzard, dat sound lak a perfect idea! I be the ninedy-year-ole man and you be de doctuh. Hello doctuh!"

"What's the matter with you, young man?"

"I ain't young, so yuh can keep yo bedside matter. I gots me a bad problem."

"Well what is it?"

"Well doctuh, ever-time I go to visit dat woman uh mine, de

first . . . is good, real good . . . At de end of de secon, I have tuf rest at least for ten minutes . . . I can get up de third, but it take me such a long time dat I sweat and get shaky . . . And de fourth be almost impossible! . . . Sometime I think I bout to die on de spot!"

"Well, nigger, how dare you, at your age, talk about making love three, four or even two times?"

"What can I do, doctuh? I got no choice—de dam building got no elevator and she lives on de fourth floor!"

"Hambone, dat's too much fuh me! We better be on our way befoe my gut fall out. You wan I should tell you bout de man in de elevator befoe we go?"

"What man in what elevator, Mr. Gizzard?"

"Dey dis man in an elevator all by hissef, Hambone. De car stop and in step dis beautiful lady wit de long hair and de nice eyes. Two floes later she reach over an push de Stop button. She takes off all her clothes and say to de man what was in dere, 'MAKE ME FEEL LAK A WOMAN!' So de man, he take off all a his clothes, throw dem on top of de woman's clothes and say, 'Okay, do the laundry!' "

"Mr. Gizzard, I do believe I hear dat wife a yo's callin yo name."

"Well, come along, Hambone. It's dinnuh time and dat chicken she fried ain't goan las long!"

They receive a standing ovation for this. Wade throws his cap out into the audience and two inspectors wrestle over it. The kitchen door swings shut on Lila Mae's back. In the kitchen, the other colored workers do not speak on what they have just seen. They stack dirty plates in the plastic tray next to the dishwasher, nibble at leftover shrimp. Lila Mae does not mention it either, telling herself it is because she does not know the silent women she has been working with, whom she has not talked to all evening for her concentration on the Follies. She tricks herself that that is why she does not mention what she has seen, tells herself it is because she is undercover and speaking to them might trip her up, a dozen other reasons. She thinks the other women are so beaten that they cannot speak of the incident, when all of them, Lila Mae included, are silent for the same reason: because this is the world they have been born into, and there is no changing that. Through the porthole in the door, Lila Mae sees Pompey rub laughter-tears from his eyes, lean against Bobby Fundle to steady himself. See, he's laughing so hard he can hardly steady himself.

Lila Mae reenters the banquet room with a glass pitcher of water.

At the Internal Affairs table, Arbergast looks up quickly. Something bothers him about the woman who just refilled his water glass. His ears stand up, angle back.

The boys are out of it at this point. Chuck, for example, passed out long ago, and his head rests on his white plate. Pink fingers grope at ties, loosen ties, unbutton the top buttons of strangling shirts. Rick Raymond treads valiantly in this dead pool of lassitude, says, "I know you boys are hungry, but we have one more act before we wheel out the troughs. May I present, gentle inspectors, without further ado, the man who made tonight possible: the Chair of the Department of Elevator Inspectors, Mr. Frank Chancre!" Groggy heads swivel toward the Big Man's table. But he's not there. They see his lieutenants, his protégés, sitting there to show the assembled who's in favor, which of their number have gained entree into the Chair's good graces, but no Chancre. The lights overhead click out except for the ones up front on the stage. The drummer, as his kind are wont to do, beats with anticipation.

Lila Mae refills water glasses.

Rick Raymond bites his nails.

Internal Affairs Inspector Arbergast leaves his seat.

In the shadows at the side of the stage, the figures of men can be observed straining. Ropes levitate from the stage, the light catches their fine hairs, describes movement right. Slowly extricated from the murky left is Chancre, standing on a wooden platform. His costume is familiar to all present from the engravings of the 1853 Exhibition of the Industry of All Nations: the clothes Otis wore when he delivered unto the world its first Safety Elevator. He is standing on a replica of that renowned contraption, his hands cocked against his hips, just as they are in the advertisements for the United Elevator Co. The men at the side of the stage grunt the elevator across by painful inches, to better spool excitement. Lila Mae can't believe he has the gall. To even compare himself to Otis, to sully their imaginations of that great day with his corpulent horror. She would have liked to see Mr. Reed's reaction to this scene, but after a few rounds of handshaking at the beginning of the event, Mr. Reed and the tireless candidate departed the Follies. She would have liked to see their faces.

The elevator is center stage now, wood and divine despite Chancre's perversion. This is the one that started it all, enabling the metropolis, summoning them into tumultuous modernity. The blueprint of the first elevation. The assembled feel tremors assail their skin. This is where it all comes from, this moment, their solemn mission through the city's unforgiving and neon boulevards, past the angry facades of tenements and department stores and high-rises and office buildings. Even after years on the street, the gradual numbing of their souls to their dirty work, seeing that magnificent creation gives them all a chill. "Gentlemen," Chancre begins, "we live in a time of great calamity. Nations clash and a great noise is heard across the land." Arbergast is a good ways from his seat, almost at the figure who intrigues him. He thinks he knows that woman, that silhouette in the darkened room who does not move. "Babies go to bed hungry. What we took for granted in our youth—safe schools for our children, safe neighborhoods, safe streets—are quickly vanishing, lost in the moral swamp our communities have become. But there is one shining light, one ray of hope in this darkness, one thing that is still safe. And it is because of you gentlemen, because of your good work." She does not notice his progress toward her, Arbergast sees, she's transfixed (appalled, actually) like all the rest by Chancre's speech. He is almost upon her, his quarry. "Fellow elevator inspectors, this night is yours. It is a dirty and thankless job, and you have performed it above and beyond the call of duty. Sirs, it is because of you that civilians," he pauses here to withdraw scissors from his jacket and poise them at the rope reprieving his platform from gravity, "can ride vertical conveyance in this glorious metropolis and say, 'All Safe, Gentlemen, All Safe.'" He dangles there, his intonation signaling to the entranced audience that he will repeat Otis's hallowed declaration once he cuts the rope and is saved by the safety spring. Arbergast grabs the shoulder of the woman, she turns, he sees the face of Lila Mae Watson. He hears a loud crash. He sees Chancre writhing in pain on the stage, grabbing his knee and staring incredulously at his leg, which is splayed out to an unlikely angle. The spring did not bite into the notches along the inside rails, and the Chair of the Department of Elevator Inspectors has fallen. The inspectors are out of their seats and launching toward the stage. Their shouts echo in the room. Chancre screams. Arbergast looks at his hand, which just a moment earlier grasped the black material of a Winthrop Hotel domestic's uniform. His hand is empty. She's gone.

*　　*　　*

In Huntley's Department Store the people need and need less once they leave. Arms full, shopping bags' plastic loops cutting into their palms, bearing gifts: new watches equipped with glow-in-the-dark radium dials so you can know the time even in the dark; cinch belts in all the rediscovered pastels from overseas, hot now, get them while they're hot; Cuban-heel pumps and alligator purses so coarse and smooth in the light, dizzying tactility; hypnotic suggestion girdles and air rifles and foxtail caps. Exhausting, all that baggage, *now* is what makes it heavy, all that invisible now-freight at the bottom of the pillage-sacks, next to receipts of purchase and coupons for the next reduced populuxe pleasure. Marvin Watson collapses the metal gate, it always sticks a bit but he knows how to ease it into itself, he knocks down the door arm and shouts, "Second Floor: Ladies Clothes, The Little Miss Shop, Ladies' Shoes and Linens." The animals push by him, jostling neighbors and friends and the Mayor's niece, trampling young children under Cuban-heel pumps to gain the floor, what the floor has arrayed out there. Two thirsty women, politely disheveled, wait to board Marvin's elevator. They are about to enter the next stage of today's spree, having finished with the Second Floor; postcoital lassitude writ in their postures, they fan themselves with advertisements, still thirsty for more, for what's on the higher floors before they must return to home and husbands and children. They want to go higher, and Marvin Watson, elevator attendant of Car Number Two in Huntley's Department Store, is the man who takes them to the next level. Down, too, if they want to, but only after he's taken his baby up to the top floor. Sometimes they ask him questions. "Where would I find a toy for my son? He's six," and "Where's the ladies' room?" Never looking at him. They are in an elevator and thus passengers and must participate in the game, staring straight ahead or up at the waffling arrow of the floor indicator, but never left or right, at the colored man who pulls the control lever. So he only sees their faces when they enter the cab, delighted for a second that their carriage has arrived and then suddenly reminded of the journey itself, rushing into the device so as to turn around and face the only exit as soon as possible. Most of the time he sets them straight, tells them first and fourth floor is where the rest rooms are, but once in a while he lies. Let them find their own way through this labyrinth. This hell of stuff.

He has worked here for twenty years, driving the control lever into its seven slots, opening and closing the doors to the floors. Studied engineering at the colored college downstate, saw North:

the big cities he knew were coming, the citadels pushed from the planet's guts like volcanoes and mountains to take the sky. He knew the next step, had a beautiful woman and a child sleeping in that woman. In magazines he'd read about the new field of elevator inspection, and it seemed like a good opportunity for a man like him, an industrious fellow like himself. The secretary handed him a package when he walked in the door. He returned it to her thin white hands and informed her he was here for an interview. Wasn't a messenger boy. When he stood before the man's desk, the professor glanced up from his papers for only a moment, the time in which it takes to say, "We don't accept colored gentlemen," not meeting Marvin's eyes and returning quickly to his paperwork.

Old man Huntley was hiring, or so the newspaper said. He needed some colored boys to run his elevators.

"Third Floor," he says to the rabid pack behind him, "Boys' Clothes, Sporting Goods and Boys' Shoes," and a flurry of multicolored hats gushes out to his left. It's not a race. Sometimes he wonders what would happen if he shoved the lever as they ran out of his cab, but knows that Number Two will not move, neither up nor down, when the doors are open. They're not built that way.

He wanted to be close to elevators so he took the position at Huntley's. Saw North vanish until the only North was the top of the road as it dipped over the hill.

The man enters the car on the first floor and declares, "Department of Elevator Inspectors." He flips open his badge, that gold nova, to the agitated wives, who suddenly see their afternoon assignation get complicated. "Everybody out." He is authority. The white men in town have their own armor as they walk through the squares and up stone steps, totems of minute affectation their wives have picked out in this very store: silk cravats from France, hand-carved walking sticks from darkest Congo, the odd ascot and plum bowtie. But this man, Marvin sees, is not from here. Look at

161

that gray fedora slashing across his brow, brim bent downward to hide his eyes, casting shadows just where shadows need to be, the sophisticated craftsmanship of his solemn pinstripe suit, cut in a Continental, the skin of his authority. Look at that. He is an elevator inspector down from the capitol to kick their hamlet into shape, taking charge, checking for rust.

Marvin stands with the visitor in the empty car. Beyond the shaft the people hustle on their angry ant errands, a legion of impulse and need. Marvin wears the same uniform he has worn for too many years now, a red double-breasted lackey's getup that radiates threads here and there and strains against his burgeoning belly. Old stains that won't come out. The defects are not visible in the poor light of the cab, so Huntley Jr. says they're good enough for now. Marvin turns to the officer and says, "She's a real beauty, this car. I've been working with this baby for over twenty years now and she's never let me down. Sometimes she catches when we pass three—I think there's something wrong with the selector. And I have to work to make her flush with the landings sometimes—I keep telling them to have the indicator adjusted, but they're too stingy to get someone in here."

"You too," the inspector says.

"What?"

"Get off. The day I need some nigger to tell me how to do my job is the day I quit. Now get off."

Marvin Watson vacates his elevator. The elevator inspector slams the door shut behind him, and Marvin hears him struggle with the inside gate. It sticks sometimes. You have to know how to jiggle it. The inspector curses and continues to wrestle with the capricious metal. Marvin considers shouting instructions through the door but thinks better of it. Bobby takes his break about this time. Bobby owes Marvin money and has been ducking him for a while now. Marvin departs for the back stairwell, whistling along to the piped-in music.

Bright day, sparks erupting off car chrome, the fins on the cars in front of her cutting through bright day. It has rained too long, the city slept in mercury light for too long. Umbrellas stand exhausted behind closed closet doors, their dripped rain puddles dry beneath disdained galoshes. The city air is sweet today.

She is in the city's car. A few hours ago, before the weary day-shift trudged into work (weary this day especially, following last night's excess and post-catastatic exhaustion), she intercepted Jimmy's legs. His legs stuck out from beneath one of the Department sedans. She kicked him lightly and heard his head bang on the undercarriage of the car. He rolled out from beneath the vehicle, his customary Lila Mae smile withering as she told him she needed a car for a few days and that he would have to cover for her. Tough sell in the motor pool this morning. She had never flirted with him before so as not to encourage him and create a situation she had little experience in. But she flirted this morning, cupped his youthful cheek in her bold hand, did not flinch at his rickety teeth (Jimmy has never been to a dentist) or avoid prolonged eye contact. He gave her the key and assured her he would square it with the garage logs. She agreed to be careful with the car, lying to him as usual.

She is not on the clock. She is not working now and is driving aimlessly on the most famous street in the world and is quite pleased with herself. Lila Mae has never taken a day off in her three years with the Department and is discovering that the city is different on weekday afternoons. That there is a secret scofflaw city within the known city, afternoons without a thought in their heads. City workers with orange uniforms repair this street, tending to broken macadam. The potholes have a new meaning this day, do not injure this city car and summon forth reams of paperwork but share with the wheels a secret. A secret that is rough and more intimate for it. She drives and looks at the storefronts, the shopkeepers' entreaties, but her eyes never stray above street level. Because that is not her job today. She need not concern herself with that different city today.

She stops at a phone booth identical to the dozens she has passed on her drive today. There is no reason she chose this one. She just felt like stopping. The booth is empty, save for a piece of paper lying on the metal sill beneath the phone. Lila Mae takes it into her hand and erases the creases. It is a drawing of a stick figure with a large round head that has no features except for a smile. She watches the people through the sooted panes. They walk slower than they do when she reports to work and when she leaves work, and differently still from weekend strolling. They are the tin men and rag dolls who wake after hours in the toy store. She counts to ten slowly and takes ten deep breaths. He answers. Today she finds that ridiculous quiver in his voice sweet. "It's Lila Mae," she says.

Chuck starts whispering and she can see him turning away from the Pit to hide the receiver. "Where have you been?" he whines. "Things are going crazy around here."

"I've been around."

"Everyone's been asking where you are. Are you alright?"

"I'm fine, Chuck."

"This place is a madhouse!" He remembers and lowers his voice again. "Last night at the Follies—"

"I know Chuck. I heard."

"He's in the hospital. His leg is broken."

"He'll live." Through the window the sleepy citizens progress up the sidewalk in trances.

"That's not the point. You don't understand. The scuttlebutt says it was Lever who sabotaged the elevator, that they were paying Chancre back for Fanny Briggs. A crash for a crash. Wade even suggested that you might have done it."

"Chuck, I need you to do something."

He sucks his teeth and is silent for a moment. Then he says, "You should really come into the office. I've talked to this guy in IAB who's covering Fanny Briggs and he wants to hear your side of the story. I think he'll listen to you. I think if you just talked to him—"

"That's why I'm calling, Chuck. What did he say about the crash?"

"That it was fishy and that you were probably set up to take the fall. He doesn't have much to go on. Look, you can tell him you've been really sick. Or that you were afraid to come in because of what the papers have been saying. He'll listen."

"Chuck, I want you to get close to him. I need to know what else he's got and what Forensics has to say."

"Where are you? Is that a fire engine?"

"I'll call you as soon as I can, Chuck, to see what you have for me. Take care."

Lila Mae closes the door of the phone booth slowly, bewitched by the different laws of this afternoon. Even the fire engine, just now out of sight, seems rushless and enervated, fighting through an aqueous lethargy. She starts the car. Drives.

The imp found her an hour after Chancre's mishap. She'd departed the Winthrop Hotel the way she came, through the service entrance after retrieving her suit from the changing room. After blocks of running (a sight: a maid who has witnessed her master's murder, or murdered her master) she leaned against the glass window of an Automat. Inside the late-night denizens, the midnight refuse, slouched over java and racing forms, tuna on stale rye and their doomed itineraries. No one looked at anyone else in this crumbling sanctuary: that would risk the perfection of their isolation, their one last comfort in this concrete city. She changed back into her suit in the women's room. She deposited her coins in the coffee machine, in the pastry machine for an arid Danish. She sat at an empty table and read the placard on the metal stand: WE CAN CHANGE YOUR LIFE FOR ONLY TEN CENTS A DAY. It was the imp.

She laughed. She laughed at Chancre's fat ass as it lolled in agony on the stage. Laughed at the drunken rallying of her colleagues as they rushed to help their leader, the foolishness of the Intuitionist campaign and Mr. Reed's Continental affectations. She laughed because Fulton was colored and no one knew and now she had an ally. Her laughter ceased at the thought of Natchez, resolving into a steady grin. The thought of him and their secret.

A groggy Mrs. Gravely (her face smeared with a nighttime beauty cream in a way that reminded Lila Mae of Hambone and Mr. Gizzard) let her into the House and she collected her things. On the dresser, a soft pyramid, was another note from Natchez. *Hope you enjoyed yourself*, he wrote, and included a phone number. She introduced the note to its older brother in a wallet nook. Lila Mae lit out of Intuitionist House.

Her place was as she left it: raped. She pulled her suitcase from under the bed and packed again, this time for a much longer stay. She did not know when she would be back. After last night, there was no telling when the Shush boys would be back to enforce Chancre's threat. She lingered in the doorway. She thought she had forgotten something. Hadn't. She did not possess any lucky rabbit's feet or childhood dolls to ward off the monsters of the adult world. Just clothes. Then it hit her—she retrieved her copies of *Theoretical Elevators*. She locked the door. It was only three flights to the street and she felt reasonable again once she stepped into the morning light. She tried to remember when Jimmy reported to work.

The afternoon light is withdrawing from the sky, and the wind rushing through the open window of the city's green sedan murmurs autumn again. Lila Mae's eyes stray above street level for the first time today. She parks beneath the sturdy square of the hotel's sign. She's a good mile up the Island from her apartment. Deep in the colored city (yet another city in this city, always one more city). The manager looks up from his desk. She says, "I need a room."

Little Pompey, that polyp, struts up the avenue with a newspaper tucked under his arm. He stops in a stationery store and purchases what appears to be a foil packet of chewing gum. He counts his change slowly and returns to the street. Past the foamy white light of Harry's Shave and Haircut, the stammering red and green neon of the Belmont Cafeteria. The office buildings burp their charges out onto the pavement and the scurrying bodies make it difficult to keep Pompey in their line of sight. Natchez asks, "Are you sure it's him?"

Lila Mae's eyes dart between the road and Pompey like a metronome. Slowly, to keep her concentration, she tells the man in the passenger seat, "If he didn't do it, he's plugged in enough to know who did. Who else would they send? I'm sure they had a good laugh about it. Like we were dogs fighting in a pit." She thinks, but doesn't say, look what they did to your uncle. Twisted his mind so that he would deny who he was.

"What if he turns down the next street?" Natchez asks. "It's one-way."

"Then you'll have to follow him on foot until I can get into position on the next avenue. He knows me, but he doesn't know you."

Pompey does not turn down the street. He continues north, chewing pink gum.

They have come to an agreement, Lila Mae and Natchez. They will help each other out: Natchez doing what he can to help Lila Mae find out who sabotaged Number Eleven, Lila Mae lending her elevator expertise to Natchez's quest for his uncle's black box. She never learned what Mr. Reed's new leads on the box were since he froze her out of the operation, so they will make do with what information they can get. "Which means the pages from Fulton's journal," Natchez offered on the phone, just before she was going to say the same thing. They'll have to figure out what they can after they obtain copies of the Fulton pages possessed by Reed, Chancre and Lift. The hope is that if they collate the pages, Lila Mae's facility with Fulton's thought will force the writings to confess, give up who has the blueprint. And with regard to Lila Mae's redemption: here they are on stakeout. Trailing their main suspect.

"Tell me about your town," she says, from nowhere, her eyes still on Pompey.

"Why don't you tell me about your town?" Natchez responds. "Or leastwise why you moved up here."

Lila Mae's small hands tighten on the steering wheel and she wonders again if the news of Fanny Briggs has reached her parents yet, the probability of it making the papers down there. If the other elevator operators in Huntley's trade in this kind of gossip, and if he has heard that way, the phone in the hallway outside her apartment ringing and her not there to talk to him. She says dully, "You don't want to hear about that. It's not very interesting."

"I do."

Lila Mae breathes silently through her nose. She eases the sedan past a double-parked ambulance. "I moved up here because here is where the elevators are. The real elevators." She points up at the jutting structures surrounding the car, the dour edifices. "Midtown is all old growth. Downtown they have highrises that are a hundred stories tall. And elevators that match them every step of the way." Conveniently reminded now of something she wanted to ask him. Reroute the conversation. "What made you think of pulling that stunt at the Follies?"

"I wanted to give them a warning, I guess. Of what I'm gonna do to them." He turns his knees toward her in the seat and leans into the crack between the seat and the door. "I wanted to get back at them. For what they did to my uncle that messed up his head. For what they did to you." Her eyes keep on the street, she feels his eyes on her. "You didn't have to leave the House, you know," he says. "I thought you would have realized I wanted you

168

to take credit for it so you could get back in with Mr. Reed and them."

"I don't want to be in their good graces."

"But they still your bosses, right? Even if they did go to your house. You have to put up with them."

She shakes her head. Pompey extricates his shoe from a tentacle of newspaper that's just attacked him. "I just want to clear my name—and for you to get what belongs to you. How did you know what to do to the elevator? To make it fall like that."

Natchez laughs. "Pretty simple compared to what machines they got up in buildings today. Did you like it?"

"You know I liked it, Natchez."

He bangs the dashboard with the flat of his hand, smiles wide. "Had to learn a lot about elevators in the last few weeks. More than I want to know. Don't know how you can do your job like you do, to tell you the truth."

"They grow on you. Like people. You never know who you're going to get to like." Stop right there, Lila Mae. "Then they pop up one day and you like them." This isn't characteristic of her at all. "You get to know them and you like them more each time."

"Like you and me, Lila Mae?" To the nervous twitch of her eyebrows, he says, "That's okay. You keep driving. When I first saw you I thought you one of them uppity Northern girls. All about what you can do for them and how much do you have in your pocket and all that. But you're not like—"

"Look," Lila Mae directs, deflects. "He's stopping."

Pompey knocks on the window of a discreet brown door. He glances over his shoulder suspiciously; Lila Mae and Natchez have pulled over on the other side of the street, on the uptown rut of the avenue. She can make out the gold stenciling, crescent-shaped, on the soaped-out window: PAULEY'S SOCIAL CLUB. The door opens and Pompey retreats into the darkness.

"It's a bar," Natchez offers. "One of them old speakeasies. Stopping off for a little rye before he goes home."

"He's not going home," she says. Lila Mae looks up at the street sign: Pompey has walked eleven blocks up from the office. Then she sees the car. "See that dark blue car parked outside?" she asks. She knows it, recognizes the blank, bovine face of the driver. "The man inside is Lazy Joe Markham. One of Johnny Shush's boys. The mob." The driver stares straight ahead, for now, looking down and beyond the hills and depressions of this busy street, past the downtown buildings, into the black river.

"A mob place? What's a nigger like that doing at a mob hangout?"

"We'll see soon enough," Lila Mae says. "Do you have the camera?"

"Got it right here."

She's relieved that Natchez does not start talking again. Not that she does not like what he says, but it is too much for her in this tiny car, and so quickly after so much time. She had entered into a contract with the city similar to the one she has lately arranged with Natchez. An exchange of services. She will keep the city vertical and intact, and the city will leave her alone. And now look at her: she let the city down last Friday, was remiss in her duties, and look at the metropolis's retribution. It has given her Natchez. When she picked him up, she looked in his face for traces of Fulton's austere intractability, something to ground him in her world. In the gentle bump of his nose, parabolic symmetry of his ears, she did not see Fulton. He was his own man. Not of her elevator world, but a traveling cable to that place the rest of the citizens live. Through a crack in the buildings' canopy, she sees a blimp, slug in the sky, primitive and unevolved. The future is in jet fuel speed, jet plane steel. There is no room in the sky for this pathetic bug.

He rouses her: "He's on the move again."

Pompey waddles away from Pauley's Social Club. Lila Mae and Natchez and Joe Markham watch him as he walks uptown in a pale gray Growley Elevator Repair uniform, a toolbox in his right hand. She starts the car.

Pompey has tools.

* * *

At intersections and crowded areas between sedans and trucks the gutter reflected the bitter pastels of metropolitan neon, rainbows hacked down to earth and dirt. Lila Mae followed a trail of cigarette butts. Up one block and around the corner and further still. She was lost. It wasn't a trail left by a single individual, for one thing, and cigarette butts aren't as reliable as footprints. They'd been banished to the pavement, dashed there by multitudes of citizens, different brands, some lipstick-smudged or saliva-damp, half smoked, dragged out, crushed under heels or left to smolder to the filter. There was always another a few steps ahead. It might lead to the subway: she needed to get home and couldn't remember where the subway was. In one respect Lila Mae was correct. The cigarettes did lead to the subway. They led to where anyone had walked. It was her first week on the job.

Later, she realized he saw her coming. Her hands fiddling anxiously in her trouser pockets, tentative footfalls, looking up at the street numbers. An easy mark. She stopped at the corner, confounded. Lila Mae was sure this was where she had emerged from underground this very morning. Chastised herself. This was a ridiculous mistake, not one she allowed herself to make. She'd spent the previous Sunday on her couch decoding the subway map, superimposing its feeble order over the few scattered sections of the city she was already acquainted with. Never mind that she found the entire mechanism distasteful. Shuffling into mole holes: aesthetically weak, not to mention just plain atavistic, this horizontal maundering about. She closed her eyes at the intersection. Lila Mae could see the map sagging over her knees in her

171

apartment, the tangled train routes—but she couldn't remember the stops. The street numbers. He was there when she opened her eyes, he said, "Nice evening," his foot on the green chipped lamppost, his hand brushing grit off his white spats. "Nice evening," he repeated.

She inspected him. Perhaps thirty (an older man), pretending to be a rogue. He wore one of the new slim suits she had observed with increasing frequency since she moved into the city, a vaguely European cut that hung close on his body, sharp along the shoulders thanks to a layer or two of padding. How many of her city paychecks would it take to get one of those numbers? The perfect point of his white silk tie was matched by the opposite-tending arrow of the handkerchief launching from his breast pocket: two halves of a diamond. He had a boy's face, she reckoned, or a man's face bulging with boyish mischief, topped by the elegant waves of an obviously well-maintained conk. These are the kind of men they have in the city, Lila Mae told herself, dispatching her daze to the back of her mind. Keep alert. She said, "I'm looking for the subway."

"Where are you trying to go?" he asked, slapping his foot off the lamppost.

"I'm looking for the uptown train," she said. The traffic light changed with an audible clunk and the downtown automobiles surged.

She could cross now if she wanted to, right now, cut off this young gentleman before he got any ideas. She looked into his face again. He had wild bristly eyebrows, a nice touch, one deliberate unkempt spot to offset his careful preening. "That's a few blocks over," he offered. "I'll escort you—a beautiful lady like yourself shouldn't be out by herself at this hour."

Lila Mae remembered that very line from the movie she had seen not two days ago. At least he likes going to the picture show, she thought. "That's not necessary," she said. Waited for the light to change.

172

"I'd curse myself all night if I didn't," he said, and when the light changed and he stretched his arm wide across the avenue, after you, she walked and did not rebuke him as he trotted alongside her. City charm, playing games. He kept talking (even though she did not answer him as she stared ahead to the next corner to see if she could sight the train entrance), informing Lila Mae that he'd just left a business meeting of some sort, and that the meeting had gone well, though he was sad that it had run so late because it was not often he had free time when he came to the city. He enjoyed the sights and the people here. They were characters. He didn't know anyone, he said, his voice falling a bit theatrically into mock woe, and she smiled at this. Despite her self and her armor. She walked quickly, out of fear, she knew. She didn't know how to act in situations like this. Last Friday at this time she was packing her few possessions into boxes, under the faint overhead bulb in her janitor's closet. Lila Mae and her new companion crossed another street. He held out his hand to traffic, stop, even though the stoplight held the automobiles still and idling. Mock gallant. She smiled at this gesture too, though inwardly now: her game face was in place. He said his name was Freeport Jackson and asked her name, although, he added, if she didn't want to tell him he understood. This was a dangerous city and you never knew. She gave him her name, in the cracked syllables she had already decided, after much practice, would be her work voice, the voice she would present to building representatives as she snapped open the gold badge of her office. He said, "Lila Mae Watson, may I walk you to the subway?" She said he already was. Past an all-night druggist, which surprised her, she'd never encountered such a thing before. But in this city people need things at all hours of the night, she thought. This place will take some getting used to.

Then there it was. The street entrance of her train. Freeport said, "Here we are. At your stop. And mine—my hotel is right here."

The grease in Freeport's hair snatched the lights from the Chesterfield Hotel and glistened like a frog's back. They were just outside the corona of the hotel, the bow of illumination that demarcated the establishment's domain from the craggy pavement of the metropolis without. Lila Mae said, "You were going my way all along."

He winked and cocked his fingers into a gun and shot her. "Would you like to have a drink?" Freeport asked. "The hotel bar is something to see," he said, "if you've never seen it." The ruby carpet, adept at keeping the city's gray encroachments at bay, climbed up steps to the Chesterfield Hotel's brass entryway, up to the light within. She'd read about the Chesterfield. Most people had. The President stayed here on his very last visit. They kept a suite open for him, the newspaper said. She didn't know they let colored people stay here. Behind Lila Mae, that sullen underground gorge, abandoned to the citizens' abuse, cracked and stained. Freeport said, "It's the least I can do to repay you for walking me home."

"I thought you were walking me," Lila Mae said.

"Exactly," Freeport said with a smile, his palm open before the carpet. Of course they let colored people stay here. This is North. She looked up at the doorman, past him and through the glass, made a wager with herself—and stopped. She'd never know the outcome, after all, so there was no point in guessing at the make of the elevators. She said, "I'll have one drink," and stepped into the light. Disdaining the hole.

He steered her quickly into the cocktail lounge, allowing her only a glimpse of the famous and fabulous lobby of the Chesterfield Hotel, which she had read about. The Maple Room was subdued that Friday night with the quiet murmuring of couples in sophisticated attire, or so it seemed to Lila Mae, who counted the furs and pearl necklaces snug around delicate female necks as Freeport ordered their drinks. The Department had a dress code. She liked her new suit but it was not appropriate here. Not that

174

she had furs or jewelry locked in a box up at her apartment, but still.

"What do you do with yourself when you're not out looking for the subway?" Freeport asked earnestly. The piano man kept his head down over his keys.

"I'm in the Department," she answered. "I work for the Department of Elevator Inspectors." The first time she ever said it. Heavy on her tongue.

"Elevators," he said, feigning interest in how she spent her daylight hours, but making a good show of it as he attempted to gauge the bulbs beneath those stark lapels of hers, the potential there, continuing to nod his head or stroke his chin as she related that it was her first week on the job and she still didn't know her way around the office but was getting the hang of it. She had learned, for one thing, that the only ladies' room was three floors below the Pit, that's what the inspectors called their rumpus room, the Pit, for reasons that were not yet entirely clear. She was getting her first case on Monday—she'd been riding with a partner all week, an owl-faced grumpus whom she didn't particularly like, and who didn't particularly like working with colored people, let alone driving with one. She guessed that some things take a little more time to change, even up here in this city. (Lila Mae did not tell him that Gus Crawford, the senior inspector in question, did not speak to her for their entire tour together. Not a single word, not even to dispatch her from the Department vehicle for a cup of coffee or rebuke her neophyte's innocent questions, not a word, referring to her only a bit wearily as "the rookie" when asked by the stymied supers and building managers, who, expecting graft as usual, inquired as to who this unexpected third party was. The building representatives left their wallets in their pockets and took their lumps.) But next week she'd get her first case, her first case file. Freeport nodded. He shared his concern that the elevator shaft must be exceedingly dirty and it must be hard to keep one's clothes clean. She assured him that she didn't need to enter the well: she could intuit it. She knew he had no idea what she was talking about, but continued anyway, dropping the names of Otis and Fulton, referring to the rival philosophical schools of Empiricism and Intuitionism. He did not trouble her with petty inquiries. He sipped his boilermaker and nodded, urged her to drink up as well, as he'd already gestured for a refill and there she was having barely taken a taste of her Violet Mary. The other colored couple in the hotel bar looked to be African. The woman wore an extravagant liquid red robe, the man a khaki suit with many pockets. They barely talked to each other and drank water.

The new citizens for the new city, the cosmopolitan darlings out on the town, tipped martini glasses and stroked silver cigarette cases engraved with their initials and called the bartender by his name. She had long reckoned on the promise of verticality, its present manifestation and the one heralded by Fulton's holy verses, but had never given a thought to the citizens. Who the people are who live here. Freeport Jackson calculated the final inch of his cocktail. The dapper men and women traded chatter over gin, white faces pink with alcohol heat in the cheeks, making toasts, discussing escrow. Rich white people, an African couple, Freeport Jackson and his evening's date. You could never build a building like a martini glass, Lila Mae observed to herself, widening as it got higher like that, it would topple over, foolish. Talk did not travel in that room. Each couple alone with itself. No rowdy groups assembled to celebrate anniversaries or alma mater championship games related over the radio. (She did not tell her companion that she was out tonight so long after the office closed because she had discovered—it was a small office and you could hear the stomach growling of the guy across the room—that the inspectors congregated at a neighborhood bar called O'Connor's on Friday nights to exchange ribald tales of various elevators and the buildings they lived in, jokes about verticality and its messy effects, to raise a glass to elevators fallen in the line of duty. Didn't tell her companion that her excitement over this weekly

176

ritual of camaraderie had sent her into the Department elevator at quitting time with the rest of them to depart for said drinking establishment, assuming, in a moment of naive joy over her new circumstances—new apartment, new job, new city—that she was welcome. She walked two yards behind them, their backs to her. Her colleagues did not invite her to sit with them at O'Connor's defaced tables, did not make any motions for her to join them at the tables, and Lila Mae sat at the bar with the civilian drunks and mumbling-to-themselves Irish nationalists, tasting beer and listening to the elevator brigade's stories of battles won and lost. No one missed her when she slipped out, abandoning half a beer soon greedily quaffed by one of the keen-eyed drunks, and tried to find the subway home. No one noticed her departure except the bartender, who kept his own counsel.) No rowdies in the Charleston Hotel Bar. Just men and women in negotiations, in smart high-stepping evening wear, careful stitches.

Who the hell is this man anyway. Freeport ordered another drink, Lila Mae demurred; he said, "I sell beauty products. Everybody wants to look good, am I right or am I not right?" He dipped his fingers through the conk waves on his scalp, caressing. "And somebody's got to give it to them. But you know that already. You're a salesman yourself. Heck, we both sell the same thing—peace of mind. I'd never try to sell anything to you. You don't need it, obviously. But most people do. I've been in sales seven years now. Seven years—jeez—it still surprises me when I think of it. Up and down the Northeast. I have a good route. I cover the distance. But I'm here now—here in the city—because I just had a meeting with a distributor. The outfit I work for, Miss Blanche Cosmetics, we started small and I've been there from the start. We've been doing so well we've decided to expand and hook up with one of the bigger distributors. We've been out there doing the footwork, putting in the long hours, knocking on doors—but a distributor, that's the big time. I'm the one in charge of getting the deal on paper. Ink. I can't tell you which company we're talking to, of course—the walls have ears, you know what I'm saying?—but we're this close," demonstrating with his manicured fingers, "this close to having it all in writing. I can feel it. You know how it is, you're in the elevator and whatnot and you know when it's right and when it's not right. Well I think I got it right now. I got it right."

"What is it exactly you sell?"

"Skin lighteners and hair straighteners mostly. Our clientele is colored, you understand, and the women we cater to want to look good. That's why I made sure from day one that I was the one who got the city. I drive up with a dozen cases of the stuff in my trunk on a Monday afternoon—you have to catch them when their husbands aren't home—and by Monday evening I'm sold out. Sold out! Like that. I don't even do any cold-calling anymore. I got my regulars and they show off for their friends and then their friends want to know where they can get their hands on it. Word of mouth. You don't see the encyclopedia and vacuum cleaner boys racking those numbers, let me tell you."

When the waiter informed them that the bar was closing and Freeport asked Lila Mae to join him for a drink in his room, she agreed. Because it had already been decided. She was an inspector. This was an investigation. Freeport extracted a bill from his gold money clip and set her still half-full glass atop it. His eyes shifted about the room, searching for thieves. "You never know with white people around," he said, chuckling. Said, "And a very good evening to you, dear chap," to the waiter as they departed the cocktail lounge, him on unsteady feet, her with sure steps. She squinted in the sharp illumination of the lobby after the intimate lighting of the bar. Freeport's fingers grabbed at her elbow. Lila Mae turned toward the elevator bank—they looked like Uniteds, she thought, from the extra-wide doors—and Freeport said, "You thought—you thought I was staying here? I could never afford this place. No, I'm staying across the street."

"Of course," Lila Mae said. As they walked down the steps to the street, the doorman wished them a good evening. Freeport nodded.

He did not lie. His hotel was right there at the subway entrance, but across the street. The night man at the Hotel Belair did not wish the pair a pleasant evening, although the rotund cadaver behind the metal grille did perhaps raise an eyebrow at them. Lila Mae and Freeport received a heartier welcome from the five inmates crouched around the lobby's radio. They turned their attention from the boxing match and watched the couple disappear up the stairs, the gentlemen's thin brown bathrobes scarred by cigarette burns and untold greasy-spoon gravies. They watched as the man slipped his palm into the small of the woman's back and led her from their collective moist-lipped delectation and up the stairs. Three quiet flights up, past racks that at one point fastened fire extinguishers but had been frustrated in their purpose by anonymous miscreants of uncertain intent. Walked past dull walls who declined comment. Lila Mae sniffed the stale air. Freeport whistled. No elevator, she thought. Freeport said, "Hold on a second, my dear," as he struggled with the lock. It wouldn't give in to his seductions. "It sticks," he said, "hold on there."

She had been in smaller rooms, lived in smaller rooms than this, and in the future would certainly inhabit rooms as suspect. The street noise returned to them after a few minutes' reprieve, through the open window, marching across the dirty green blinds: honks, catcalls, collisions. The city's raspberry. She saw the bathroom and its cold tile: Freeport was drying three pairs of exhausted socks on the shower rod. Freeport darted to the table by the lumpy bed and removed the bottle from its brown bag. Crumpled the brown bag and tossed it to the metal basket beneath the single window. "Like a nip?" he asked. "A little nightcap?" he offered, rubbing his handkerchief across a tumbler rim and holding the glass to the light.

She told him she would undress in the bathroom. The door wouldn't shut for warping or too many ambitious paint jobs, thus allowing a ribbon of white light at the frame through which she could hear his quick fumbling movements out of fabric, the rasping and squeaking of the tiny bed as he mounted it. Lila Mae hung her pants on the shower curtain next to the man's socks and laid her jacket and shirt and bra over them. She felt the sweat on her feet make the hotel disinfectant on the bathroom floor tacky. She checked her face in the silver glaze of the mirror: Lila Mae had her game face on, that rigid concoction of hers. Holy, it seemed to her, because that's how she designed it. It accorded with her own definitions.

He said stuff but she ignored it because it did not pertain to the case. She did not concern herself with his breath, corrosive and slow to dissipate, a low foul cloud. She recorded the details of the investigation, his fingers and kisses, his slow tumble on top of her, which was awkward, as if he were a seal and did not possess arms to steady himself. Her first investigation. Lila Mae made a file for her first investigation and recorded the pertinent details. The language of the report was drawn from the lumbering syntax of bureaucracy. It preserved the details but did not retain the other parts, the ones this language did not have words for. He didn't wake when she dressed and departed, as she knew he wouldn't.

* * *

A week ago at this time, the night of the accident, she sat in a rocking subway car, returning from O'Connor's and staring at a newspaper headline. The late edition carried the Fanny Briggs story on the front page. Rosacea squatted on the face of the man who held the paper, making his skin as rough as tabloid paper. His eyes scanned the cheap print. He turned the pages slowly, moving on to other metropolitan catastrophes, the next mithridatic outrage, the pages fluttered behind the front page but the headline remained the same, in the same place hovering across from her. CRASH.

Now things are quite different. The headline is there, bed-clothes for bums, dancing on the plume of a midtown wind tunnel. But she is advancing on it, for it contains her name and she is reclaiming her name.

She arrives a half hour early and parks the sedan across the street from Bickford's shiny windows. When she makes out Chuck's distinctive walk (an idiot choreography of shoulders and hips, sockets working overtime), she searches the street for signs of his shadow, the silent men who might be following him. Waits another ten minutes after he sits down in one of the window booths (exposed), then enters Bickford's: he has not been followed by Chancre or Internal Affairs or who knows.

"So what do you have for me, Chuck?" she asks briskly, squeezing into the booth.

" 'So what have you got for me?' " Chuck complains. "That's all you have to say for yourself? I haven't seen you since last week."

She imagines this the voice he reserves for domestic mishap. Marcy-tone: whining, angry. "I'm sorry, Chuck. There's a lot going on right now." She takes the napkin into her lap. The restaurant has recently upgraded to stiff cloth napkins in an attempt to lure some of the theater crowd. Bickford's is in a weird place: two blocks east from the warehouses, two blocks west of the Big Houses. Bickford's humble days as a greasy spoon are waning, the nice money is in family fare, snaring the gullible and aimless tourist crowd as they bumble lost. No more haphazard blue-plate specials, no more handwritten signs describing the cook's daily whim. Better plates, even-tined forks, opaque globes over the fly-specked bulbs. She doesn't recognize the menu anymore.

"You look good, at least," Chuck says, a sucker for an apology. "For someone on the lam."

On the lam: she is that, she thinks. "What's the mood around the office these days?"

"It's been pretty hectic since Chancre's accident. Hardwick's really been driving us, which isn't helping things. Chancre's still in the hospital so it's got them worried about losing election momentum. It was a real blow to their morale."

"I saw it made the papers." And seeing it cheered her. Bad ink goes both ways.

"It was a pretty spectacular fall," he says. "They were sitting pretty after Fanny Briggs—put the Intuitionists in their place and all that—but with the Otis routine, Lever's regained some support. Some people are even saying that Reed and Lever were behind it." It's not much of a stretch, Lila Mae thinks, to see Reed taking credit for Natchez's prank. "With that and the Fulton rumors," Chuck continues, "the election is up in the air again. Have you heard about the Fulton stuff?"

She can't remember what face she's supposed to have on. "The rumors about the black box?" If Reed and Lever have leaked to the rank and file that the box is out there, they must be confident that they'll find it soon. Or perhaps they already have it. She'd know if she were still on the inside. Lila Mae wonders what their response is to her disappearance from the House.

"Right," Chuck says. "Apparently *Lift* was supposed to run a story on it this week, but it didn't appear. There's all sorts of speculation about that, of course, but the bottom line is that some of us have hope in Lever again, and some of the fence-straddlers are coming around to our side. Do you think it's true, Lila Mae? That it's out there?"

"It could be."

"Just think of it—Fulton's black box. Do you know what it means? The second elevation is coming. Everything around us, all that out there, will come down. All of it," animated, looking at Lila Mae for a companion in his romance of the future. She is, to say the least, subdued. Chuck slides his finger into his coffee cup and withdraws a long black hair. "Some of the guys were mumbling that the perfect elevator might put us out of work, but there are always maintenance issues and all that. It should be pretty interesting come Tuesday night. Are you going to vote?"

"I'll have to see how things are faring. Has Forensics come back yet?"

He shakes his head. "No autopsy yet. You know how they are—they're so happy to get some work that they got to milk it and keep everybody in suspense. But it looks like they're going to release their findings on Monday morning."

Monday morning is perfect for her, is what she thinks. By that time she should have what she needs from Pompey, and that, coupled with the forensics report, should clear her. Forensics is capable of being bought off—they work for the city—but they report to the Mayor's office, and no matter what else the Mayor and Chancre have cooking, the Mayor knows better than to mix with the elevator inspectors' election. The election is a family matter, and the inspectors take family matters very seriously. "What about this man Arbergast?" Lila Mae asks. "How's his case going?"

"That's the bad part, Lila Mae," Chuck frowns. "He's got nothing from what I can tell. Not with you gone. Nobody's talking. When Forensics comes back with their report—and I think we both know it was sabotage—you're still the number one suspect. You haven't been heard from in a week." His voice squeaking. "After that report comes in, he's going to have to bring in the cops because it officially becomes a criminal case. And you look guilty, Lila Mae. You look guilty."

"I was guilty before. Now they just have an excuse to get the rope."

"Why don't you come in, Lila Mae," Chuck says. Almost pleading.

"Let's not start that again."

"I can help you. Talk to Arbergast. He'll help you out. You're one of us."

She considers, for a second or two, if they've gotten to Chuck. It could be any number of parties. But she has called him because she trusts him, and she needs that trust. She's ready to accept the consequences. "It'll all be okay come Monday," she says, believing it to be true.

"You're not going to let me in, are you?"

She trusts him: just look at him now. Nobody's gotten to him. She wishes she could let him in, but there will be time next week to share all she has learned . . . No. Not all. She knows she's not going to tell him about Fulton. She can't. It is in his face now: that faded look, the uninteresting flatness of a background object in a photograph. Their friendship, so real a moment ago, is remote. She's left him behind. She won't be telling him anything. "It'll all be over in a few days, Chuck," she says. "Then I'll tell you everything."

"And the police?" Chuck asks.

She purses her lips, then remembers. "One more thing, Chuck—what do you know about 366 Eighth Avenue?"

"366 . . ." He presses out his cheek with his tongue, a habit Lila Mae has always found vaguely repulsive. "I know that building," he says finally. "I saw it on the Board this morning. I think it's set up for inspection next week. Marberley has it."

"It's a new building. No one from the Department has seen it yet?"

"No, it's a checkup. Marberley wrote it up for some violations a few weeks ago."

She's in her car five minutes later, uptown in her room at the Friendly League Residence half an hour later. This is the smallest room yet. Liverpool's "moving drawing rooms" of the turn of the century, steeped in Victorian largesse, spacious enough for a hundred passengers and decorated with smoked mirrors and yielding cushions, could have fit three of this room inside (an elevator in an elevator, an elevator-passenger). The basement coffers of the Friendly League Residence, unofficial repository of the city's outcast furniture (rescued from the dump, rescued from burned-out tenements), have outfitted this room with one chair of leprous upholstery and a writing table more than suited for the sober composition of suicide notes. Tall brown cabinet doors hide the Murphy bed, up now, tilted in its hinges and half-stuck after years of wrangling by haggard guests.

She has not seen any of the other guests but can imagine them. The city's tidal forces wash the weak-treading citizens out here, to the edge, to pitiless crags like the Friendly League Residence. Old men in gray clothes with beards like dead grass, stooped and shuffling. The alibiless. Jagged coughing haunted the halls last night, stealing out of multiple rooms, a sodden death-chorus. It kept her awake, to say the least, manifested in her dreams when they finally came as thunder and wet rain over her childhood home. She couldn't go outside for the rain, in her dreams. She shook the night off quickly this morning, after finding the sun peeking over the low rows of tenements, which trooped off to the far north of the island, into the black river. Not a lot of elevators in this neighborhood. This is the place verticality indicts, the passed-over flatlands, what might as well still be forest and field. No, Chancre and Lever will not find her here. The other guests' invisible shuffling-out-of-rooms ended around ten this morning and she waited another hour before venturing out of her box, figuring then it was probably safe. The manager downstairs did not look up from the comics as she pushed aside the front doors and let them slam behind her. He has seen many things.

She spent the afternoon on the city's turf. In the Hall of Records downtown, on the other edge of the island, right across from the Fanny Briggs building. She walked quickly through the shadow the new building spat across Federal Plaza, eyes away from that structure, quick into the revolving door of the Hall of

Records. Lila Mae offered her badge to the clerk, a short old crone who did not even bother to check her identification, so preoccupied was she on stamping, with a gleaming steel device, the seal of the city on a heathen mound of paperwork. Lila Mae could clearly discern, upside down, the holy seal convert that bureaucratic rabble. If the Department had issued a warning out on her badge, it had not reached this office yet. When she was finished with the broad ledgers of the Hall of Records, she went to meet Chuck at Bickford's, and Fanny Briggs's long shadow had seeped into the air, indistinguishable from night.

In her room at the Friendly League Residence, she reads *Theoretical Elevators*, Volume Two. Reads, *The race sleeps in this hectic and disordered century. Grim lids that will not open. Anxious retinas flit to and fro beneath them. They are stirred by dreaming. In this dream of uplift, they understand that they are dreaming the contract of the hallowed verticality, and hope to remember the terms on waking. The race never does, and that is our curse.* The human race, she thought formerly. Fulton has a fetish for the royal "we" throughout *Theoretical Elevators*. But now—who's "we"?

She is teaching herself how to read.

At the pounding on the door, she closes the book (the pages resist each other, so jealous and protective are they of Lila Mae's touch). She is expecting Natchez, who is to deliver his update on his search for Fulton's journal pages (and perhaps more). But it is not his knock, nor his low voice heard now croaking, "Amy, Amy baby, I'm sorry," that last word trailing away, dripping down the door like spittle. "I'm sorry I did it. Open up and I'll show you. It's just that sometimes when I get in that place . . . it's so low, so low and I can't see up out of it." This incident is over. The man slaps the door with his hand, and she can hear him walk down the hallway, slowly, soft clothes, a bathrobe maybe, sliding on the dirty tile behind him, a tail or a broom.

When Natchez's knock finally rattles the old door, she does not need to confirm through the peephole. She withdraws the chain, opens up and he's staring off down the hallway with distaste and—she sees Fulton's profile there, the lightly angled brow, knob chin. He wears a light blue suit of plain cut, the kind of suit she associates with the men of colored town, a church and wake suit, probably the only one he owns. Out of the House servant uniform. He says, turning to her, "Nice hotel you picked, Lila Mae."

"You're a sight for sore eyes," she says.

Natchez plucks nervously at his lapels. "I didn't bring much up here. I don't know why I brought this along," shrugging, looking up at the yellowed ceiling. He prestos a bunch of flowers from behind his back, a splash of violets. "I saw these on the way. I thought you might be needing something for the room, and it looks like I was right."

No, she can't remember the last time someone . . . has anyone ever? She can't recall at all. She locks the door behind him and surveys her tiny room. Doesn't take long. "Thank you," she says. "You can put them on the sill. I haven't anything to put them in."

He places his hat, a dusty black homburg, on the sill next to the swaddled violets. Natchez drags the chair away from the table with a long screech, sits. "You could have done better than this. Even my room's better than this and I didn't have no money for a decent place. I mean—I didn't have any money for a decent room."

"You don't have to act any way for me, Natchez." He's taken the only chair in the room. She struggles with the Murphy bed and glides it to the floor. "We come from the same place," she adds, sitting on the atoll lumps of the mattress.

He looks nervous, rubs his palms across his knees. "Did you find anything today? I mean when you went downtown."

Perhaps he really is a bit nervous, Lila Mae thinks. She has never thought of herself as an imposing person (that's how little self-perception she has), but he is new to the city and maybe that

187

explains it. "I think I know why Pompey went to that building last night," she says. 366 Eighth Avenue, where the two of them tailed Pompey after he left Pauley's Social Club. "The building is owned by Ponticello Food—they own a tomato canning factory across the river. I'm pretty sure it's a Shush front. I have enough to confront him, anyway. With the pictures we took. Maybe I can get him to admit he sabotaged the Briggs stack."

"I'll go with you," Natchez responds. "What time?"

"I don't need your help—I mean I can do it myself. I work with him. I know him—inside and out. I can handle it."

"What time? I'm coming with you." His hands are folded across his chest.

"You have your own errands to do." His motives are good, but she is no child. "How did it go at the House today? Did you get it?"

"Man, they didn't think nothing was up. I waited until Mrs. Gravely went out to do her shopping for dinner. Reed and old Lever were out all day. Took all of five minutes to find his notes. For people who think they pretty smart, you think they would keep that drawer locked—it was right in the drawer where you said it would be." He pulls out the small black camera from his jacket and shakes it in the air. "Once I recognized his handwriting on it, I took the pictures."

Lila Mae leans forward, excited. "Can I see them?"

Natchez replaces the camera. "I haven't taken them to the drugstore to get them developed yet. I was going to wait until I got the ones from the Department and the ones from that elevator magazine."

"Maybe you should develop what you have," Lila Mae says, "and use different film for Chancre and *Lift*. That way you won't lose everything if something happens."

His face shrinks a little. The red neon of the liquor store sign across the street flashes on his face, off and on. "Yeah, you're right. I'll take this down tomorrow."

Did she sound like a scold? Lila Mae thinks. She was only trying to be practical. "Just in case," she says in soft tones, "is all I'm saying."

"No, you're right. I'll do that."

"Are you sure they're in the Department? They might have taken them somewhere."

"I'll find them," Natchez says. "If they're there, I'll find them, and if they're somewhere else, I'll find where that place is. You worry about what you got to do and I'll worry about what I got to do."

"I'll tell you what—after I talk to Pompey, I'll go to *Lift* and try to find where their copies are. That way, we'll save time."

He looks cross, Lila Mae thinks. As cross and defiant as she looked when he insisted on coming to Pompey's with her? He says, "I'll do it, Lila Mae. That's the agreement, right? You got enough to do. When I get the film developed, you can help me figure out what my uncle was saying. Okay?"

She wishes she hadn't tried to tell him what to do. She has been misinterpreted. "Natchez—do you want to get something to eat?"

He frowns. "I'd really like that," he says, "but I have to get back on the train. I have a long day tomorrow." He stands and pushes the chair back to where he found it. "I know you one of these modern city gals, Lila Mae, but me, I like to take it slow. You know? It's just how I was raised. Let's—let's go out tomorrow night for real. After we finish our business let's go out and do it right. No elevators, no black box, no uncle. Just us. We can go out to dinner and then maybe you can take me out to one of these clubs you go to." Natchez smiles. "I got all this salary from Mr. Reed and it's just been burning a hole in my pocket."

"I'd like that," Lila Mae says.

In the doorway, he quickly kisses her cheek. "Good night, Lila Mae," he says. "And keep this door locked if you ain't going to move to a nicer place."

The modern city girl locks the door behind him.

189

"I know what you did," she tells Pompey. "I know what you did to the Fanny Briggs stack."

She has been here since this morning, kneading the rubber grooves of the floormat with her shoes. Lila Mae was surprised to learn that Pompey lived only two blocks from her apartment, but in their history they rarely exchanged beyond terse office communiqués (never have *Done with that stapler?* and *The new Board up?* been pronounced with such venom). Just two blocks away from her apartment at the Bertram Arms and it could be a different neighborhood. The life here, the ambient cheer of this easy Saturday afternoon: she associates it with her childhood, Southern skies above the myriad taffy pleasures of colored town. On her street she is anonymous; the Caribbean immigrants share a code, a broad and secret choreography she is excluded from. But these are American colored. As the afternoon unfurls outside her car window, each neighbor greets a neighbor, hats are doffed extravagantly, smiles are currency, no strangers. A toddler strays two steps from her mother and almost falls, virgin knees to the pavement, if not for the sure hand of Mr. So-and-So from up the street, who never leaves the street, who always has a redemptive hand or hard candy or arcane wisdom for the children. The mother thanks him, promises a pie. (All nefaria kept behind apartment walls, saved for inside. The neighbors hear everything but do not interfere, squirreling away every curse and blow as gossip for lean hours.)

The street's breezy vignettes divert Lila Mae on her stakeout outside Pompey's tenement. The man in the red hat who leans against a lamppost on the corner, his quick hands. The average time it takes for a shopper to complete transactions at the corner grocery (seven minutes). He does not leave his house. She knows he's in there because he answered the phone. (She let him hear her breathe.) She spends hours gathering herself: imagines vaulting up the gray stone steps, ringing the buzzer for apartment 3A.

A stickball game erupts out of nowhere, quick as a summer shower, in the time it takes her to glance from Pompey's stoop to her pocket watch. Ten screaming kids, half a broom, a stained canvas ball. Apparently her car is third base, she discovers when one of the boys slaps her trunk, safe. Startled, she turns in her seat and his round, dizzy face is in the window: "Sorry, lady!" he squeals. Your mama's so black she, you throw like a girl, nuh-uh he didn't tag me I got there first.

The stickball game disappears as fast as it came, the boys skid off to some new and suddenly pressing pastime. Lila Mae has decided, *now*, when the door to 327 opens. Pompey holds the door for a squat, round woman in a bright blue dress and two young boys who swat each other noisily. The Family Pompey. She'd assumed he was married—Pompey has a good city paycheck and is not the type to raise hell of any kind, adulterous or alcoholic or what have you—but hadn't factored in the kids. They look about five or six, short-limbed kinesis. Mrs. Pompey is in the unfortunate habit of dressing her loins' issue in the same-colored clothes, just one size apart. Perhaps that is why they beat at each other, slapping each newly undefended quarter on his antagonist's tiny person. Pompey looks down, scowls and clenches his sons' shoulders. In unison their heads incline toward his hands, a common response to shoulder pinching, Lila Mae has noticed, instinct ushered in aeons ago by the opposable thumb of some slope-browed hominid patriarch. They stop fighting, stop squirming once their father releases his grip and instructs them to behave. The boys make it down the stoop to the sidewalk without incident as Pompey kisses his wife goodbye on the lips. She hadn't considered that either, a tender side to Pompey, her prey today. It affects her somehow, she pushes the image aside. She has business with the man.

While his family makes their way around the corner, Pompey sits on the front stoop and withdraws a cigar from his shirt pocket. She allows him two blue drags, then eases out of the Department sedan and climbs the steps before he can notice her approach. She's standing over him when she interrupts his unknowable petty meditations with a terse "I know what you did."

"Watson? What are you doing here?" He chokes on the smoke, as surprised by the sight of Inspector Watson at his front door as by the unlikely image of her in a dress. (Her mother made it years before. Large roses float on white fabric, tight on her body without a single unseemly curve. She hasn't worn it in years, never had occasion to. Never met someone like Natchez, whom she will meet later this evening after they have finished their missions. If she presses her nose to the dress, Lila Mae imagines she can smell her mother's sweat, deep in the cotton.)

"I know what you did to the Fanny Briggs stack. I know Chancre ordered you to do it," she says flatly.

"I don't know what the hell you're talking about, girl." His face curdles. "Now why don't you get away from my stoop before I get on the phone to IAB and tell them that their public enemy number one has finally shown up?" He glances quickly up and down the street to see which of his neighbors is cataloging this incident.

She thinks, he's probably wondering if he has time to sneak inside his door and slam it behind him. Nope. "Now you listen to me, old man," leaning over him, "I'm the one in control here now. I saw you go into Shush's clubhouse and I saw you in your little repairman's uniform go up to 366 Eighth Avenue. You've been cleaning up after Shush's maintenance gang, making sure they pass inspection so that Shush's criminal activities don't attract any undue attention from the Feds." Pompey leans back beneath this barrage, and Lila Mae leans even closer, tart smoke scoring her nostrils. "I know Shush owns 366—and the shoddy work his boys do on elevators would be just the FBI's perfect excuse for a raid if he's not taking care of Department citations." She drops the pictures of him leaving Pauley's Social Club, entering and leaving 366 in the Growley Elevator Repair uniform, into his lap. "You're Chancre's boy. Now if you don't give it up on what went down at Fanny Briggs, I'll be the one calling IAB. And the Feds."

"I didn't have anything to do with Fanny Briggs," he says, head shaking furiously, trying to shake away what he sees in the photographs. "I didn't have anything to do with it."

"You know what, Pompey? I'm really tired of people telling me lies. I'm through kidding with you people."

" 'You people'? And just what people would that be?"

"You don't have to shuffle for me, Pompey. I know your game."

"I didn't do nothing to Number Eleven. I don't know what happened. If you want to call IAB or the police, you go ahead and do it. Because I didn't do anything to Fanny Briggs."

She pulls back. This man is incredible. "You'd cover for them? You'd go to jail to protect them, after all they've done to you?"

He pulls his suspenders off his flesh as if they were chains, lets them snap back. Pompey holds his cigar in front of his eyes and stares at the smoldering red tip. "This is one of Chancre's cigars," he says. "Chancre's. They taste like shit but they got a Spanish label so no one says anything. We all know they taste like shit but we smoke them anyway because he gave them to us." He looks up at her now. His eyes are cracked with red lines. "I do his work. We all do. Three months ago, the man calls me into his office. I don't know what he wants. I've never spoken to him even though I been there longer than most of those white boys. He asks me if I need money. I tell him, sure—he's the boss, maybe he's going to give me that raise I been asking for. He asks me if I heard anything about his friendship with Johnny Shush. 'Friendship' he calls it, with his big feet up on the desk like I don't know what's going on. Like I'm some dumb nigger. I say yeah, there are rumors, the boys talk about it. Then he asks me again if I need any money and how I could make some looking after Shush's maintenance crews, because they always do a bad job—none of them seen a machine room in their lives before they became repairmen—and Shush's got to keep a low profile because of this federal probe. He can't afford to bribe anyone in the Department, not now. All I got to do is look after the buildings that have been red-coded and make sure they make muster when the Department does the follow-up. If Shush's boys have messed up, which they usually do, I clean it up because I know what the Department is going to be looking for. I needed the money, so I took the job. Been three months I been doing it. Chancre says just three more months and things will have cooled down. So I did it."

"It's against the law," Lila Mae barks. "You took an oath."

"Don't talk to me about oath," he spits. "I got two boys. One five, the other seven. I was raised in this neighborhood. It's changed. You've been watching me all day, I figure. You see them kids play ball? Ten years from now half of them be in jail, or dead, and the other half working as slaves just to keep a roof over they heads. Ten years from now they won't even be kids playing ball on the street. Won't be safe enough even to do that. Walk down this street, you can smell the kids smoking that reefer. Right out in the open like they got no shame. You see that young man on the corner in that red hat? He sells it to them. A few years from now, it won't be reefer he selling but some other poison. My kids won't be here when that happens. I need money to take them out of here."

"Why should I believe you, Pompey?" she demands. "You've been just as bad as the rest of them ever since I joined the Department. Worse. Laughing at me with them. Most times you laugh harder. If you didn't do it, then who did Chancre send in?"

"I don't know anything about it!" He almost stands up, but catches himself and settles for deep glowering. "And you, how am

I supposed to act, the way you carry yourself. Like you some queen. Your nose up in the air? I got two kids."

"Yeah, I heard you. You got two kids. And you shuffle for those white people like a slave."

"What I done, I done because I had no other choice. This is a white man's world. They make the rules. You come along, strutting like you own the place. Like they don't own you. But they do. If not Chancre, then Lever. I was the first one in the Department. I was the first colored elevator inspector in history. In history! And you will never, ever know what hell they put me through. You think you have it bad? You have no idea. And it was because I did it first that you're here now. All my life I wanted to be an elevator inspector. That's all I wanted to be. And I got it. I was the first colored man to get a Department badge. They made shit of what I wanted and made me eat it. You had it easy, snot-nose kid that you are, because of me. Because of what I did for you.

"Come up here and piss in my face. I don't know what you're looking for, *In*spector *Wat*son, but I don't have it. It's not here. You have to go someplace else to find it, and that's your bad news. I remember when this was a mixed block. Had that polack deli on the corner. Now it's closed down." He returns his gaze to her. He taps the light ash from his cigar and takes a deep drag. "You can tell them about me. Call the cops or IAB, whatever you want. I'm gonna be here on this stoop until I finish this here cigar I got. And I'm gonna go to work on Monday like I always do and see what happens. Lila Mae Watson or no Lila Mae Watson."

When she wrenches the car away from the curb, he's still in the same position. Staring up at the tenement across the street, hands resting on his knees. A thin old gentleman with a wooden cane, on his interminable progress up the street, stops to wave at him, and Pompey returns the greeting. The photographs lie at his feet. Flakes of ash from Chancre's cigar hitch a ride off the wind, pirouette up and away.

ST. ROLAND THE CARPENTER, b. Taranto 1179; d. near Naples, 1235. One of the primary sources for Roland the Carpenter's life is his letters and drawings of fantastic contraptions, of which many were preserved until they were destroyed in a fire in 1873; they give a picture of the man and the conditions in which he worked so unassumingly and selflessly. He was ordained a priest among the parochial clergy at Bologne. He made aborted attempts to become a missionary among the Moslems. This desire had some fulfillment in 1219 when he accompanied the crusaders of Gautier de Brienne to Egypt; he made appeal in person to Sultan Malek al-Kamel, but had no success with either Saracens or crusaders, and after visiting the Holy Land he returned to Italy.

In 1225, while praying in the church of San Febronia, he seemed to hear an image of the Virgin Mary say to him: "Lift the people to His Kingdom." He took the words literally and developed the belief that churches should have two floors, the bottommost for sacrifices and alms-giving, and the uppermost reserved for prayer. The next year he founded the Order of the Gradual Stair but had little success in finding converts. In search for sinners he penetrated the prisons, the brothels, the galleys, and continued his mission into hamlets, back lands and at street corners. He converted none save one spectacular penitent, a Spanish woman who had murdered her father in a gambling dispute and then disguised herself as a man and served in the French army. It is said he once rescued a family of chickens from a burning barn. A saying of his that has rarely been repeated since is: "Let us take one leg up, and He will carry us the rest of the way." In 1235, he fell afoul of the local governor for aggressive proselytizing and it was decreed that he should be put to death by a battering of cudgels. His wounds were healed after every blow, whereupon he was burned at the stake. At his funeral all the poor of Naples surrounded the coffin that contained his heart, which had been recovered from the ashes; the peasants had mistaken his procession for that of another holy man who had died the very same night. His emblem in art is three stairs. He is the patron saint of elevator inspectors.

* * *

Such modesty, she thinks. No one wants to take credit for such a handy piece of sabotage. She believes Pompey, and his story jibes with Chancre's. (She's a good mile away from her destination, she drives slowly, no rush, only half her mind on the angry vectors of city traffic.) If they didn't do it, she muses, then who did—because if no one is responsible then she was negligent. And she is never wrong. Considers: Chancre had no reason to lie. If he was brazen enough to have her kidnapped, to make plain his alliance with Johnny Shush, there is no reason not to admit tinkering with Number Eleven. (Number Eleven, the forgotten victim in this drama, a cab so full of promise, taken from us at such an early age, in the prime of life. Who cries for Number Eleven? So preoccupied is she with how the accident impacts her that Lila Mae never gives a thought to the bereaved, the sobbing assembly line who has lost one dear, who never had a chance to say goodbye.) Pompey. She was so sure about Pompey, that shuffling embarrassment. She files her botched interrogation away. She has an engagement to keep. Lila Mae notices a long black hair lying like a snake on her dress. Drops it out the window.

Pompey is a small man on a dirty stoop in an endless city. She files it away for later. She has a date, and an errand to run before that date. The modern city girl has chosen a restaurant she remembers Chuck describing to her once, a Tiki joint with (reportedly) Hawaiian grass hanging from bamboo fixtures, and lights covered by multicolored globes. They have dancing after midnight, and Lila Mae hopes that this will fulfill Natchez's expectations of her social life, despite the fact it has been cribbed entire from Chuck's adventurous forays into the city he has made his new home. She catches her eyes in the sinister rectangle of the rearview mirror: tiny and cold, ancient black meteorites peering out of dirt. She could have been nicer to Natchez last night—after so many poses, couldn't amiability be a guise as well, removed from the closet hook when necessary? Natchez is new to the city and she remembers her first slow steps on this concrete, looking up at the scuffed knees of the structures girding above her. (The very same buildings that at this moment accelerate sunset. City night precedes real night thanks to these grim monoliths, the merciless fortification they have erected against nature.) Lila Mae thinks, she should be to him what she never had when she arrived here. Simple kindness, a helping hand—so before they meet for dinner she will infiltrate *Lift* and find Ben Urich's pages of Fulton's journal. Red stoplights warn. She stops at the intersection, thinks, she will do what she can to make his mission easier, the discovery of his birthright.

At the corner to her right is a building condemned. Small and understated red signs announce its demolition, cheap plywood in a perimeter to keep the citizens away from the damned edifice. There is time to think, as the green light germinates, what need shaped this being, now husk. Its desiccated skin has been sooted by decades of automotive bile. Hard to see beneath it. Warehouse, office building, sweatshop. Obsolete and doomed, soon to be replaced by one of those new steel and glass numbers. Chuck is right, she thinks. She hadn't considered all the implications of the second elevation. They will have to destroy this city once we deliver the black box. The current bones will not accommodate the marrow of the device. They will have to raze the city and cart off the rubble to less popular boroughs and start anew. What will it look like. The shining city will possess untold arms and a thousand eyes, mutability itself, constructed of yet-unconjured plastics. It will float, fly, fall, have no need of steel armature, have

198

a liquid spine, no spine at all. Astronomer-architects will lay out the heliopolis so that it charts the progress of the stars through heaven. The demolition man's hand is on the detonator. Scarred around the knuckles by forgotten cigarettes. All the people are gone. Deliberates: a cigarette before or after? After the explosion the sky will fill with dust. Decides: now.

When Natchez and Lila Mae find his black box.

Honking behind her. It is time to move away from the dying spot, leave the animal to die in peace. On to more practical matters. What will *Lift* favor, she wonders, these guardians of the elevator industry? Rustic Grummans with their filigreed cabs, quaint molding encoding the history of the sacred machine, or antiseptic Arbo Executives, sheer and spartan, born of the exigencies of speed, jet plane elevators? She picks the latter, and will find she is right when she gets past the *Lift* night watchman, Billy, who is distracted now by the final leg of his college correspondence course, specifically his latest assignment, a five-page paper on courtship and Victorian mores.

She parks, looks at her watch. It is seven-thirty on a Saturday evening. The citizens plan their weekend rites of expiation. *Lift* is a monthly and their latest issue has just hit the newsstands; she hopes there will be no one upstairs. Most of the windows are dark on the silent floors above her: as she looks up, the face of the *Lift* building is a plank extended over the starboard side, over a sea thick with sharks. Pushes open the doors.

The night watchman sits behind a gray curvilinear desk. Sweat beads on his wide forehead and the brown hair above his craggy face is damp. Furious concentration. He seems out of breath from his mental strain, definitely out of shape physically: the buttons of his dark blue uniform allude to an ongoing border dispute with his soft belly. In his hands is a dime paperback his eyes do not stray from. On its cover a young chimney sweep digs in his pocket for pence. She says, "Lila Mae Watson. I'm here to inspect your elevators."

Billy holds his paperback in the air and asks, "What's 'paraffin'?"

"A waxy substance used in candles. Mostly. Do you want to see my badge?"

Still distressed over the paraffin dilemma, Billy says, "Isn't it a little late?"

"Night shift. Neither rain nor sleet. Wherever there's an elevator in trouble, we're there." She holds her badge closer to his face. "That better?"

"I need glasses, to tell you the truth. Reading glasses, anyway." He frowns at his book and waves her on. She picks out *Lift*'s name from the white letters in the occupants' registry next to the elevator: eighth floor. She tries to imagine what his expression will be when she tells him she has the *Lift* pages. Natchez wished to accompany her on her visit to Pompey's, told her to stay out of this sneaking around out of protective impulse. She wants to see his eyes when she slides the film across the dinner table, past the miniature Hawaiian god, which glows in solemn power from its proximity to the candle. It arrives, an Arbo Executive all right, trim and lucent.

It seems, she notes, to be operating at optimum performance levels.

On the eighth floor the Executive's sleek door recedes and she sees the *Lift* logo levitating on glass. The outer room is lit by three ceiling lights set above a wide and solid desk, presumably where the receptionist sits in workday hours, filing her nails with a rustless implement (that fine white dust floating in the air, nudged by ventilation grates). She pushes open the glass doors: she does not hear a sound.

Lila Mae creeps to the white stucco wall separating reception from the long newsroom beyond and peeks behind it, scanning quickly. There is no one to see her. Like sneaking a glass of water. Twenty or so desks lined up to the (north, she notes) wall, islands inhabited by paper fauna, and not an inquisitive critter in sight. All the typewriters sleep, clacking ceased. Mum's the word. Over one desk, a good two thirds into the room, a small desk lamp with an emerald glass shade adumbrates a busy desk and a vacant chair. Was the light left on accidentally or is someone here? The building, walls and floor, hums. Then she sees eyes watching her out of the darkness, from the west wall, and she retreats behind the receptionist's bulwark. She stares without interest at a ball of red paper in the secretary's wastepaper basket. It looks like a valentine but it is not the season for valentines. She does not hear anything behind the partition. Her left hand traces a ridge in the stucco; invisible scar beneath her fingers, an old wound with a tale behind it, no doubt, but there's no one to tell her and it will not speak for itself. The elevator shaft is waiting a few steps away, just behind the office doors, and elevator potentiality waiting for her summons. But she doesn't hear a sound, and after the thought of relating to Natchez her botched mission repulses her, she peeks again behind the wall, her eyes have adjusted to the murk, and sees that what she took for eyes is a trophy. An Otis, to be exact, honoring vertical excellence. Two gold call buttons float in quartz, spaced apart according to the industry standard. The trophy rests on its side atop the listless dais of a black file cabinet. Some reporter's coveted Otis, the surety of cheap grandeur: an exposé on graft, a report on shoddy and hazardous suspension gear in a faraway kingdom's shafts. No, there's no one in the newsroom except the damned industry. She is alone with an unattended desk light whose electricity is an expenditure waiting to be itemized and eliminated in the next budget of *Lift* magazine, Covering the Elevator Industry for Thirty Years.

She trips through the magazine's masthead, which is corporealized now as a series of black nameplates on the reporters' desks. She recognizes some of the names from articles. They are the chroniclers of her mission: the bards compose their tales here, on these typewriters, versifying the inspector's glum adventures into darkened shaft. She searches for Ben Urich's name on the desks—she remembers Mr. Reed identifying Urich as the author of the squashed article. She has never liked his articles, which seem unduly obsessed with the dingier aspects of her enterprise, fixate on the backroom deals and betrayals she has done her best to stay out of during her Department tenure. (And here she is on tiptoe now, a center stage in that intrigue.) If his desk does not contain Fulton's notes, she will move on to the editors' offices. Travel up the masthead to those tiny specks at the top. The ones who know.

There. His desk is clean and organized, a standout from his fellow scribes' tabletop anarchy. Lila Mae digs into her purse (another neglected artifact from her closet dusted off tonight) and finds the miniature camera. Cups it in her hand as if it were a beautiful black frog she discovered in a creek. Lila Mae bought the camera this morning with sixty dollars she discovered in the breast pocket of her Friday suit. She'd forgotten about the miscalculated bribe—so much since then—but was glad she got to put it to good use. And her hand is on the first drawer when Ben Urich says, "You must be Lila Mae Watson." Which, needless to say, disturbs her plan.

*   *   *

Big Billy Porter laughs and raises a mug to his comrade's escapade. "You think that's gross, Ned my good man, let me tell you about the first time I ever saw the bastards. My first month out— this is Before the Code, I'll have you know, and the Department didn't even have the motor pool yet. We had to take the bus or the subway—they send us out in the morning with a pocket full of change and three index cards with our cases on them. Had to find our own way around, mates, and it was a damned mess. One thing after the other. So it's my first month out, right, and I have to inspect the old Jenkins Textile Factory downtown. I know it has to be one of those early Otis machines, you hear me, from how old the building is, but I don't know how old. Jenkins, Jenkins Junior, I don't know who the guy is, but he greets me on the loading dock. Like he's been waiting for me a long time, like I don't have anything better to do than check out that ancient rig he's got up there, right? You know the type, boys. So he says to me, 'We're having a little problem with the freight elevator,' timid like a schoolteacher. Like I don't know that. Anyway, he drags me inside and we go up to the machine room and I'm telling you boys, you have never seen anything like this. For one thing there were no windows and you knew no one had been inside there for years. Mouse droppings all on the floor, spiderwebs hanging from the ceiling. And the dust! I thought I was going to choke to death. Anyway, I see the cables coming out of this big wood contraption, looks like a big crate. But no motor. So I ask the little guy what the hell that is and he's talking through his handkerchief 'cause of the dust and he tells me his dad didn't like the sound the motor made, so he had them cover it up so it wouldn't make as much noise. And I'm thinking to myself, it was just a few years ago that United made all that money for coming up with the same innovation and here the damned owner of a rag factory has done it long before. You get patents for something like that and here it is locked up in this dump downtown. I don't tell him that, but that's what I'm thinking. So I tell him I'm sorry about his dad's delicate sensibilities and all that but I'm gonna have to take a look inside it. Junior hands me an iron pipe that's laying in the dust and I start having at the box. I'm straining and I'm trying to find a purchase point and then suddenly it gives—and they all come streaming out it, thousands of the little black bastards. And I know what you're thinking—oh, yeah, Billy, what are you whining about, we've all hit a roach bomb before. But you have never seen anything like this, fellows. Thousands and thousands of them, they're running up the bar to my hands, they're running across the

203

floor like water out a fountain. I jump back and I look down and they're all up my pants and I can feel them underneath my clothes, on my skin. The other guy is screaming—he backed up against a crate and slipped, and they were all over him. Screaming like the devil. Well, I was screaming too, if you want to know the truth. They must have been breeding in there for decades, eating that old Otis wiring and having just a high old cockroach time. We didn't know they liked to eat elevators back then—there were stories, of course, but the Department study was still years away. I almost shit my pants. I ran out that room, shut the door behind me and got the hell out of there. Hours later I still had roaches crawling out of my pockets. I don't know what happened to Junior. Maybe the little black bastards ate him."

* * *

She tugs the metal beads dangling from the light shade. He sits on the edge of the desk, ass a paperweight. The right sleeve of his powder-blue seersucker is rolled up in an unruly bunch to the elbow, where his arm transforms into an odd white appendage that ends in tiny pink fingertips. A stained cast. His face is slack and exhausted, dusted with tiny gray scrub-hairs. She says, "You know who I am."

"I figured you would come sooner or later," he tells her. "Once I got the other parts of his journal. You haven't been to the office so you must be up to something. Your file says you're one sharp cookie—I figured you'd be coming around. Do the same thing I would do in your position."

Even with his injury, Ben Urich attempts a pose of metropolitan bachelorhood. His left index finger hooks into the cuff of his pants, easy baby, just passing the time. "You look confused," he says. "I have been too, over the last few days, to be perfectly honest. Ever since I finished the article on the black box."

204

"Which never came out." She replaces the camera in her purse and zips it shut.

"My editor was convinced that we shouldn't run it." He raises the white club that is his right hand. "And I was soon persuaded that his decision was right. Or, attempts were made to persuade me."

"Johnny Shush," she offers.

"How much of his journals have you seen?"

"None yet. I was just about to take my first look."

"Yeah, like I said, I figured you'd be around soon. You or someone else. They're in the bottom drawer. Beneath last year's pinups."

The drawer slides and shudders. Bangs loud in the deserted newsroom. Lila Mae lifts two calendar pages featuring two famous picture-show starlets in erotic repose, finds the goods beneath them, split in shadow. "You can take them out," Ben Urich tells her at her hesitation. She recognizes the cramped handwriting, the internecine, slashing script. She has studied it under the gaze of the Institute librarian, in locked rooms—she even, in the early, giddy days of her conversion, practiced Fulton's handwriting for hours. Knows the ink. For one entire semester Lila Mae wrote her class notes in that hand, believing it would bring her closer to him. As if the mechanics of delivering the idea to the physical world were half the process. She mastered his hand, its reticent parabolas and botched vowels. Here it is now, on the familiar notebook paper Fulton preferred. She tracked down the manufacturer once; they have a plant across the river where they still turn out the Fontaine line. The teeth along the inside edge complete the tableau: they have been torn out of his notebooks.

Says to herself, "It's his." She could be in the Institute stacks, she could be in her old room above the gymnasium, in her converted janitor's closet. It is that real. She decodes that scratch, tumbles down its slopes and sudden cliffs, halfway down the page past a series of glyphs she doesn't recognize: *Anymore tests at this point would be redundant. It works, and all that is left is to deliver to the cities.* It works.

"Is it what you wanted?" Ben Urich drawls.

"It is it exactly." She doesn't lift her eyes from the pages. "Who sent them out?"

"If I knew that, we wouldn't be talking. If you knew, you wouldn't be here," rubbing his good hand over the dirty cast, "so I guess I'll have to scratch you off the list."

She barely hears him. The cream-colored paper is in her hand. She could memorize it and transcribe it later. Place her re-creations next to Natchez's photographs and see where they lead. She'll present her copy at the dinner table and slide it to him. Her present. Still looking down . . . *it required principles—a way of thinking—I thought I had abandoned.* She repeats the phrase to herself, making it indelible. As cover she asks, "How did you know I was coming?"

"It was written, you might say. Like my fingers. I assume from the reports that you've been staying at Intuitionist House. That you're working with Reed and Lever to make sure Chancre and his masters don't get it first. . . ." He trails off. "Which means that the Intuitionists don't have it yet."

"I left the House." *I have walked away from it, only to return and find that it has not changed. It works.*

"Didn't like the food?"

"Didn't like the conversation."

"Then you've found a different partner. I thought for a minute that you might be Arbo's way of telling me they're still watching me."

What he said: Chancre's masters. Finally, after too long pondering the minutiae, she looks up from Fulton's notes. "Arbo? What do they have to do with this?"

His eyebrows jumping. "I thought you were smart. A hundred-percent accuracy rate." The highest in the Department, Lila Mae adds to herself, not that anyone would ever mention that. "Until Fanny Briggs anyway. Who do you think really needs the black box?"

She stares at him, the pages in her small hand bending to the floor.

"I can see you're genuinely taken aback," Ben Urich says. He reaches into his pocket and withdraws a shiny dime. "Arbo and United—they're the real players here. I see I've upset you. Why don't you have a seat?" She sits down slowly in Ben Urich's seat, where he muckrakes, where he exposes. Through the windows in the north wall, she sees the dark windows of the offices across the street. No one there.

"This is a real surprise," Ben Urich says. "You're the key, after all." He flips the dime in the air, as is his habit, but he's not used to his left hand yet. He misses the silver on its descent and it rolls away into the darkness.

"What are you trying to tell me, Urich. What the hell are you trying to tell me?"

She's talking to his back. He's on his knees trying to retrieve his dime. "Who else needs the black box more than United and Arbo," he asks a ball of dust, "the biggest elevator manufacturing concerns in the country? The world. Arbo broke my hand to make me back off the story, for Pete's sake."

"Arbo. Arbo's dwindling markets."

"They're in bad shape, that's for sure. Overseas sales down forty-five percent, domestic thirty. Ever since their Jupiter line never took off and United came back swinging. Got it!" he says, returning to his desk. "Christ, you want some water or something?"

"Ever since United got Chancre to endorse their line," Lila Mae considers. Her voice is faint, as distant as the quiet rotors in the machine room above her.

"Of course," Ben Urich confirms. "Every major elevator market in the world looks to this city's Department for guidance. This is the most famous city in the world. The Big Skyscraper. I don't have to tell you that the whole world, every contractor and two-bit real estate tycoon, comes here first. This city."

Remembers Reed, that first day in Intuitionist House, telling her that Lever was out of town talking to the good people at Arbo, that's why the candidate could not meet her. "Arbo," she says, "is bankrolling their campaign." Whoever owns the elevator owns the new cities.

"I should hope so. It's not like the Intuitionists are rolling in dough. Those dues don't add up to much after you deduct all those wine and cheese symposia. Shoot, you only have that House because crazy old Dipth-Watney was feeling generous to the underdog. Arbo owned the Department when Holt was Guild Chair, and it was United's money that won the Chair for Chancre. You know that story about Holt and the chorus girl?—she was one of United's Safety Girls. Did you think this was all about philosophy? Who's the better man—Intuitionism or Empiricism? No one really gives a crap about that. Arbo and United are the guys who make the things. That's what really matters. The whole world wants to get vertical, and they're the guys that get them there. If you pay the fare."

He's missed the dime again. This time it bounces and jets off to the left of the desk. He crouches again, asks, "Who do you think was behind your accident last week? United. Chancre might have done the dirty work, but only at United's direction. Those are Arbo elevators in the building. Then there was that incident at the Follies, when Chancre fell on his ass. Had to be Arbo dealing out payback for Fanny Briggs."

"It wasn't them."

"Then who was it? The ghost of Elisha Graves Otis?"

He doesn't know everything. "You said Arbo broke your fingers," Lila Mae says. "Why would they try to stop your article from coming out? If they're backing the Intuitionists—and Fulton's box is most assuredly an Intuitionist creation—then why wouldn't they want the truth to come out? It doesn't make sense. The Guild hears about it, they vote for Lever, and Arbo has their man."

"They've won the hearts and minds?"

"They've won the hearts and minds, yes."

Still looking on the floor. "You want to give me a hand here?" She ignores him.

"Let me ask this, Miss Watson: who has the blueprint?"

"I don't know."

"If they don't have it, they don't control it. Suppose it's not Intuitionism-based. Suppose, for the sake of argument, it's Empirical. Or it's Intuitionist but Chancre finds it first with his Shush and United muscle and keeps it under wraps. Destroys it. Where does that leave Arbo?

"I'll tell you where," he says, "with their peckers swinging in the wind. Pardon my French. My article announces to the community that the Intuitionist black box is coming and that it'll be found soon. Build up the hopes of the inspector electorate, that bunch of bitter bastards, and then it doesn't show up. They'll show their displeasure on Tuesday, in the polling booths. Here it is," he says, standing again. To the dime, as he returns to the light: "Trying to hide from me, little buddy?"

"They have to do what they can to keep your story under wraps until they have it."

"Otherwise they're screwed. Chancre can spin it any way he wants. Even from his hospital bed. The rumor escaped anyway. 'Another Intuitionist hoax.' My sources tell me he's already got a press conference scheduled for Monday. 'If my opponents have the black box, let them show it to us.' Put up or shut up."

"Where is it?"

"Exactly."

"Your hand."

"They nabbed me right outside the office," Ben Urich says, wincing for a moment in recollection. "I put up a fight, I did my darndest but the next thing I knew they had me in the back of a car. They started to break my fingers one by one. It was two guys, two blockheads. Trying to come off like mob guys, but I knew they weren't mob. Could tell by the shirts. They were corporate boys, wore the downtown uniform right down to their cotton oxford shirts. Mob guys, Shush's boys, they got their own style. Buy the same expensive suits their bosses wear, with the same tacky lapels, and their shirts are cheap blended fabrics. Get them all from the same store—Finelli's on Mulberry."

"They broke your fingers."

The pink fingertips at the end of the cast wiggle. "Last Saturday. They got me right outside this office and got tough, telling me to lay off the story or else. Messed up my hand—my writing hand, mind you—and dropped me off at my apartment like I was their prom date. To send me a message. But then I remembered the shirts and started doing some legwork."

"You found out they were Arbo." Of course, of course.

"I got out some old surveillance photos I took a few years back. When they started selling their new undercarriage brakes to overseas firms, bumpkins who didn't know that they hadn't been approved in the States yet." He places the dime on the desk and rummages through another drawer. "The pictures are here somewhere," he says. "Here they are." He flips through a stack of glossies. "I found the men pretty quickly. That's them leaving the office with the rest of Arbo's muscle. Right there."

She is afraid to look. It is a grainy black and white photograph capturing one minuscule segment of city. Five solid men stand around a dark sedan. She angles the photo beneath the lamp, sees her hands are shaking and commands them still. "Jim and John," she says.

"You know them?"

"They were in my apartment last Friday. Searching it."

"Makes sense, considering what's in the Fulton pages our anonymous mailer sent to them." He juggles the dime in his good hand, gathering his courage for another go at his favorite pastime. "Jim Corrigan and John Murphy. On the Arbo personnel files, they're listed as 'consultants,' but the police have jackets on them. Breaking and entering, aggravated assault, industrial espionage, what have you. United has Shush's boys and Arbo has these guys. Jim's even got a murder charge under his belt, but Arbo's lawyers got him off. You remember the LaBianco case a few years back?"

"Who's this?" She taps the photo. Her hands do not shake.

"That's Raymond Coombs. Another 'consultant.' Mostly does strongarm work for them because he's a big colored guy and intimidating. Wait a minute—I think I have a better shot of him." He shuffles through the photos. It is a head shot. The man's eyes look off to the left, soft and lost. "You know him?" Ben Urich asks.

"He told me his name was Natchez."

"Wouldn't want to meet him in a dark alley, from what I've read. One tough customer. Guess he'd have to be—a colored man working in a white outfit. Like you, I guess." The dime is in his hand, inviting, taunting. "But I don't know why I have to tell you all this. With what you appear to know, I would think this old news."

She can't think. Asks Natchez's photograph a question.

"Because your name is in his notebooks. You're the link."

"I don't . . ."

"Look back in the drawer. From my photos of the Fulton pages sent to Arbo."

Underneath the pinup calendar are more photographs. She holds them under the lamp. Her head hurts.

Ben Urich decides to go for it: tosses the dime into the air. "Wasn't easy getting these, let me tell you. It's on that page, in the margin," he says. His hand darts. It snatches the dime.

She sees her name.

"Heads," Ben Urich says.

Lila Mae Watson is the one.

211

"Now maybe you can tell me what that means," Ben Urich says.

"Hey, can we get in on this?" John Murphy asks. "Or do we need, like, an engraved invitation?" Jim and John stand behind them, just a dime's throw away. Jim leers at them, John has his hands on his hips as if mildly vexed. He says, "Because we've come a long way and it would be downright rude for you to turn us away."

She runs. Jim lunges for Ben Urich, who has been jerked out of his suave recline. As he falls back on the desk, he aims one foot at the back of his chair and launches it, skidding on its wheels, at the legs of John, who stumbles in his pursuit of Lila Mae and smashes his head into the corner of a desk. Which leaves Ben Urich pinioned on his desk with Jim's fingers on his neck. Ben Urich takes his lumps. Ben Urich always takes his lumps.

The elevator's door opens, conjured from tranquil quiescence, the vehicular ether, by Lila Mae. She slams her palm against the Lobby button (black mottled with gray, sure and firm plastic, Arbo Floor Button, Motley Black, City Series #1102), sees John emerge, rubbing his head, from around the partition, she reaches for the Door Close button (initiating a signal to the selector in the machine room a hundred feet above through the amiable copper of the traveling cable inside the Arbo Router, City Series #1102) and leans against the dorsal wall of the Arbo Executive. John does not pick up the pace. He sees the black rubber lip of the elevator door start its progress across the entrance of the cab. He nods at Lila Mae and pivots towards the fire doors.

* * *

It is not difficult to outrun an elevator if the competition is only a few floors. The elevator moves deliberately through the shaft at a speed approved, after tense summit hours, by both the Depart-

212

ment of Elevator Inspectors and the American Association of Elevator Manufacturers. The box is safe, but the box must also feel safe when the passengers observe the doors slide shut and they dematerialize into the nether space of the shaft. As they lose their world and gain another. But Lila Mae does not see her pursuer when she runs out into the bright fluorescence of the ground floor. It is not difficult to outrun an elevator, but a recent head injury can make it difficult, particularly when careering down from cockeyed landing to cockeyed landing.

Lila Mae jumps over the legs of Billy the night watchman, who is out cold on the clean white tile, a navy-blue porpoise. She gains the street. Behind her, she hears the stairway doors slam open. On the other side of the street is the Department sedan. She would have time to get in the car—the keys are in her hand right now, cool and solid—but the automobile is boxed in by a large van, out of which hunched colored men ferry clean tablecloths into the service entrance of Ming's Oriental. Instinctively she jets right, and makes it a few steps before she realizes that left is where the populated avenues are, the theater crowds and cops. But she's already committed. Calculates her lead on John: not much. She jumps right, into a doorway that opens up to steps. Wants to get out of plain sight before he reaches the street. Too bad it's only a few doors down from the *Lift* building and an obvious refuge. Unseen above her head, elegant loops of red neon declare, HAPPY-LAND DIME-A-DANCE. She's up the stairs.

Lila Mae hears music.

She pushes against the scratched swinging doors at the top of the dirty staircase and lets the music out.

She walks slowly, like one who emerges from a downpour, acclimating herself to sudden warmth and the receding storm. She barely sees the two bouncers, two gorillas in lime sports jackets, who perch on metal stools by the door. Thick black mustaches shrub beneath their nostrils, intrepid vegetation on petrous faces.

They nod at Lila Mae and do not speak. Their elbows rest on their knees, they stare at the crack between the doors. There is no need to keep her out.

On a round wooden platform at the far end of the room, so distant as to be a distant city on the horizon, the conductor's arms glide. His back is to the dancers, and all are left to imagine his face from the stringy gray hair drooping unruly over his jacket collar. The tails of his tuxedo jigger. He waves his hands through humid air and the musicians' eyes flit between the sheet music and his rapier's tip, the incisions he makes in the humid air. They do not look at the dancers either, at their languid movements, the inevitably perverted manifestations of their work. For they understand that the dancers are flesh and weak and can never live up to what the musicians deliver from their gravid instruments. Understanding that something is always lost when it comes to human beings.

The men who do not dance sit along one wall, in a line of red seats that have been retrieved from the rubble of a demolished theater. In opera seats, one seat or two or three between them, they watch the dance floor, regretting incidents. The women here have been instructed against aggression, the hard sell. There is no need—these men, in their threadbare suits, choking on fat neckties, with their broken postures, are easy sells. The management knows that they scurry here out of the rain with ideas and will approach, in due time, the women when their moldy ideations have settled on a suitable vessel. The women have sifted through bargain racks in bargain districts, chosen polka-dot prints and obscure flower patterns. Fat arms and thin arms, swollen thighs and emaciated necks. The men choose from the bargain racks. The music urges and a man chooses a woman and they dance for a dime.

She looks at the door. John has not stabbed the bouncers yet. The bouncers stare at the doors, their backs to the dancers. They reserve their attention for manic bruisers and juiced-up hopheads who do not understand the nature of this particular establishment. She can envision John mangled at the bottom of the stairs, where all the rough trade ends up. Unless, she thinks, he kills the gorillas or incapacitates them, distracts them with two slabs of raw beef.

He is the only colored gentleman waiting to dance. He watches the dancers, the aloft couples, through fixed eyes. His suit is shiny, returning light in patches on his elbows and knees. It is an old suit. He does not see her until his dry hand is in hers and his arm sockets surrender to her tugging. He is up on his tentative feet, led by her to the dance floor.

The first song, caught halfway through, swiftly indoctrinates them. They are new to each other. Stiffly, gingerly, he places his arm around her waist, the other clasps her hand. She is rigid. Their feet obey the music and she fears he will fall, he is so frail. His gray and black hair is glued to his scalp by punctilious application of grease, a stream of static waves. She understands it is the style he has preferred for years, decades. His hair gradually falling into gray, as if age were the beckoning bottom of the shaft. Dust and mice. He smells dimly of smoky cologne. His pinstriped suit is patterned with crimson lines alternating with gray lines. Her partner is thin and disappearing. A ruby flash of handkerchief pokes from his chest pocket, perhaps at one point the same color of the suit but it has not faded, now a flare in her eye, an echo of finer times and better circumstances.

She does not know this song. The other dancers do, or pretend to, marshaling limbs and hips in a way she has never understood. Like the rest of her brethren in the Department, she does not like to dance. He leads. His arm braces her back. His hand is rough in hers, a working man's hand, crenellated by toil. She remembers her childhood chores, running out with a bucket to the outside pump. It has been a long time since she worked with her hands. He looks up at her. His skin has a reddish tinge, maybe some Indian in there, maybe he's from the Caribbean. First generation.

Around them the dancers are balloons, directed by unseen currents, slow and bright in this dry refuge, a panoply of trajectories. They are loose, cut a rug. The women are pros, the men driven. The men think, this is the last night on earth and I am spending it in the arms of a beautiful woman. The women are not necessarily beautiful, but anything is possible. The women count dimes, ponder the bills waiting on top of the icebox. The bills are gratified a dime at a time, steadily.

Her face is not painted like the other women's, but he doesn't seem to mind. His teeth are amber and cracked. He leads, she follows his lead and looks at the bouncers, who have not moved. The bouncers stare at the doors like she stares at her partner's scalp: into blankness. His ears are brown and pink, a baby's ears, and him so old. Hairs stick out.

The first song ends. He looks up at her and then digs in his pockets for coins. The fare. She shakes her head. The next song begins and he holds his hands open to her: Shall we? Her partner likes this slower tempo. His step is more confident, his grip a pinch. It reminds him of another song. *It's our song*, calcified by incident into pure memory. It's a powerful substance, pure memory, it irradiates. (She does not hear the commotion at the door. The bouncers have beaten an interloper, someone who did not understand what this place is.) Who is she now to him: his wife, his daughter, that old sweetheart, all lost now. What remains of them is this, this song. Over his shoulder, the other dancers reenact their elemental dramas. Arguments over nothing. Incandescent lovemaking. Who are they to each other, the women who work here (blistered feet, down payments on better futures), the men who come here with loose change (what is lost will be regained). The conductor's back is turned, his arms sprites.

Who is he to her? A ghost. She asks her partner, who is not her partner now but someone who is dead and will not answer except in what remains of him, his words, "Why did you do it?"

"You'll understand."

"I'll never understand."

"You already do."

Another mid-tempo number begins. The ballroom is appreciative. Without knowing when, she has taken the lead from her partner and now she guides their steps. His eyes are closed and she sees the small brown bumps on his tight eyelids. It is safe in here in the eye of the storm. Outside, down the stairs, out on the street, the city retreats under angry wet assault, high pressure. Low spirits out in the city tonight. It came unexpectedly. The news said a little rain, that's all. Not this. The sewers are full, the gutters are drowned and disgorge litter, doctor's bills and bank statements, they float higher, to the sidewalk levees and over them. The citizens pull the shades back and wait for the end. Lobbies and delicatessen floors wet now.

In here it is dry, in these red walls fading to pink. This new song is slow. She feels rain on her bosom but it is not rain but his tears. His chest shudders against her chest. She says, "Let it out." She can see every distinct hair on his head, the veins of blood vivid beneath the scalp. She leads. Her feet are sure on these warped wooden floors. It is safe in here. Out of the metropolitan welter. She has been leading them in an irregular square, repeating the pressure in this one area as if repetition will make them real, wear down the barrier into the next world. The other couples sway. They revolve around her and her partner, shuttling near and far in private orbits. Each partner, thrown against the other, is shelter, a polite warmth. The city is gone. This room is a bubble floating in the dark murk. The ballroom lights still warm the soul, the band continues to play through some mysterious dispensation. The bodies of the others move gently around her and her partner. A reprieve for those here tonight in the Happyland Dime-A-Dance.

Part **TWO**

From the lost notebooks of James Fulton:

By the ninetieth floor, everything is air, but that's jumping ahead a bit. It starts with the first floor, with dirt, with idiocy. As if we were meant for this. As if this is what fire meant, or language. To crawl about, prey to the dull obviousness of biology, as if we were not meant to fly. To lift. It starts on the first floor, with the grub's-eye view of the world: dirt. What will happen: it will move from the first floor, from safety, from all you've ever known and that takes a bit of recalibrating your imagination. To recognize that come-hither look of possibility. Trust in the cab, made by people like you, trust is the worst of it: it was made by people like you and you are weak and you make mistakes. They have incorrectly imagined this journey, misfigured the equipment necessary. By the fifth floor, the unavoidable consideration of physical laws, the slender fragility of the cables holding the car. Your own fragility. The elevator does not complain, climbs in a bubble of safety, fifteen and sixteen and twenty-six floors and no mishap: well that's no comfort, the accident could come at any time, and the higher up the worse it will be. Could anything survive a fall from this height? They say they have safety devices but things can go wrong and things often go wrong. Giddy at forty—made it this far. And yet still so much to say goodbye to if this is the end. This floor, fifty, where they all wait, those who will not receive apologies, the dead, those who have been wronged and are too low now for reconciliation. Those broken by your passage, the odd ricochets of your passage to this ride: there's nothing to be done. There is only the ride. At seventy-five no turning back. No need for safety devices because there's only up, this ascension. It is not so bad, this thing, that world falling away below and there are sturdy cables and a fine cab, dependable allies. Even the thought, *if there were only more time,* possesses no weight here, for nothing has weight, it has all been taken care of, the motor can handle any mass differential between the cab and the counterweight, that's its job, and what wish could possibly weigh so much that the machine could not accommodate it? Half enjoying it now. The walls are falling away, and the floor and the ceiling. They lose solidity in the verticality. At ninety, everything is air and the difference between you and the medium of your passage is disintegrating with every increment of the ascension. It's all bright and all the weight and cares you have been shedding are no longer weight and cares but brightness. Even the darkness of the shaft is gone because there is no disagreement between you and the shaft. How can you breathe when you no longer have lungs? The question does not perturb, that last plea of rationality has fallen away floors ago, with the earth. No time, no time for one last thought, *what was the last thing I thought last night before I fell asleep, the very last thought, what was it,* because before you can think that thought everything is bright and you have fallen away in the perfect elevator.

*　　*　　*

The grid is quiet this Sunday morning. The citizens do not live this far downtown. Too much power in the lattice. Some tried. They discovered their hair on the pillow upon waking, fingernails and teeth loose and swimming in their flesh. Never mind the impossible prospect of organizing complete sentences. (She tightens her tie, tinkers with her collar.) So no one lives in the financial district anymore, no one lives too close to the humming municipal temples. The streets of Federal Plaza are deserted and there are no shadows for the clouds, which snare the light and stain every ray silver. She parked outside Mama's Bakery last night for a few hours, clambered over the upholstery into the back seat, nestled into a corner but did not sleep. At the first alarms of dawn she pulled her dress over her head. Armed herself in her Monday suit—not the right day, of course, but her calendar's been scrambled of late. A manufacturing defect. It is not as crisp as she likes it; the erectile reserves of Chinese laundry starch have been woefully depleted. Her suit is good enough for what she needs to do, however, as far as she can tell from the automobile's tiny mirrors. She rubs spit into a dry patch of skin below her right eye. She drags her fingers through her hair.

It started here. A week ago. It is in its guts.

Lila Mae pounds on the door for ten minutes (she counts) before the sleeping guard steps out of the darkened lobby and up to the glass. His tight brown curly hair points in wild directions and is firmly matted on the right hemisphere, the same side of his face, it turns out, that is bloodless and etched with odd wrinkles.

223

Lila Mae presses her badge up to the glass. He pauses to scratch his right buttock before unhooking the wide loop of keys on his belt.

"I thought you guys were all finished with Number Eleven," he says.

"It's never finished," she says, halfway down the lobby, brogues clattering on the faux marble like hooves, charging like a bull.

She hears, distantly, the keys rattle as the guard locks the front door. His voice in the fog: "You need me to let you into the basement?" She does not look back. He's already been ejected from consciousness, got the bum's rush from her psyche. Lila Mae stands in the middle of Elevator Bank B. This is the longest she's gone between inspections since she joined the Department. Never taken a vacation, and here she is a whole nine days since she departed 125 Walker. She lays her palms on the first floor entrance of Elevator Number Eleven of the Fanny Briggs building. She feels the metal beneath the green industrial paint. It is black and cool. Ambient temperature. From far away, she hears the guard ask a question but she cannot make it out because it is so far away.

Nothing.

At first she decides on Number Ten, next-door neighbor to the dear departed. She presses the call button and can hear, she thinks, the selector rouse groggily, still damp from dreaming. A click. Then she changes her mind and goes for Number Fourteen, Eleven's opposite in Bank B. Fourteen is also flanked by two elevators, and must share that distinct middle child anxiety. A bell rings, cheerful and pert: it will never get more cynical and embittered, that bell, never flag in its cheer through hundreds of thousands of chimes. It wasn't built that way. Number Fourteen welcomes its passenger and the passenger boards.

Arbo recalled their Metropolitans a year after their heavily promoted release to fix a small but eventually significant cosmetic problem. Seems the cleaning agent used by the city's maintenance army didn't sit very well with the cab's inner panels of simulated wood: after a hundred applications or so of Scrubbo, the panels began to take on a green-brown color in odd patches, in shapes that reminded more than one person of mold. Disease. In short, the cleaning agent and the paneling didn't take to each other. One approach might have been to instruct the owner of the new, deluxe Metropolitans to use a different cleaner, one less caustic and reactive to the sensitive skin of the elevators. It was not to be. The city had purchased, at a very reasonable price, at generous man-handled discount, a lifetime supply of this certain Scrubbo. What "lifetime supply" entailed exactly when it comes to a city was never fully hammered out; suffice it to say that there are crates and crates of the stuff in basements of government buildings, in janitors' closets throughout the municipality, and they all proudly display the beguiling purple smile of the Scrubbo mascot, for whom no job is too dirty. The politicians refused to budge on this Scrubbo matter. It had been paid for. Indeed, it was agreed that the incident was Arbo's fault for not properly testing their equipment for possible safety hazards (there is not, and has never been, any evidence for a link between the cab's unsightly dermatological problem and human illness), and, in addition, there might be a lawsuit on the horizon. Even up in their towers, behind reinforced glass, Arbo knew which way the wind was blowing. They changed the panels for free, and to this day the Arbo Metropolitan is the elevator most city employees associate with their hapless drudgery, a fact supported over the years by polls solemnly conducted by the United Elevator Co.

These are new Arbo Metropolitans, Lila Mae notes: the inside panels do not betray the characteristic scratch marks left by the less than circumspect Arbo repairmen when they replaced the blighted panels. She noticed this fact on her first visit to Fanny

Briggs. She tells herself, do not look at Number Fourteen. She is in this car to help recall, completely, her inspection of Number Eleven, which now sits in the morgue a few buildings away, in grotesque shards on metal trays. She does not wish to taint her reenactment. The reverberations of Number Fourteen's idling drive insinuate themselves through her shoes, sing up through the muscles in her leg. She shuts them out. She does not feel them. Closes her eyes. Lila Mae reaches out into the darkness and presses the glass convexity of a button.

Number Fourteen's counterweight begins its decent into the shaft, diffident and wary.

This is the wrong darkness. It is the darkness of this day and this time and this elevator and Lila Mae needs that further-back darkness, the one she encountered on her first visit to Fanny Briggs. She can't touch the walls of this elevator as she did those of Number Eleven, for fear of taint. She imagines her hand extending out to the unyielding solidity of that dead elevator's walls, the way the inner paneling embraced her hand's curves. She's, she's almost at that darkness now. It is a slow curtain dropping before this day's darkness. There. This new darkness is the old darkness of Number Eleven. She watches the sure and untroubled ascent of Number Eleven. The genies appear on cue, dragging themselves from the wings. The genie of velocity, the genie of the hoisting motor's brute exertions, the red cone genie of the selector as it ticks off the entity's progress through the shaft, the amber nonagon genie of the grip shoes as they skip frictionless up T-rails. All of them energetic and fastidious, describing seamless verticality to Lila Mae in her mind's own tongue. They zigzag and circle, hop from foot to foot, fluctuate for her, their only spectator, the only one who's ever in the seats out there. They gyrate for her and reenact without omission their roles from last Thursday's performance. The genies never forget their lines. Lila Mae rises steady, Number Eleven is a smooth ride, alright. The genies bow and do not linger for her lonely applause.

She opens her eyes. The doors open to the dead air of the forty-second floor. She hits the Lobby button.

Nothing.

*   *   *

And if nothing and Chancre are telling the truth (she now believes he is, mistrust now as useless as trust), then this was a catastrophic accident. That is what the remains will give up to Forensics' latex probings: nothing. No telltale incision scar on an innocent inch of coaxial cable, no wires corkscrewing off the famously dependable antilocks. Nothing at all. (A few days from now when this is all over, Lila Mae will think to call Chuck for the exact wording of Forensics' findings, and his confirmation will seem to her remote: without meaning.) You don't expect them in the early failure phase; they usually pop up during the random failure phase, in adolescence, the fruit of malevolent pathology. Something gave in the elevator for no reason and its brother components gave in, too. A catastrophic accident. The things that emerge from the black, nether reaches of space and collide here, comets that connect with this frail world after countless unavailing ellipses. Emissaries from the unknowable. (The security guard assigned to the Fanny Briggs building watches her stumble from Number Fourteen, proceed across the lobby, blind, and tug on the locked front door.) She is never wrong when it comes to Intuitionism. Things occur to her. What her discipline and Empiricism have in common: they cannot account for the catastrophic accident. Did the genies try to warn her, were they aware, twitching at times, forbidden to make plain their knowledge but subtly attempting to alert her through the odd wiggle and shimmy. She wouldn't know what to look for. Whatever signals the genies may or may not have dispatched through her darkness went unread. She imagines the proximity of the catastrophe sending ripples through the darkness from the future, agitating the genies with impending violence. It's irrelevant. She didn't see it. (She doesn't appear to see him. The guard watches as she continues to pull at the front door even though the lock does not give. She keeps trying.) Chancre and Pompey did not lie, and no one else sabotaged Number Eleven, she's sure of that too. How often do catastrophic accidents touch down here. The last one in this country was what, she searches after it, thirty-five years ago, out West. The ten passengers (midjoke, aimless perusal of the inspection certificate, fondling house-key weight in trouser pockets, trying not to whistle) had time to scream, of course, but not much else. The investigators (and what a hapless bunch they would have been, the field so young) never found any reason for it. Total freefall. What happens when too many impossible events occur, when multiple redundancy is not enough. Scratching heads over this mystery of the new cities. The last recorded incident of total freefall happened in the Ukraine, and was eventually traced to an inept contractor's failure to properly install the progressive brakes in the undercarriage. Five died. She can't remember the make of the elevator—what company was most popular in that region at that time. Can't remember. (Finally the guard unlocks the door. She still doesn't see him. He watches her stagger down the broad stone steps, about to fall any number of times.) Nobody in her business would wish a catastrophic accident on their worst enemy. They're a superstitious lot, and envious and bitter of every colleague's success, but wish a crash like this on a nemesis and you're just asking for one yourself—with you in it, hollering against probability all the way down. It's not even probability because it's beyond calculation. It's fate.

They won't find any reason for this crash, trace the serial number back to the manufacturer, interrogate an arthritic mechanic's trembling fingers. This was a catastrophic accident.

"Poor Number Eleven," Lila Mae says—one moment of feeling for the unfortunate victim, that's all, before rerouting the incident to her own purposes: it was a catastrophic accident, and a message to her. It was her accident.

The elevator pretended to be what it was not. Number Eleven passed for longevous. Passed for healthy so well that Arbo Elevator Co.'s quality control could not see its duplicity, so well that the building contractors could not see for the routine ease of its assembly coeval doom. So well that Lila Mae Watson of the Department of Elevator Inspectors, who is never wrong, did not see it. Did it know? After all of Fulton's anthropomorphism: did the machine know itself. Possessed the usual spectrum of elevator emotion, yes, but did it have articulate self-awareness. Erlich, the mad Frenchman, of course, posited such but he never gets invited to conferences and his monographs wilt on the shelves of his relatives' libraries. Did it decide to pass? To lie and betray itself? Even Fulton stayed away from the horror of the catastrophic accident: even in explicating the unbelievable he never dared broach the unknowable. Lila Mae thinks: out of fear.

She has not realized her destination, what she is driving toward, despite the fact there is only one place she will reach on this route. Out of the tunnel now, her destination could not be more obvious: still, she hasn't realized it yet. Distracted as she is by this latest inspection currently underway in her head.

Is his black box immune to the comet of the catastrophic accident. It is all jumbled now, machinations eclipsing machinations. For a second, she doubts that Fulton was colored: it could have been another one of Natchez's lies. Something he and his masters cooked up to reel her in. She sees the scene, hovering above the highway a few automobile lengths ahead: Reed and Natchez in the downstairs study of Intuitionist House, sipping smoky antique scotch as they check their net for frayed strands. Natchez knows the open windows of a colored girl's heart, he's had many, Reed knows the attended latches of the Intuitionist mind, his weaknesses are hers. The progress of their scheme: Natchez hadn't developed his film of the Intuitionist pages because he had never taken any photographs; he had been studying them all along. Tried to keep her from going to the *Lift* building for fear she might discover their plan. *I've been reading a lot about elevators since I found out about my uncle.* He knew all he needed to know about elevators for some time now.

No traffic on this Sunday morning, which is fortunate because she's not paying a whit of attention to the road. She's been this way many times. She will not take the wrong exit.

If she had met him for dinner, he would have detailed, fork jabbing above their medium-rare steaks and umbrella-adorned cocktails, his infiltration of Chancre's office, the close escapes, how swiftly he discovered Fulton's notes. His colleagues at Arbo, no doubt, obtained copies of whatever material had been sent to the Empiricists and United as soon as they discovered they were not the only ones to receive the mysterious dispatches. Trash her apartment when they suspect her of collaborating with Chancre, force her into Natchez's company: if she does not trust the Intuitionists, perhaps she will trust one of her tribe, his story of correcting the injustices done to her race.

No, Fulton was colored. She understands this luminous truth. Natchez did not lie about that: she has seen it in the man's books, made plain by her new literacy. In the last few days she has learned how to read, like a slave does, one forbidden word at a time.

She is driving on this Sunday morning to her alma mater, the Institute for Vertical Transport, to find out why her name is in Fulton's journals. To question the only person she can ask now, the one who can explain why Arbo needed to win her confidence. Why a man she never met willed her into his death.

Catastrophic accidents are a-million-in-a-million occurrences, not so much what happens very seldom but what happens when you subtract what happens all the time. They are, historically, good or bad omens, depending on the time and place, urging in reform, a quest for universal standards of elevator maintenance, or instructing the dull and plodding citizens of modernity that there is a power beyond rationality. That the devil still walks the earth and architecture is no substitute for prayer, for cracked knees and desperate barter with the gods.

She does not hear the car horn, let alone the urgency of the car horn. She drifts into the right lane and almost sideswipes the mock wood paneling of the station wagon. The kids in the back-seat scream, pink lungs heaving, father's hands grip the steering wheel, but for all the commotion of this few seconds there is no accident. Lila Mae's automobile and the family's automobile do not crash. She decelerates and eases into the shoulder of the highway, gravel popping on the undercarriage. Rests her head on the green rubber of the steering wheel.

Arbo and Natchez are merely unanswered questions. Their intrusion into her life is a matter of cause and effect, prospering along logical trajectories of greed, and only require adequate information to explain them. Time to sift the facts through her fingers and shake out the fine silt until what is left in her hand is what happened. But there is still this matter of Fulton and Intuitionism. She thinks, what passing for white does not account for: the person who knows your secret skin, the one you encounter at that unexpected time on that quite ordinary street. What Intuitionism does not account for: the catastrophic accident the elevator encounters at that unexpected moment on that quite ordinary ascent, the one who will reveal the device for what it truly is. The colored man passing for white and the innocent elevator must rely on luck, the convenience of empty streets and strangers who know nothing, dread the chance encounter with the one who knows who they are. The one who knows their weakness.

She believes the documentary evidence Natchez showed her, even if his blood tie to Fulton has been exposed as a lie. (Back on the highway now: she hadn't pulled over to ponder the accident that didn't happen but the one that did, ten days before.) Fulton was colored. In his books, the hatred of the corrupt order of this world, the keen longing for the next one, its next rules. He was the perfect liar the world made him, mouthing a supreme fiction the world accepted as truth. (Back on the highway, going where she's going.) In constant fear of that shadow, the shadow of the catastrophic accident that would reveal him for what he was. The shadow that envelopes and makes him dark.

Almost there, Lila Mae.

The black gates of the Institute for Vertical Transport are open. On Sunday, the students depart campus to attend mass at the neighborhood churches. The churches of this town welcome all fellow believers, no matter where they were born, what circumstances and choices have led them here. She drives around the east side of campus, duly noting the squat edifice of Fulton Hall, the Engineering Building, even her old home, the Gymnasium, always quiet on a Sunday morning. Trees cluster respectfully at the side of the road as she approaches the declivity that marks the faculty housing. She parks. She closes the door of the sedan. It only takes a minute for Mrs. Rogers to answer her knock. Lila Mae says to the old woman, "He was joking, right? About Intuitionism. It was all a big joke."

*　*　*

Sometimes when the wind drove the rain beneath the roof of the porch, when the wind was particularly upset at something or other, the rain would hit the front edge of the couch and wet it. That's why the old brown couch always smelled so sour: old damp and mold. They never lifted it into the back of the truck and doomed it to the rotting piles at the town dump. It was an old couch and treasured for the solid parity it had achieved between its comforts and defects, so the Watson family kept it on the porch. One example of its magic: the porch paint did not peel if it was underneath the couch. And another: the right side had formed a perfect bucket for Marvin Watson's behind, widening over the years, incredibly, as Marvin's behind widened. Marvin sat in his groove that day and tapped the envelope against his thigh. He told his daughter when his waiting ceased, when she cracked down on the first steps of the porch, "Your mother went to the store. She gave me this."

Lila Mae had hoped to intercept the letter at the mailbox and have time to read the words and consider them for a few days before she would tell or not tell her parents. Her schedule at Mrs. Applebaum's made it impossible. She never knew when she was going to get out. She had considered bribing Mr. Granger, the mailman who served colored town, but had decided it too complicated. She saw the red crest of the Institute for Vertical Transport, which she had seen first a few months before in the town library, and saw the soft shark teeth where her mother had opened the letter, probably with one of the Watson household's many dull knives. As her father extended the envelope to her he said, "You didn't tell me you had applied." The envelope was good paper. The thick, elegant paper they have up there. No broken mills, cheap mills, there. She withdrew the letter, it was still light enough to read without getting a headache. Her father watched her eyes. He wore his house clothes, the coarse trousers and heavy shirt he wore on the weekdays, before and after work. When he was out of the Huntley's uniform. The house clothes changed. They were replaced every few years by new versions in different colors. The Huntley's uniform, however, remained the same. Lila Mae saw it once. He snuck it out of work one day to show Lila Mae and her mother. Colored people were not allowed into Huntley's if they wanted to buy things. Only if they worked there. She read the letter and replaced it in the envelope.

Her father asked, "What are you going to tell Mrs. Applebaum?"

"I told her I might be leaving to go to school. I told her that when I started."

"You didn't tell us," her father answered. Then he said, "There's no shortage of people who could take your place with Mrs. Applebaum."

She had decided when she saw him on the couch. When she knew he knew. Lila Mae said, "I hate to leave you and Ma all by yourselves."

Her father leaned back, to a verse of metal growling from inside the couch. He said, "You don't worry about us. You worry about yourself. It's not so different up there, Lila Mae. They have the same white people up there they got down here. It might look different. It might feel different. But it's the same."

*   *   *

He lived here, assembled his vehicular epiphanies here, mulled over the bolts and pins of his mythology in this very house. Mrs. Rogers leaves her in the ruined parlor. Beneath her, an angry slash of ripped upholstery grins ticking. The fireplace mantle has been swept clean—she can see the coat sleeves of the men who trashed her own apartment brush across it—and her host's collection of ceramic horses are dashed to the floor, broken heads and limbs. The men's fingers groped inside the couch and chairs after Fulton's notebooks and Mrs. Rogers's loose change, smashed the two emerald lamps to see what may or may not have been inside them, cracked the frame of Fulton's portrait over taut knees. Lila Mae rubs her hands on her thighs and surveys the damage. The odor of cigar smoke lingers in the dull air and she can see a cigar butt ground into a photograph of Mrs. Rogers and her children, in happier times, not here. They didn't find anything but must persist, a determined gang thundering through the houses of those who might possess the object. Their violent blundering seems so pathetic to Lila Mae now, a child's plea for attention, a good hug. They'll never find it.

Mrs. Rogers returns from the kitchen with tea and thin butter cookies. Lila Mae reads the old grooves in her skin, the ripples around her eyes and mouth, the after-images of old expressions. The human face is only capable of two or three real expressions, and they leave their mark. Lila Mae thinks, she only has one expression and what will her face look like forty years from now. Eroded rock, a wall of dry canyon. Mrs. Rogers sighs, "They gave this place a real going over. Just a fine mess they made. Broke all of my horses. Broke they legs off." She doesn't look at the mess on the floor, busying herself with the delicate disrobing of a sugar cube. "I was in the city visiting my sister and I come home to this."

"Last night?" Lila Mae asks. "What time did you get back?"

"About eleven last night."

Then they hit the place right after she left Ben Urich. When they realized she knew. Lila Mae's been a practicing solipsist since before she could walk, and the days' recent events are doing irreparable damage to her condition.

Mrs. Rogers points to a bucket in the corner. A gray dishrag slithers over its lip. Preoccupied, she says, "One of them relieved himself on the floor. You can't smell it, can you?"

"I don't smell a thing," Lila Mae lies. "Did you call the police? Institute security?"

"What for? They probably the ones that did it."

Lila Mae leans forward in her chair. "This is the first time, right? When you told the Institute that this place had been broken into after Fulton's death and his notebooks stolen, you made that up, correct?"

"It may have been a lie," Mrs. Rogers shrugs. Stands. She hasn't touched her tea and snacks. It's all ritual, Lila Mae appraises. Her host says, "I did most of the upstairs, but I haven't finished down here. Do you want to give me a hand?" An old house and an old woman. She needs to preserve the rules of this place, the order she keeps beneath the pitched roof. Even though they have pissed on it. She bends over slowly before the fireplace and picks up one of her fallen horses. It kneels on its stomach in her rough palm. No legs. Mrs. Rogers gets down on the floor and looks for its legs.

Lila Mae grabs the broom that leans against the back of her chair. She picks an area, sweeps couch innards and shredded paper into mounds. The old woman says, "To answer your question, yes, he was having a joke on them at first, but it wasn't a joke at the end. It became true." She discovers one of the tiny thoroughbred's legs under the newspaper rack and holds it up to the window. "You have to realize something about James," continuing, tilting the leg in the sunlight. "Deep down he was real country. No kind of sense at all in his head except his own kind of sense. That's what made him what he was."

After all that has happened, Lila Mae figures she can put up with the woman's drifting explanations. There's no rush. Lila Mae says, "But he wasn't who he was. He passed for white. He was colored."

"Well look at you," Mrs. Rogers says with exhaustion, sparing a second for a quick glance at her visitor. "Not the same girl who was knocking on my door last week, are you? With your chest all puffed out like a peacock. You've seen something between now and then, huh?" She places the horse on the mantle, where it rolls over on its side and exposes its white belly and manufacturer's lot number. "I didn't even know myself until his sister come up to visit one time, and I lived under the same roof with the man. I knew he wasn't like no other white man I had worked for, but I didn't think . . . She came up to the door one night—I don't know, fifteen years ago? Twenty? Whenever it was, it was right before he wrote the second one of his Intuitionist books."

This information isn't hard to recall for Lila Mae. There was an eight-month break between the publication of *Theoretical Elevators* Volume One and Fulton's embarkation on Volume Two. It was twenty years ago when Fulton's sister knocked on his door. What did she look like. What do you say to a brother you have not seen for decades. Lila Mae can barely speak to people she saw last week.

"She shows up at the door," Mrs. Rogers continues, "and tells me she has to see James. She was one of them down-home women. You could see she made herself the clothes she got on her back. I look her up and down because I don't know who this woman is, and say I got to see if Mr. Fulton is receiving visitors. You should have seen his face when he walked down the stairs. His pipe fell right out of his mouth onto the floor—you can still see the carpet where he burned it. He starts fussing and telling me to go out to the store—suddenly he got to have fish for dinner. So I leave, and when I get back, she's gone and James is sitting in his study reading his journals like nothing's strange. Asks me what time will dinner be ready, just like that. He told me who she was later, but that was after."

Did she bring photographs or bad news: the death of their mother. Money for burial costs. What do you say to your brother who you have not seen for many years. She can see them talking in this room. The furniture is the same, the day's light thin and cold. He sits in the chair Lila Mae sat in, hands kneading the armrests. It is the moment he has feared since he left his town. When he will be revealed for who he is, the catastrophic accident. But his sister does not expose him. She did not make him crash. He was saved.

"It wasn't soon after that he started acting funny," Mrs. Rogers says. She has now retrieved four horses and eleven legs. They lay on the mantle as if on a battlefield. Their masters dead and dying. "Just little things a body wouldn't notice at first, but then it creeped up on you."

"Like when he dunked the provost's head in the punch bowl at the groundbreaking ceremony."

"That was later, but you on the right track," Mrs. Rogers tells her. "He'd been in a pretty good mood because his first Intuition-ist book was doing alright. It had been hard on him but now he was getting what he deserved. When he finished that first book he showed it to them up on the hill there. His colleagues. And they just tossed him out of there—he couldn't get anyone to take it seriously. None of them wanted to touch it. So he paid for it himself, and it started. They believed it."

She can't decide which porcelain limb belongs to which porcelain horse. "I remember when the first reviews came out in one of those elevator journals," she says, placing the leg next to a small white pony caught in fractured gallop. "He sits down right in the chair right there and starts reading it. I was in the kitchen cooking. I didn't hear anything for a long time, and then I hear him laughing. You see, James was a very serious man. He had a sense of humor, but it was his own sense of humor. We lived in the same house for years and I don't think there was one time when we both laughed at the same thing. That day I hear him laughing from the kitchen. Like I ain't never heard him laugh before—like it was the biggest, best joke he ever heard. I come running out and ask him what's so funny. And he just looks up at me and says, 'They believe it.'"

She must be referring to Robert Manley's famous mash note in *Continental Elevator Review*, which, if Lila Mae's memory serves, anointed Fulton "the field's greatest visionary since Otis" and "hope's last chance against modernity's relentless death march." It was the first review to describe Fulton's approach as "Intuitionist": postrational, innate. Human. No wonder he laughed. His prank had succeeded. From that review's cornices, the gargoyle of his mythology shook its stiff, mottled wings and conquered, city by city, whispering heresy, defecating on the robust edifices of the old order. No wonder he laughed.

Mrs. Rogers pulls Lila Mae back from distraction. Mrs. Rogers says, "I never seen him happy like that. He was happy for a whole week, and that's the longest time I ever seen him happy. Then one night I'm down here doing my crosswords. I couldn't sleep so I was doing my puzzles. James comes down from up there, wearing his robe—I thought he was in bed. He comes downstairs looking confused and upset and he says to me, 'But it's a joke. They don't get the joke.' "

"He thought that someone would understand but they didn't."

She nods. "They had all their rules and regulations. They had all this long list of things to check in elevators and what made an elevator work and all, and he'd come to hate that. He told me—these are his words—'They were all slaves to what they could see.' But there was a truth behind that they couldn't see for the life of them."

"They looked at the skin of things," Lila Mae offers. They couldn't see his lie. It was Pompey that allowed her to see Fulton's prank. The accident resounds in her still, the final notes of the crash the new background music of her mind. She had been so sure that Pompey had sabotaged Number Eleven—it appeased her sense of order. If Chancre wanted to set her up, any number in her Department would have been happy to oblige. But Lila Mae fixated on Pompey. The Uncle Tom, the grinning nigger, the house nigger who is to blame for her debased place in this world. Pompey gave them a blueprint for colored folk. How they acted. How they pleased white folks. How eager they would be for a piece of the dream that they would do anything for massa. She hated her place in their world, where she fell in their order of things, and blamed Pompey, her shucking shadow in the office. She could not see him anymore than anyone else in the office saw him.

Her hatred. Fulton's hatred of himself and his lie of whiteness. White people's reality is built on what things appear to be—that's the business of Empiricism. They judge them on how they appear when held up to the light, the wear on the carriage buckle, the stress fractures in the motor casing. His skin. Picture this: Fulton, the Great Reformer, the steady man at the helm of the Department of Elevator Inspectors, gives up his chair when the elevator companies try to buy his favor, place him in their advertisements. They have already bought off many of the street men—building

239

owners lay cash on inspectors in exchange for fastidious blindness to defect. Their sacred Empiricism has no meaning when it can be bought. When they can't even see that this man is colored because he says he is not. Or doesn't even say it. They see his skin and see a white man. Retreat behind the stone walls of the Institute does not change matters. He is still not colored. *There is another world beyond this one.* He was trying to tell them and they wouldn't hear it. Don't believe your eyes.

Mrs. Rogers says, "He was making a joke of their entire way of life and they couldn't see. The joke wasn't funny to him anymore. Once he realized that—that it was a joke but they didn't see it like that, it wasn't a joke anymore. His sister come to visit soon after that. He told me later she saw him in the newspaper. Like I said, he got strange after that. He started writing that second book. He'd lock himself in his study and he wouldn't come out. I had to start leaving his dinner outside the door because he wouldn't come down to eat. This went on for months and months. Then one day he comes down and says he finished."

Lila Mae knew he was joking because he hated himself. She understood this hatred of himself; she hated something in herself and she took it out on Pompey. Now she could see Fulton for what he was. There was no way he believed in transcendence. His race kept him earthbound, like the stranded citizens before Otis invented his safety elevator. There was no hope for him as a colored man because the white world will not let a colored man rise, and there was no hope for him as a white man because it was a lie. He secretes his venom into the pages of a book. He knows the other world he describes does not exist. There will be no redemption because the men who run this place do not want redemption. They want to be as near to hell as they can.

Lila Mae looks at the old woman. She busies herself with her collection, attempting to right those mangled equine forms. They will not stand. The kind thing to do would be to put them out of their misery, but she will not do that. She hangs on to them. Perhaps one day they will be right again. Mrs. Rogers and Fulton living together in this house, as employer and employee. She tends to the colored business and he tends to his white business. Secretly kin, but she does not know that. So no, Lila Mae sees, he does not believe in the perfect elevator. He creates a doctrine of transcendence that is as much a lie as his life. But then something happens. Something happens that makes him believe, switch from the novel but diffuse generalities of Volume One to the concrete Intuitionist methodology of Volume Two. Now he wants that perfect elevator that will lift him away from here and devises solid method from his original satire. What did his sister say to him. What did he wish after their meeting. Family? That there could be, in the world he invented to parody his enslavers, a field where he could be whole? A joke has no purpose if you cannot share it with anyone. Lila Mae thinks, Intuitionism is communication. That simple. Communication with what is not-you. When he gives lectures to his flock, years later, they are not aware of what he is truly speaking. *The elevator world will look like Heaven but not the Heaven you have reckoned.*

Lila Mae hears a car door slam outside. Through the window, she sees her old Engineering professor Dr. Heywood lock the door of his car. Returning from church and prayer for the next place. Beyond. It is need. She has always considered herself an atheist. She has knelt beside her mother and father in church and said the words she was supposed to say, but she never believed them, and when she came North she stopped going. She has always considered herself an atheist, not realizing she had a religion. Anyone can start a religion. They just need the need of others.

They haven't made much headway into the mess left, presumably, by Arbo and their bruiser army. Lila Mae, for her part, has spent the last few minutes sweeping up a mound of grit and then brushing it out into a thin layer before gathering it again. Mrs.

Rogers has been fussing over her silly tchotchkes, her broken horses. It's useless. Lila Mae asks, "Why did he put my name in his notebooks?"

Mrs. Rogers sits down on the couch. Too tired. Touches the side of the teapot and frowns. Cold. "Toward the end he knew he was going to die. He spent his days and nights all running around trying to finish his last project. Nights he went over to the library they named after him—he said he liked the peace there." She's looking at her hands. They're palm-up in her lap, dead, over-turned crabs. "He said he saw a light on in the room across the way, and one day he asked me if I knew what the name of the colored student on campus was. I told him I didn't know, and that's all I know about it." Looking now in her visitor's eyes. "You should take what's left. I don't want to hold on to it anymore. It's too much."

She rises and walks into the kitchen. Lila Mae can't see what she's doing. But she hears it. Hears squeaking, it takes her a few seconds to place it. It is an old pulley, doing what it was meant to do. There's a dumbwaiter in the kitchen. A primitive hand eleva-tor containing all the principles of verticality. She hears rocks scraping.

When the old woman returns, she holds a stack of notebooks, Fulton's cherished Fontaines, wrapped loosely in a shred of stained leather. The sacred scrolls, of course. What did she do? Lila Mae can see it: she's removed some bricks from the back wall of the dumbwaiter shaft and opened up a shallow dark hole. Where the texts waited. They stand for a minute, the two colored women, face to face, a generation and two feet apart, djinns of dust whirling in the shafts of afternoon light between them. Lila Mae takes the notebooks into her hands. It's a good weight. She asks, "What made you send out the packages?"

The old woman says, "He left instructions. He said when I sent them out, someone would come."

She got lucky the first place she checked out. She wanted to live in the colored part of the city after so long in the pale alien territory of the Institute. Graduation exercises done, Lila Mae was on her own. She needed a place to live because she had a job in the city. The first colored woman in the Department of Elevator Inspectors. She wanted to tell all the people on the sidewalk of her accomplishment, that old dignified lady on the stoop fanning herself with a newspaper, the steel-eyed cop on the corner with the sun in his buttons. That she'd made it through. The first woman of her race to earn a badge. Grab their shoulders and shake them. They wouldn't care, of course. No one knew what kept this city up and climbing. They didn't know her and it was the first hot day of summer.

It was the island's colored neighborhood but it was not the colored town she'd grown up in. It had come into being overnight when the industrialists' tunnels broke the surface and they laid a sign: SUBWAY STOP HERE. These rowhouses, tenements, the lines of them across the Island from river to river. That's how the first tenants found this neighborhood and that's how she found it. She emerged from the heat of the underground tunnel and pondered the intersection. Any street as viable as any other. Lila Mae randomly picked one amiable block. Halfway down, after dodging the white spray of an open fire hydrant, she saw the sign. ROOMS FOR RENT, the little afterthought VACANCY swinging on two iron hooks beneath it.

The real estate speculator who had staked out this street's acres had opted for six-story tenements with Italianate facades, gray and sturdy. Rooms for whole families; later, two or three families in one apartment. A good investment. A skinny white man with damp black hair sat on the stoop listening to a horse race on his small radio. He mopped his brow with a rag as he yelled at the announcer, ladling out invective. Lila Mae patiently waited for the race to end and hoped that the man's fortunes would not have an impact on his answers to her queries. He wore gray trousers held true by red suspenders and a dirty white sleeveless T-shirt. She noticed the engraving in the arch above the door: THE BERTRAM ARMS. He didn't wait to hear the end of the race, suddenly clicking the knob with another volley of curses. Lila Mae said, "Excuse me, sir, I'm looking for the building manager."

He looked her over. "You want a room?"

"Yes. The sign says—"

"I know what it says. Come on up," he told her, scooping up the radio, "I'll show it to you."

The lobby still had its first coat of paint, queasy green coated with a healthy layer of dust trapped by congealed grease from apartment stoves. She didn't like the smell but figured she could get used to it if she had to. "It's on the fifth floor," the man said. "The windows face east, and that side of the building gets a lot of light in the morning." She followed him up the smooth steps. "No pets. Some of the tenants got pets but they're not s'pposed to." The heat of the day waited inside the halls. Some of the doors to the apartments were ajar to allow cross-ventilation but Lila Mae could not get a good look inside them as they climbed higher. The rooms were quiet. "There are pay phones on each floor. People generally get their messages, but you have to be nice to your neighbors."

He opened the door to apartment 27. "See for yourself," he said. He waited outside.

It wasn't that big but it was clean, more or less. She could still see the vague outlines of the previous tenant's pictures dust-scored into the walls. She saw that there were two rooms, a large main room and a smaller one that might fit a small bed. She didn't have many things. They've probably cut up these apartments a bit, Lila Mae thought. She could fit a bed in there. Bigger than her room at the Institute, anyway, and she'd lived in that box for three years.

It was stuffy because the windows were closed. Lila Mae walked to the window and let the air in. She could see pretty far east, until a couple of large buildings cut off the view of the river. She'd rather face the really tall stuff downtown, but there was time for that. Without turning from the window she yelled, "How much did you say this was?"

"Fifteen dollars and forty-five cents a week," the man said. "Due each Monday. And a three-dollar key deposit."

She considered the room. It was a good deal, she thought. She could swing it on her salary. A new start. Lila Mae thought, she could make a home in the city.

* * *

She has been here before. In the hard plaza, among the stone animals. Whether the granite menagerie was Arbo's idea or the sculptor's vision is not clear. The animals—a baby rhino, a lion, a hyena, on cocked forelegs, with drooping necks, irisless eyes— watch a horizon that does not exist for the buildings, stoop to drink from an oasis that does not exist for the concrete. Any symbolism intended to illuminate Arbo's corporate mission or personality is lost on Lila Mae. The animals don't move. Men and women in conservative businesswear keep their distance as they navigate the plaza, towards subways and watering holes and lunch establishments. Prey, afraid deep in the strata of their consciousness of the predator's waking, improbable and impending.

Lila Mae has been here before. In her last semester at the Institute for Vertical Transport. Arbo invited the graduating class to a recruitment meeting conducted in a long room with glass walls high above the street. As Lila Mae and her fellows sipped coffee and nibbled at French pastries, the tall man from Arbo, in his dark and expensive suit, described the nurturing atmosphere and opportunities for advancement the elevator manufacturing concern could offer graduates of the most prestigious elevator inspection school in the country. At one time he, too, was fresh out of elevator school and eager to rescue the cities. At one time, he revealed, he was lured by the romance of life in the trenches, the dizzy rush of wrestling the devices to the ground until they confessed, the holy crusade against defect. Arbo offers more, he said, his hands wide across the vista behind him, the low countries beyond the city, the very clouds palpable. Arbo creates the future, he told them, inspectors serve the future. The students considered their shabby clothes and the grimy institutional yellow of Department offices. These recruitment sessions at elevator companies were a ritual. Lila Mae considered them a final test of their commitment to public service. Temptation. In all the years of the process, not one student had ever forsaken the lure of the streets, the moral imperative of the good work. They trickle to the corporate world only after a tour of duty down there, in the shadows, dodging rats. Only after being tested, after considering the grim pennies of a city paycheck, do they return to Arbo and United and the rest, defeated, hats in hand, begging for release and better suits. Near graduation time, the elevator concerns extend invitations, and the students listen to the devil and hold their ground.

The Arbo Building is one of the tallest in the city, as befits a company whose prosperity is an index to verticality. As big as they are, they cannot fill the building: they enable the city and leave it to others to fill, as it has always been. Lila Mae has to ask the security guard at the front desk where the man's office is. He consults a ledger. He directs her to Elevator Bank C, the express elevators. Arbo cannot fill the entire building, but they've got dibs on the top floors. It keeps them on their toes: no matter how high they are, the sky still distracts and reminds that there is always higher.

The express elevator is empty, one of the latest Arbo models, and silent as it disdains the low floors. Ignores them. Lila Mae rides alone. She so rarely rides with civilians, the people who justify her profession. Or former profession. She's not on the clock today. Not this Monday.

On the eightieth floor, the receptionist asks if she can help Lila Mae, her voice cheer in a vacuum. Lila Mae says she's here to see Raymond Coombs. She gives her name. The receptionist enunciates into the squat gray intercom. Coombs is startled, words crackling into the flat air of the office. He instructs the receptionist to let her pass.

The carpet is pliant under her feet, chewing up those brogues of hers. In the hallway she passes a display case containing a miniature replica of Arbo's first machine, the Excelsior. The brochure reprinted on a placard behind the glass promises "a delightful marriage of luxury and industry, where passengers can ride comfortably, ferried to the destination by the very best of today's mechanical conveyance." The hallways are silent, everybody's in their offices or out somewhere. Lila Mae stalls out before the antique device. It seems sad to Lila Mae. They do not care about comfort anymore. There's no more hiding the machine's purpose, out with the couches and engravings of griffins and nymphs. Below the manufacturer's oath, Lila Mae sees an endorsement from the management of the Charleston Hotel, the recipient of the prototype lift. It says, "The upper floors can now be the most desirable in the house, whence the guest makes the transit in less than half a minute of repose and quiet, and, arriving there, enjoys a purity and coolness of atmosphere and an exemption from noise, dust and exhalations." They took the wrecking ball to the old Charleston years ago. Wasn't tall enough.

Raymond Coombs's office lacks one wall. Substituted is glass; but for the blinds stacked up by the ceiling, Coombs's back could be to air. His sleeves are rolled up to his elbow. He wears a crisp white oxford shirt punished by gold suspenders—corporate creation as opposed to the coarse fabrics of the man's former disguise. Those struggling working-man stitches. His tie is red and green and shiny. She says, "Nice office," looking beyond him to the dirty river hundreds of feet below.

Coombs says, "I've paid my dues." He closes a file on his desk. To be truthful, he is more surprised at being interrupted at his paperwork than at her appearance in his office. He removes his tortoise-shell glasses and places them in his shirt pocket.

Lila Mae notices a photograph on the east wall of the room, a head shot of the famous reverend. The man who is so loud down South. She says, pointing, "They let you have his picture up."

"My employers allow me a certain latitude," he responds, shrugging. "I do my job and that's all they care about. Would you like a seat?"

She stands. "When did it start? That Friday or before that?"

He purses his lips and considers. "As soon as we saw your name in his notebooks. Personally, I didn't think much of it. The codebreakers downstairs spent two days working this column of numbers we found in the margin of one of the notebook pages. Didn't get anywhere. It turned out Fulton was just trying to add up his dry cleaning bill. He put all kinds of shit in there. So, no, at first your name being in his notebooks didn't mean anything in and of itself, but the guys upstairs wanted us to follow up every lead."

The intercom buzzes. Raymond Coombs instructs the young woman at the front desk that he doesn't want to be disturbed.

Lila Mae nods toward the photograph on the desk. "That your wife?"

"Married for twelve years. Works over at Metropolitan Hospital. She's a registered nurse."

"Kids?"

"A boy." Coombs turns the photograph from view. His voice is an octave or two higher than it was in Intuitionist House, in her hotel room. He says, "We didn't know what you knew, if anything.

We'd already dispatched Jim and John to your apartment, but once we heard about the accident at Fanny Briggs, I thought it might be wise to send Reed up there to intercept. I figured the news of the black box might be enough to flush you out. See what you knew. The accident changed everything. It was a bonus. That made it personal. Yes," he says, fingers flitting on his club tie, "I'd have to say that the accident helped things considerably."

His eyes travel slowly down her body, rest on the brown leather satchel she holds across her abdomen. "Do you want me to go on?" he asks.

She nods. No one could foresee the accident.

"At first we really did think that Chancre had sabotaged Number Eleven," he says, finishing-school diction all the way, "but our spies informed us that he was as surprised as we were. Luckily, you were fixated on the idea, with our encouragement, and that Pompey fellow. At least you were predictable that way," he says, grinning. "Let one colored in and you're integrated. Let two in, you got a race war as they try to kiss up to whitey."

She doesn't take the bait. "Keep talking," Lila Mae orders.

"Once we knew we had you," he continues, "I saw that you could still be useful, even if we weren't sure about what you knew about the notebooks. You certainly didn't give up any information, but we just chalked that up to what we'd read in your Department file—that you didn't trust anybody. I told Reed to send you to see Fulton's old maid—the old bat wasn't responding to any of our overtures. But when you didn't come back after that, I had to turn on the charm. It threw us for a loop."

He no longer speaks like a colored man from the South. Like Natchez. Nor is his face the same as it was, in this fluorescent light, in this circulated air. The leather is sure in her hands. She traces the zipper's serrations with a fingertip. "How'd you find out about Fulton?" she asks.

"A few years ago when we realized his later stuff was missing,

249

we just did the legwork no one had had a reason to do before. Found out where he came from. His sister had just died. She didn't have any heirs, so we just bought her estate. Using the term loosely, of course."

"No one cares where he came from."

"Not particularly. Colored people think two of our presidents were colored. We make noises about it, but nothing ever comes of it. The rank and file in the industry won't believe, and those who know care more about his last inventions. His color doesn't matter once it gets to that level. The level of commerce. They can put Fulton into one of those colored history calendars if they want—it doesn't change the fact that there's money to be made from his invention."

"You certainly earn your pay." The gold lettering outside his door read, RAYMOND COOMBS SPECIAL PROJECTS.

"I try. If I were really that good, my sabotage at the Follies would have kept you in Intuitionist House. Make you feel safe because I could protect you, where we could keep tabs on you and keep you away from Chancre. I was trying to square things—but you got your own ideas. Independent Lila Mae." He stops to consider Lila Mae's satchel. She sees it dawn on him that she might have a gun in there. "Can I ask you something?" he says, wheeling himself back in his chair to be free of the table. "For future reference on my Natchez disguise."

"Shoot."

"What made you go to *Lift?* Did you think the dumb country boy would mess it up, or did you just want to give your new beau a present?"

"I just wanted to help."

"I'll keep that in mind next time."

Just one or two matters left to clear up. The elevator inspector wants to know for sure, even though Lila Mae understands all she needs now. The elevator inspector inquires of the man from Arbo,

"What are you going to do about the election tomorrow? You seem to be in a stalemate at this point."

Coombs watches Lila Mae rub the edge of the satchel; his eyes dart to the doorway behind her and he considers angles, distances. He says, "Chancre's holding a press conference from his hospital bed tonight. I'm sure he'll address the Fulton rumors—everyone knows about the black box at this point. But we'll take care of it. I'll take care of it." He braces himself slowly, takes stock of his desk and what implements might come to his aid. "And you, Lila Mae, what are you going to take care of?"

"I have something for you," she says. She drops it on his desk.

"What's this?"

"It's Fulton's notebook. It's what you've been looking for."

"Why?"

"I just wanted to help," she says.

On her way to the elevator, she considers for a moment breaking the glass protecting the small Arbo Excelsior. Carrying it under her arm and setting it down in the stone menagerie outside the building. Freeing it to take its chances in the new city it was never designed for. Into the wild. But it would never survive out there. She kisses the glass instead and walks on.

* * *

What floor?

* * *

How could he have expected them to be ready for it? They can barely make sense of the cities they have now. The ones Otis gave them. They bump into each other going through doors and execute ridiculous pratfalls. He wants to be there now, in the places they will build when they have the perfect elevator. He won't be there.

251

He knew that as soon as he started to believe in it. He had never allowed himself to believe out of fear. So of course when he started to believe, it was too late. He could only describe what he thought it would look like and give them the means.

It cost him three dollars to get his shoes resoled. He remembers that. Some might find it funny that he's the one to give it to them. After all they put him through. But he didn't have a choice, did he? Once he started. He started with a different idea but then the idea got to him and it made him do it differently than how he started. It got under his skin, one might say. Now he's almost finished, if his body will let him finish. Where was he? Something about the thinner air up there and how to deal with it. He notices he's written *three dollars* in the margin of his notebook. He's always writing things in the margin.

Now that it's getting warmer outside it is not so cold at night in the library they named after him. Some time ago he stopped wearing anything except his night robe. No one says anything because they consider him a great man and allow him his eccentricities.

He's thought it through as far as he can see. It will be up to someone else to execute the plan. Maybe the wrong person will come. They'll think the time is right when the time is actually not right, and that would be terrible. Or they might wait too long. Well, he truly can't see what evil will come if they wait too long but he would definitely prefer it if whoever comes for it has a good sense of timing. Whoever that is. It might even be one of the students out there on the campus right now, those sleeping know-nothings snug in their elevator dreams. Maybe one of those jerks will find it.

So much corruption in the world today. Oh hell that's the way it's always been, old fool. Let it lie. Get back to work. All this work to do. If only he'd started sooner. But he had no way of knowing what he needed to do until he started it.

It's late. He writes the elevator.

His handwriting has gotten worse since he started. He sees that. It worsens the closer he gets, as if his words are being pinched and pulled by the elevator on the other side of his writing. Like they were being pulled into the future. He can still read it.

He remembers he ran into the Dean this evening on the quad, that self-righteous old clown. Nattering on about his dinner date with some other yahoo they got around here. He asked the Dean if he knew the name of the student exiting the gymnasium, the young colored girl who always walks fast with her head down to the cement. The Dean said her name was Lila Mae Watson and that she was a credit to her race.

He sees her through the window now, as he has for many nights recently. She studies in the small room across from the library. A converted janitor's closet, if he recalls correctly. Hers is the only light on in the whole building. Just like this light. This light is the only one on in the whole library. She doesn't look like she eats much. She looks so frail and slight through the window. He wishes she had better sense. But he cannot concern himself with her. The elevator needs tending. He lifts his pen. He notices he has written *Lila Mae Watson is the one* in the margin of his notebook. That's right. That's the name of the only other person awake at this hour of the night. She doesn't know what she's in for, he thinks, dismissing her from his mind. He's always writing things in the margin.

His work summons him. He's almost done. He has given Marie Claire her instructions and trusts her to carry them out. Someone will come. Someone will take care of it. This thing he's writing.

Maybe he'll start bringing the lantern up here at night and use that to work by. It would make the light really dramatic. That would really start people talking.

It works, but they are not ready for it. They will not be ready before his time runs out. He wishes he could be there with them. But he is not for that world. He's in this one.

Seven, please.

Lila Mae has a new room. It's a good size. Enough room for a desk anyway, and that's what is important. It looks out on a factory.

She writes a sentence and then scratches it out. Sometimes she almost gets his voice down but then it flutters away and it takes her some time to catch it again. The biggest problem, she finds, is nailing Fulton's voice as it appears in Volume Three of *Theoretical Elevators,* as opposed to the arid academic voice of Volume One and the aimless mystic voice of Volume Two. The rhythms of the first two books have been scored into her brain. The optimism of this new book is taking some getting used to. She has to recalibrate. Luckily, she's just filling in the interstitial parts that Fulton didn't have time to finish up. She knows his handwriting. The most important parts are there. They just need a little something to make them hang together. Seamlessly.

She stretches in her chair. She likes this new room. They might find it, they might be coming for her once they figure things out. But that won't be for a while. There's time to move on and find another room. And there are other cities, none as magnificent as this, but there are other cities. They're all doomed anyway, she figures. Doomed by what she's working on. What she will deliver to the world when the time is right.

They are not ready now but they will be.

The elevator in the notebook fragments Marie Claire sent to them is not perfect, but it's pretty good. After Marie Claire gave her the rest, the former elevator inspector sent them the parts they didn't have. Once they break Fulton's code and hieroglyphics, which should take them a long time without the key she possesses, the elevator should hold them for a while. It is not perfect but it's pretty good. She particularly likes the cab design, which takes care of engineering necessity without sacrificing passenger comfort. Just like they did in the old days. This third volume of Fulton's truly understands human need, she's found. The elevator she delivered to Coombs, and then to Chancre and Ben Urich, should hold them for a while. Then one day they will realize it is not perfect. If it is the right time she will give them the perfect elevator. If it is not time she will send out more of Fulton's words to let them know it is coming. As per his instructions. It is important to let the citizens know it is coming. To let them prepare themselves for the second elevation.

The windows of her room look out on a factory. She likes that. She feels bad for the buildings these days when she sees them. Because they are nothing like what is coming.

She's the keeper.

Sometimes in the room she thinks about the accident and its message. Much of what happened would have happened anyway, but it warms her to know that the perfect elevator reached out to her and told her she was of its world. That she was a citizen of the city to come and that the frail devices she had devoted her life to were weak and would all fall one day like Number Eleven. All of them, plummeting down the shafts like beautiful dead stars.

Sometimes in her new room she wonders who will decode the elevator first. It could be Arbo. It could be United. It doesn't matter. Like the election, their petty squabbling feeds the new thing that is coming. In its own way, it prepares them.

She returns to her work. It didn't have to be her, but it was. Fulton left instructions, but she knows she is permitted to alter them according to circumstances. There was no way Fulton could foresee how the world would change.

She returns to the work. She will make the necessary adjustments. It will come. She is never wrong. It's her intuition.

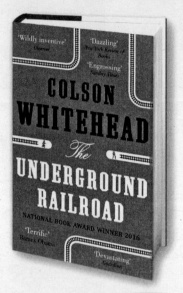